INTO ORBIT

Into ORBIT

ADVENA ABDUCTIONS
BOOK TWO

HOLLIE HARTWRIGHT

PINDIKA PRESS
CANBERRA

Into Orbit (Advena Abductions Book Two)

Published by Pindika Press
Canberra, Australia

Paperback ISBN: 978-0-6456731-1-1

For Hannah, the best sister in any universe.

Author's Note

INTO ORBIT IS THE second book in the high-heat *Advena Abduction* science-fiction series, which began with the short novel *Count Down*. Though each book features a different human heroine and a resolved why-choose romance with a HEA, the series is intended to be read in order and has an interconnected series arc.

Into Orbit is a super spicy, fast-to-medium burn, insta-connection alien romance where the lucky human heroine will not be choosing at the end. It contains F/F, M/M, M/F, and group scenes, along with alien *bits,* and a whole lot of swearing. It is suitable for adult audiences only.

Content warnings include personal violence and injury, space violence, allusions to r*pe and forced breeding, kidnap, incarceration, medical scenes, and doctor-patient relationships (consensual). If you think I've missed anything from this list, please, *please* contact me and I will update it; I am committed to keeping my readers safe.

This series is written by an Australian author, using Australian English. Formal Australian English is largely based on the spelling and conventions of UK English, though sometimes US spellings will slip through for certain words, depending on which TV channels our parents let us watch when we were younger.

Terms & Definitions

POD: A SMALL, TWO-BEING craft used by the Tirian peace-keeping force. There are two kinds: those used for short-distance transport, and those flown into battle as part of a larger fleet.

Hamadryad: the spirit of the heartree within a Tirian Forest. Hamadryad are born Tirian and discover their dual nature later in life.

Karia: the dominant female of a Tirian family; its leader.

Bond/bondship: an emotional link between two Tirians, so strong it alters their very nature. Bonds are unbreakable and for life.

Elya: a fundamental energy force existing throughout the known universe, seen and channelled only by a rare few.

MAEVE

'There's nothing more I can do, Maeve.'

Rian Wilding's voice was apologetic. Sorrowful, even.

'There must be something,' I insisted. 'Something that hasn't been done yet. *Anything*.'

'Maeve,' he said gently. 'Your local officers searched your apartment. They went to Tessa's work. They spoke to all her co-workers, all her friends, all her social media contacts. They called me. They called my mother. They searched the parks near your apartment and contacted every hospital in the city. They've done door knocks, reviewed CCTV, taken forensic samples. They've run two media campaigns, one local and one country wide.' He paused. 'I've done some slightly dodgy things to check that they're doing everything in their power, and they are. I'm worried, too, but short of quitting my job and pursuing less legal avenues, I've done everything I can.'

'That,' I said immediately. 'Do that.'

He sighed. I imagined he was doing something with his hands to alleviate his frustration – pinching the bridge of his nose, rubbing his eyes, running his fingers through his hair. I had no idea what Tessa's cousin looked like – I'd never met him – but I'd sent enough calls, texts, and emails over the past month to know that I was seriously testing his patience, not to mention his boundaries. Our contact wasn't above board; he wasn't supposed to speak with me at all, but he'd bought a burner phone once it became apparent that I wasn't going to leave him alone. His willingness to bend the rules – along with his obvious tolerance for a strange woman harassing him constantly about her missing friend – made him seem like a decent enough human, and I had the feeling that we would have gotten along, in different circumstances. I'd learned a few sparse details about his life – that he'd spent a good deal of his childhood in Ireland, that he ate takeaway more than was healthy, that he went to the gym between the hours of 6:30-7:30pm every evening he wasn't working – but, more importantly, I'd become familiar with the way he *thought*, which was carefully, analytically, unemotionally.

And I knew what he would say next.

'The note, Maeve. The text.'

'You know that note was bullshit,' I said furiously. 'Tessa walks out of Advena with a strange man and just … *disappears*? *Tessa*? Are you fucking joking? Plus, our apartment stank of sex and … *male*. Has she texted you again? Because she sure as fuck hasn't contacted me. Something happened, Rian. Tessa wouldn't just go.'

'As I said, you're not the only one worried.' His tone was maddeningly even. 'But are you so sure? Tessa loves you, Maeve, but she doesn't have many friends. She was working in a job she didn't like and living in a city she didn't care about. Would you truly say she was *happy*? I agree it's out of character, but what did she really have to stay for?'

Me, I wanted to shout, but I suspected his words hurt so much because they were true. If Tessa had been offered adventure, excitement, and a whole lot of smoulder wrapped up in that beautiful, dark-haired man, perhaps she would have just ... gone.

'She wouldn't do it,' I said stubbornly. 'I *know* she wouldn't. Something is fucked up about this, and if you won't help, then I'll find someone who will.'

I ended the call before he could respond and stuffed my phone angrily into my jeans pocket. It buzzed a moment later, but I ignored it.

Splaying my hands on the office desk, I took a deep breath, trying to calm myself down.

'Maeve? What are you doing here?'

I exhaled, then pasted a smile on my face, turning around in time to catch Claire's worried frown. 'Just ... taking a break.'

She blinked. 'A break? But you weren't rostered on today.'

'I'd better get out of the office so you can start your shift, then,' I said brightly.

She pursed her lips. Claire had gorgeous lips, the kind that caught your eye on the street, so the effect was rather less *disapproving* and rather more *sex goddess*. Despite the expression, her voice was kind. 'You're seeing someone, yeah?'

She didn't mean *seeing someone* in the fun way. Claire had been gently encouraging me to make an appointment with a counsellor ever since we realised Tessa was missing.

I waved my hand. 'I will.'

She gave a barely-perceptible sigh but didn't push. 'I better start,' she said reluctantly. 'Jessa wants to do an audit before the end of the tax year, and I have more work than I know what to do with.'

I forced another smile. 'I'll see if Belle needs any help.'

'You could go home instead,' she said pointedly.

Hard pass on that. 'Good luck with the audit.'

'I'm watching you, Maeve,' she grumbled, taking her place at the desk and opening the work laptop. 'Don't make me get Anna to do her puppy-dog eyes thing.'

'Cruel woman,' I muttered, and forced myself into the chaos of the Advena dance floor.

Business was booming, and the bar was packed; we looked to be close to capacity. I shot a frown at the doorway, catching one of the bouncer's eyes. Jason held up three fingers, letting me know how close we were to closing the doors. I gave him a nod, then eyed my precious bar.

Belle had it under control, even though we had two brand new staff on tonight. The line was minimal and continually moving, and everything was clean and ordered. I hated to admit it, but they didn't need my help, not even a little bit.

Anna came out from the kitchen, depositing a bowl of hot chips behind the bar for the staff. She caught sight of me; her nostrils flared in a rare show of irritation. *You promised*, she mouthed. She pointed a stern finger at a free stool at the bar, then disappeared back into the kitchen.

She'd try to feed me; it was what Anna did. I fought my way through the line, wondering when I'd eaten last. A broad-shouldered man taking up far too much space glared at me when my elbow found his rib; I stared back at him, one eyebrow raised, until he crumpled like a used tissue and pretended he'd never scowled at me in the first place.

Coward.

After a month of constant worry, no sleep, and no sex, I may have been spoiling for a fight.

That was an understatement. I was a warehouse full of gunpowder, and I was praying for someone to throw a lit match.

'You said you wouldn't do this, Maeve.' Anna plonked a basket full of chips down in front of me with a *thump* that was audible even over the noise of the crowd and the pop-punk blaring through the speakers. 'You said you'd stay home.'

Home, where it was empty and silent and where Tessa was still present in a hundred tiny ways.

'I know, but –'

'Do I need to call your mum?'

I blinked at her; she lifted her chin defiantly in response, the tiny woman in an apron a thousand times braver than the limp-dicked fool in the bar line. Everything about Anna – from her tiny stature to her delicate features – screamed *fragile*, but her doll-like appearance hid a will of steel.

I narrowed my eyes. 'You wouldn't dare.'

Anna pushed her blonde braid over her shoulder and set her jaw. 'I will. If you'll listen to her, I will.'

I gave a mock pout. 'I'm twenty-eight years old. I don't need you to tell on me.'

Anna leaned forward, getting up in my face. 'Yes, you do, Maeve.' She held my gaze. 'You're not thinking straight.'

'I never think *straight*, Anna.'

She rolled her eyes, completely unimpressed by my obviously hilarious pun. 'You're being rash and impulsive,' she said. 'You're not making considered choices. You're not sleeping, you're not eating. When was the last time you went to a cross training class? To the pool? And Maeve, I say this with all the love in the world, but when was the last time you washed your hair?' She reached out and took my hand. 'Please eat. I'll get you a drink and make you something better than chips to take away. Then *go home*. I'm asking you to take care of yourself.' She paused. 'Actually, I think I might be *begging*.'

'Yes, Anna,' I said meekly.

She made an exasperated sound and threw up her hands. 'That's what you said last time.'

She got me a drink – I was eyeing off the whiskey shelf, but she gave me cranberry juice instead – then disappeared back into the kitchen, throwing a stern *stay there* look over her shoulder. I took a sip of my juice, studied my chips, then a movement caught my eye in the mirror behind the bar.

A woman was staring at my reflection.

I stared back.

She was dressed oddly, but I'd never minded odd. Her torso was wrapped in what looked like a breastplate, but it seemed to be made of *bark*, its seams held together by thick thread somehow made to resemble tiny vines. Beneath the breastplate was a simple, long-sleeved white top – too warm for late summer on the Australian eastern seaboard – and her legs were encased in high-waisted leathers. Around her neck was a beaded chain of polished wood, and the rings on her elegant fingers showed the mottled marks of bark knots.

It wasn't her clothes I stared at, though.

She was beautiful as hell, with waist-length hair that shone silver under the dance floor lights. Her features were sharp, her face made of symmetrical planes and angles, balanced out by small, full lips. Her skin was browner than mine, and her eyes were a deep, warm hazel that flashed forest-green when the lights changed. Between her heart-shaped face with its elven features, her slender curves, and her silver hair, she was a Tolkien fan's every dream come true.

Okay, she was mine, too.

Her lips parted.

Maybe I will go home, after all.

I gave her my best heavy-lidded smile, then leaned back in my chair, my stomach stirring with interest as her gaze didn't shift.

Yes. A night with her was *exactly* what I needed.

I took up a chip and bit into it, making a show of licking the salt from my lips.

I had never been accused of subtlety.

Her eyes didn't leave my face, but she didn't come closer either, so I raised my eyebrows and gave her another smile, this one encouraging. She tugged at the hem of her shirt and wove her way through the bar line.

'Hi,' I said when she reached my side, still watching her in the mirror.

Her lips curved. 'Hullo,' she breathed.

A shiver ran over my skin at the sound of her voice, or perhaps because she stepped closer. She smelled like flowers and rain, and I licked my lips again, this time without thinking. 'Can I buy you a drink?'

Her brow furrowed. 'You wish to provide me with nourishment?'

I laughed. 'Yes?'

Her gaze flickered to my drink. 'There are many different kinds.'

Okay. Definitely odd. 'Would you like the same as me?'

She sucked her bottom lip between her teeth, and I realised she could be the oddest person I'd ever met, and I wouldn't care as long as she did *that* again. 'Yes. That could be wise.'

I got up and offered her my chair, then went behind the bar. She studied the stool for a few moments before climbing up. She was a good deal shorter than I was, another thing I liked.

'Is there a Con on?' I said, pouring her a cranberry juice.

She frowned. 'Con?'

She was *adorable* when she frowned.

'You know, like a Comic Con, or maybe a Renaissance Faire, or ...' I trailed off as she looked blank. 'Nope? Um. Are you from here?'

She shook her head; it was my turn to frown. For a moment, it looked like there were leaves growing through the strands of her hair. I reached over and grabbed another chip; it must have been longer than I'd thought since my last meal.

'I'm from quite far away,' she said, her tone thoughtful. 'I've never seen anything like this before.' She made a graceful gesture with one long-fingered hand, encompassing the bar and the dance floor.

If she'd never seen a bar before, then she certainly *was* from far away. 'Do you have a name?'

She studied me closely. 'Yes,' she said at last. 'But it's been a while since anyone used it. Elswyth.'

'Elswyth,' I echoed. I set her juice down on the bar. 'Lovely to meet you. I'm –'

'*McCarthy Sixty-Nine*,' she said with a tiny nod. 'I know.'

I stared at her, my stomach twisting with sudden wariness. 'I beg your fucking pardon?'

'McCarthy Sixty-Nine,' she repeated, as if I hadn't heard her. She pulled a smartphone – or a small tablet, I couldn't quite tell, only that it was thinner than any phone I'd ever seen and looked fuck-off expensive – from somewhere and turned it to show me one of my own social media accounts. It was one of the embarrassing years-old ones, remaining as a humiliating testament to my years after high school, full of pictures of a drunken me pouting alongside over-filtered shots of food.

My last post on it was recent, a share from one of the media campaigns about Tessa. I'd tagged that account because most of the contacts were people I'd met in Europe on various tours, and I'd figured it couldn't hurt to share the posts about Tessa outside Australia. There'd been a lot of sad reactions and a few comments, but no leads.

Not yet, anyway.

Elswyth waited, her eyes on my face.

I slipped my own phone from my pocket and opened the lock screen, bringing up Rian's number. 'What do you want?' I said roughly.

She frowned. 'From you? I don't think I want anything. But you asked for information about this female, and I may have some.'

'About ...' I trailed off. 'You have information about Tessa?'

'I was scanning some Earth systems and saw this post, so I ran the image of your friend through the peacekeeping security feeds. I didn't expect it to come up with anything, but it did. There was a female on board a DarkStar six-three-zero-four luxury model fitted with significant customisations that left Earth's orbit on the date you specified, just a few hours later than the time you gave. Another Tirian ship passed them on the outer orbital ring and took a standard scan.' She gave a slight smile, as if pleased. 'The database listed the female on board as Darnagh, rather than human, which is why their guards didn't investigate. She was with three others – a starling, a cephalopod, and a cyborg. The starling matched the description of the male your friend left with.'

I stared at her, speechless. I wasn't entirely sure what the emotion churning in my stomach was – rage, perhaps, or grief, but either way it was hot and angry and burning my throat. I grabbed the edge of the bar, half to hold myself up, and half so I wouldn't be tempted to commit assault.

'Enjoy your drink, asshole,' I said calmly, and I made myself turn and walk away, my feet heavy with the knowledge that a complete stranger thought toying with someone trying to find a missing loved one was an acceptable way to use their time.

I wished she hadn't been quite so beautiful.

'Wait!'

I ignored her.

'Please wait!'

I stilled. There was something in the plea that caught at me, making my stomach twist. I spun around, only to find her directly behind me.

'Do you know how fucked up you are?' I hissed. 'You have a serious fucking problem.'

Her brow crumpled, like *I'd* hurt *her* feelings. She stepped back, holding out her fancy screen. On it was an image. Not quite a photo – more like an infrared image mushed with a shot taken by someone with shaking fingers.

For all that, Tessa was still recognisable, with her hourglass curves and her mane of curls. She was hand-in-hand with a man – one with a crew-cut – and they were gesturing to some kind of equipment that looked like a machine at a gym. Another man was by her side, the one from Advena with the dark hair and devouring smile; I could tell by the waving shadow of curls around his face.

And his shoulders. It was pretty hard to forget *those*.

Tessa's body language was relaxed. She wasn't hunched, wasn't tense. And even in the fuzzy image I could tell that she was wearing her favourite stiletto-heeled boots.

I looked up at Elswyth. 'Where the fuck did you get this?'

She blinked. 'I told you. It's a scanning still from a DarkStar six-three-zero-four luxury model a peacekeeping ship passed in outer orbit twenty-nine days ago.'

'Are we speaking the same fucking language?'

She tilted her head; her silver hair rippled with the movement. My fingers itched with the sudden need to touch it, to lace through the soft-looking strands. I pushed the thought away. 'I believe so. It is one of my gifts.' She looked down modestly. '*Elya*, you see. As it is part of me, so too am I part of the universe.'

I pinched the bridge of my nose, just as I'd imagined Rian doing. 'I don't understand anything you're saying. Except that's Tessa, with those two men. This was taken a month ago?' I stared at the screen. 'So where is she now?'

'Two *beings*,' Elswyth corrected. 'Only humans have men and women. The third male – the cephalopod – was out of shot. The ship was headed on a trajectory straight for Natare. It's where my ship is heading, too. There's a Seventh-Quadrant Peace Summit to try to deal with the Roth issue.'

'Your … *ship*. Seventh-something-summit?' I paused. 'Are you in a cult?'

She mouthed the word. 'Cult? No, I'm Tirian.'

'Tirian,' I repeated. 'Okay. Let's brush past that. Are you telling me that you're going where Tessa is?'

'If this is the female you're searching for, then I'm going where I think she *might be*,' Elswyth corrected.

I raised an eyebrow. 'And how can you help me?'

She gave a half-shrug. 'I'll take you. If you'd like, of course. As a Category-3 planet, Earth isn't a signatory of the universal pact, but because we're headed to a cross-Sector Peace Summit, there's a legal loophole. You could claim diplomatic immunity on behalf of a planet with a vested interest in the Summit's outcomes, and my Captain couldn't refuse you passage. I could take you there without breaking any laws, either intergalactic or Tirian.'

'That seems like a lot more words I don't understand, and a lot of trouble for a stranger to go to,' I said.

She gave another slight smile; it quivered, and I had a mad urge to take her in my arms and make whatever she was feeling better. 'The messages you wrote on your posts,' she said. 'They were so lovely. I don't...' She trailed off, her eyes flicking back down to the sticky club floorboards, then up to fix on mine. 'I kept thinking how nice it would be to have someone who cared about me that way. Just for *me*, and so completely. I couldn't get the words out of my head. I couldn't stop thinking about who Tessa might be, who you were, and the relationship between you. So I came here.'

I was a fairly good judge of character; I'd want to be, after working behind a bar for ten years. I had to be able to tell when someone should be cut off; had to be able to tell which group would push through *rowdy* into *violent*; had to be able to spot the creepers so the bouncers would keep an eye on them; had to be able to tell when someone needed a cab called, or saving from a dickhead who wouldn't take no for an answer. For my own part, I had to be able to tell when I could take someone back to my apartment, when it was safe to go to theirs, and I had to know who wouldn't get attached, because I wasn't the sort to settle.

Elswyth was strange; most people wouldn't need my instincts to recognise *that*. But her eyes were clear and her gaze direct; she seemed entirely genuine.

I hadn't written much about Tessa, really, just re-posted the official media releases with a message to Tessa beneath. *Tessa, if you see this, come home. You are loved. You are missed.*

Surely it wasn't enough to warrant this woman's concern; maybe my judgement was off.

Time to test her, then.

I folded my arms. 'Fine. Take me to Tessa.'

Her brows rose in surprise. 'Really?'

'Really,' I repeated, daring her preposterous story to unravel. 'Take me to your ... ship. Take me to your captain.'

I'd expected her to waver; most people did, in my experience, when you called them out directly on their bullshit. Their smile would freeze, their lips would twitch; they'd stammer their next sentence, then try to wriggle their way out of the mess they'd caused like a worm caught on a hook.

A full, beautiful smile spread over Elswyth's face instead, and it was *me* who did a double take, *me* who swallowed nervously as her teeth sank lightly into her full lower lip in a way that sent heat straight between my legs.

Nope, I told myself. *Hard nope. Don't do it, Maeve.*

'Are you ready now?' she said.

I pulled my phone from my pocket and sent Anna a message.

If I don't come back, go to Rian, love ya xx

My finger hovered over the text Rian had sent me.

Take care of yourself, Maeve, he'd written, after I'd unceremoniously hung up on him.

I could be about to do something stupid, I wrote, then a moment later, deleted it.

I appreciate everything you've done, I sent instead, then stuffed the phone back in my pocket.

'I'm ready,' I said.

MAEVE

Elswyth led me out of Advena. Jason – the head bouncer – watched me warily as I strolled out the red doors; I hadn't gone home this early for weeks. Claire was with him, dragging on her vape; she eyed Elswyth and shot me a small, knowing smile.

Yeah, I wish.

I gave her a smile in return, and ignored my phone, which was buzzing in my pocket. I didn't know whether it was Anna or Rian, but either way, I wasn't going to be talked out of this.

The night had cooled. I pulled my leather jacket more tightly around me until I noticed Elswyth shivering. I twisted my lips, fighting against the immediate compulsion to help her. I was – and always had been – a complete sucker for a damsel in distress. I wasn't successful in my struggle; a moment later, I stripped my jacket from my arms and draped it carefully over her shoulders.

She shot me a startled look. 'You would offer me warmth and shelter?'

'Um. I'm giving you my jacket, sure.'

She seemed pleased by that, settling into my jacket and pulling it close about her neck. I forced my gaze away from her, swallowing.

At first, I didn't worry. Elswyth was walking down streets that I knew had security cameras; Advena had paid for their installation and our security company monitored their feeds. I turned towards one, pausing to give it a clear shot of my face.

But after we turned two corners, my skin began to prickle. She was leading me into a black spot.

The club knew it was a problem, but our clientele tended to walk towards the main road, not further into the suburb. We'd petitioned the local council to install their own cameras here, but they'd decided to spend the money closer to the city centre, where there was a long line of clubs and a history of trouble.

I glanced across at Elswyth, wondering if she knew that there was no one watching us here.

She wasn't looking at me; her face was turned to the sky. Her nose was slightly wrinkled, and damned if my lips didn't twitch into a tiny smile. Even if she was in a cult, or perhaps just operating on a different plane of existence, the expression did lovely things to my insides. The starlight suited her; her hair became liquid silver, and I really did need to get more sleep, because I could see the impression of leaves through the silky strands again.

'It's so different,' she said wonderingly. 'I can barely see your stars.'

'It's a city,' I said.

She shot me a questioning frown.

I raised an eyebrow. 'Light pollution?'

She pursed her lips, her frown deepening.

Okay, then. 'There's so much light coming from the city that it brightens the sky and the stars seem muted. When you go into the country you can see the stars clearly.'

'What is *the country*?'

I stared at her, then rubbed my nose. 'Um.'

She grabbed my arm, and a sudden shock ran through me at the contact, my core clenching. I'd never felt anything like it. It wasn't lust, not exactly, though it was difficult to convince my body of that fact. It was warmer and *larger*, as if my limbs had been submerged in something deliciously tingly, something that set my every nerve ending alight.

No, Maeve. Absolutely fucking not.

'There it is,' she said. 'The Pod.'

My eyes followed her finger to a thing that did, indeed, look like a giant seed pod, nestled between two garbage bins on the sidewalk. 'Um,' I said again. 'What the fuck is that?'

'It's a Pod,' she repeated. 'A small craft built for a maximum of two. This one is used for ship-to-surface transport, or short trips from ship to ship.'

'It doesn't look big enough for two people.'

She tugged me towards it. A soft thrum went through the air and the Pod split in two, the top half sliding backwards to reveal a small control panel and two simple, sleek-looking olive-green bench seats. The whole thing looked as if a modernist furniture company had started making spaceships by somehow growing them on massive trees.

'It's not exactly spacious,' Elswyth said apologetically, her fingers tugging nervously on my jacket hem. 'But the trip won't be long, and the peacekeeping ship is ... well, pretty much exactly the opposite of the Pod in every way.'

My heart started to pound in my ears. 'Ohh-kay.'

'You take the back seat,' she said kindly, as if I'd been thinking anything different.

Everything in me was shouting *don't do this, you fool,* but I was stubborn. There was no way this weird thing was getting off the ground; surely her entire ruse would fall apart the moment the Pod failed to fly.

I climbed inside.

My knees pressed against the back of the front chair and I sat slightly hunched until the bench slid back, giving me more room. The chair felt firm, but as I wriggled, it moulded itself to my body.

'Uh,' I said, significantly more comfortable but infinitely more freaked out.

Elswyth climbed in the front and settled in her seat. 'Ready?'

I think I may have made a mistake.

I swallowed. 'Yep.'

She pressed a button on the control panel and the top slid over us soundlessly, trapping me inside. I inhaled deeply, then blew out my breath in a slow, controlled exhale as fear crawled up my spine.

'I should tell you that I'm very new to flying,' Elswyth said, 'but it wasn't too hard on the way down, so surely it can't be *that* much different going back. Don't panic.'

I snorted before I realised she meant it seriously, and not as a reference to one of my favourite novels. 'I didn't bring a towe – *holy shit,*' I squeaked, as *vines grew from the fucking chair* and wound themselves around my chest and shoulders, pinning me in place.

I could see that the same thing was happening around Elswyth, swamping her slender frame in green. Her arms were left free from the elbows, allowing her fingers to race over the control panel, which was covered in glowing lights. A series of low, growling noises filled the Pod; I twitched when Elswyth responded, her soft voice mimicking some of the sounds and adding new ones.

The Pod began to rumble.

Fuck.

'I found it a little unnerving the first time,' Elswyth said over her shoulder. 'Just remember to breathe.'

'I – *motherhugging fuck nugget!*' I shrieked as the Pod shot up in one smooth, too-fast movement, like a ride at an amusement park.

'Breathe,' Elswyth called over her shoulder. 'You're all right ...' She trailed off and paused. 'Is *McCarthy Sixty-Nine* your full name?'

A hysterical giggle tore its way from my throat. 'It's Maeve, actually. My name is Maeve. Maeve McCarthy.'

'Then breathe, Maeve McCarthy.'

She all but sang my name; I liked the way it sounded, so I did as she told me. I'd left my stomach on the ground and I could see the city streets receding beneath us as my fingers dug themselves into my chair. I needed to do something to remind myself I had other body parts, so I concentrated on filling my lungs with oxygen while I was still capable of conscious thought.

Don't pass out. Don't pass out.

This was happening.

Maybe passing out would be okay.

I made a wild grab for rational thought. If we had Pods on Earth, I sure as heck hadn't heard of them. Surely rich people would use them instead of cars – the rate we were rising was terrifyingly fast and there was zero air traffic this far from the airport; you could use one of these to get around the city in minutes.

'Are you breathing, Maeve?'

'Mmph,' I answered, as clouds began to wisp around us.

Time slowed, as it always did when adrenaline flowed through my veins. The world took on a special clarity in those moments – the times when I was afraid, or training, or fucking, or fighting – like I could suddenly see everything in high definition. I could make out the streets as they started to disappear into the cloud, see that the shine of Elswyth's hair wasn't coming from any external light, but rather from her hair itself, as if she was crowned in ropes of the world's tiniest LEDs. I could see that what I'd taken to be thick green thread stitching her bark-like armour together was, in fact, vine-like shoots; one of them was curling over her shoulder and growing a row of rose-like buds, delicate and beautiful, their petals blooming the softest apricot-pink.

I may have said an internal prayer as we rose above the clouds – the words I could remember, anyway.

If I live through this, I'll go to church, I promised whatever god might be listening. *For a visit, anyway. Just to say hello.*

'The pressure will change in a moment,' Elswyth said over the tiny garden on her shoulder. 'The control panel says we have to pick up speed to break atmosphere, and I assume it knows what it's doing. Remember to breathe.'

'Breathing,' I muttered.

I couldn't see the stars any longer. Everything was black, and the black went forever. My body was slowly pressed back into the seat, and I guessed that our trajectory had changed and our speed had increased. The chair seemed to shift, moulding further around my body, creating a sense that I was safe – even when I could see out into motherfucking *space* and I knew that I very much wasn't.

Stupid chair.

'And *out*, Maeve,' Elswyth said, and I realised I was holding my breath. I concentrated on the tiny line of blossoms on her shoulder as their petals continued to slowly unfurl, and I forced myself to breathe normally.

For a few tense minutes, the only sound was the whoosh of my breath and the beat of my heart. I watched the tiny flowers, wishing I could reach out and touch them.

When Elswyth made another low, growling sound, I started in surprise. The rumble of the Pod changed slightly, slowing.

'We'll dock in a minute,' she said, her voice tense. 'I've let the guards know you're coming. There will be a decontamination process before we can board properly, and they might fit you with a translator.'

'You sound worried,' I said warily.

She gave an almost-silent sigh. 'This is the freest I've felt in years,' she said sadly. 'I don't want it to be over.'

I didn't have time to process that comment before I realised what she meant by *dock*, and I saw the ship.

I tried to swear, but I couldn't find the words.

There was one main ring, made of a sleek, flawless silver. There was a second ring beneath it, around half the size, positioned towards what I imagined was the front of the ship, if something round could have a *front*. Linking them was a square, box-like protrusion; it seemed as if we were heading there.

But inside the main ring was a dome of glass, or some other clear material, and inside that was *green*. As in, *organic* green. Trees and plants and a slash of blue that looked like a stream full of running water, with one huge, sprawling central tree overlooking the rest like a protective mother.

'What the ever-loving *fuck*,' I hissed.

Elswyth said nothing; her shoulders tightened.

You've finally done it, Maeve; you're finally in over your head.

A series of growls rolled through the Pod once more, and silver swallowed the black as we flew into what I assumed was the larger ship's dock. The Pod's quiet rumble changed to a whir; there was a soft bump as we landed, followed by a whine as the Pod gently lurched to the side and was repositioned in a series of small, smooth movements.

Silence.

Elswyth took her own advice and dragged in a long, ragged breath.

The Pod roof slid back, and I blinked at the sudden light. Elswyth's blossoms closed their tiny petals and budded tight as the vines around me loosened and my seat shifted. I moved my arms and rolled my shoulders.

And found something brown and knotted like an ancient branch – something that was unfamiliar and yet somehow unmistakably a fucking *gun* – pointed straight at my face.

Elswyth began speaking – well, growling – softly, her hands held out in a universal gesture of *calm the fuck down*. She stepped gracefully from the Pod, growling all the while. I followed her out – significantly less smoothly – and found myself face-to-chiselled-chest with the wielder of said branch-gun.

I tipped my chin up to see a pair of beautiful brown eyes glowering down at me, lit from within by anger and worry.

For the second time that night, a jolt of *something* ran through my body, as if I was a wire and I'd suddenly become live.

He might not have been human, but he was very definitely *male*, with a square jaw, shoulders so wide they were a threat to doorways, and a pair of pecs that gave my rack a run for its money. His mahogany hair was pulled back in a half-braid, long enough for the remainder to brush his shoulders, and his breastplate and leathers matched Elswyth's. The delicious sharpness of his high cheekbones was emphasised by an arrangement of small, sharp-looking triangular plates that I assumed were some kind of cosmetic enhancement and made him look all kinds of badass; my fingertips tingled with a sudden desire to trace those tiny plates just to see how sharp they were.

His jaw tightened; he moved closer, his eyes never leaving mine. Fear and arousal flared together in my stomach. It was a pairing I wasn't normally into, but judging by the clenching of my core, my body did not care for what was *normal* and had zero consideration for the insanity of its current situation.

Elswyth gave a louder growl, the sound shot through with frustration. 'Are human males so thick-headed?' she muttered to me.

'Yes,' I answered, not taking my eyes off him. 'Is he going to take that gun away?'

'Oh, by the green gods – *Ashton*,' Elswyth scolded, then fell back into a series of growling sounds that he returned. After a moment, he shoved the gun reluctantly back into a holster at his hip.

'I'm trying to tell him you need a translator,' Elswyth went on. 'He's telling me that I can't bring strange aliens aboard the ship.'

'That does seem like a sensible rule,' I said. 'Could you maybe tell him that I don't mean any harm?'

Elswyth shot me a look that said *what do you think I've been doing*, then resumed her growling at a slightly more aggressive pitch. The male – *Ashton* – stepped back, away from me, and I felt a pang of regret before I shook myself out of it.

I used the moment of space to look around. We were in a huge hangar, filled with craft. Some were the tiny Pods, positioned around the walls on small platforms. The craft taking up most space in the hangar were larger; I bit my lip so I didn't laugh. There were two kinds, and one was shiny silver and half-spherical – just like the UFOs from b-grade eighties films.

The hangar wasn't empty: there were twenty or so people – not people, not humans, but *Tirians* – working, some with screens in their hands, others with tools. They were clearly fixing or checking the different types of craft, though most of them had stopped to watch the scene between Elswyth and Ashton.

They were watching me, too, though with less surprise than I'd expected. Perhaps they'd seen humans before.

'Finally,' Elswyth muttered, and I turned back to her in time to see another male approaching.

I really need to get laid, I thought, as my body perked up again.

This male was shorter than the gun-wielder and more slender, though he was still half a head taller than me. Instead of the breastplate, he wore a sleeveless tunic of forest-green over his leathers; his arms were so perfect they deserved their own wing in an art gallery, all undulating muscle that slid beneath his skin when he moved. Unlike Elswyth and Ashton, his skin was pale; his hair fell in loose waves around his face, a shining dark blonde under the hangar lights, curtaining his moss-green eyes.

Elswyth took my hand; a bolt of feeling – and heat – raced through me again.

Get a fucking grip, Maeve.

'This is the ship's Head Doctor, Willow,' Elswyth said. 'He's going to insert a translator so you know what's going on.'

I eyed the doctor warily; he stared back at me, expressionless. 'What does inserting a translator entail?'

Elswyth gave a soft growl, which the doctor answered. 'He said it will mesh with your eardrum,' she explained when he'd paused, 'and amend the sound waves you hear into something you can understand. The translators on the ship haven't been updated to include Earth languages yet, which is why they can't understand you. But once the translator is in, it won't matter – you'll be able to understand our language.' She cocked her head as the doctor kept growling. 'He said that the insertion will hurt. He doesn't think he can give you a painkiller, as he's not familiar enough with human biochemistry. He also said that you will experience a slight delay in the translation for a few days, until the device has properly meshed with your system. After that, it's almost instantaneous.'

'Can it be removed?'

She conferred with the doctor, then nodded. 'Yes. He said he'd like you to be unconscious for *that*, though; taking them out is trickier than putting them in.'

That didn't sound amazing, but I didn't know what else to do. If Elswyth was the only one I could communicate with, it would severely limit my ability to find any other information that might help me find Tessa. I wouldn't usually put anything into my body I wasn't sure of, but this wasn't exactly a situation that allowed me to be picky.

'Okay,' I whispered, my stomach churning.

Elswyth raised my hand and cupped it between hers. Her skin was cool – cooler than mine – but my body warmed instantly at the gesture, then grew hotter as she pressed my fingers to her cheek in a gesture that was unexpectedly tender. 'I won't let them hurt you, Maeve McCarthy.'

The doctor and Ashton watched. Willow's face stayed expressionless, but the big male glowered before glancing away.

I gathered my courage. 'Do I need to sit down?'

'No, you –'

The doctor stepped forward and shoved something in my ear.

It burned like seven bloody hells and I gave a pathetic-sounding yelp before my instincts kicked in and I spun, slamming my palm straight into the doctor's unprotected throat. He reeled back a few steps, his eyes going wide and his blank expression giving way to one of shock. Ashton slid forward a bare moment later, and with a swift, unnerving grace, spun me around and locked me against him, his arm around my neck, all before I could stammer out an apology.

Unfortunately for Ashton, I didn't like that very much. I wrenched my body around to face him, jabbed him once in the stomach and once in the crotch with my fist, then shoved him backwards, pulling free from his hold. He didn't fall, but he did stagger, so I followed up with a punch to the jaw that sent a shockwave of pain through my hand and arm.

His eyes lit with challenge, the rich brown burning gold, and I realised that he didn't have a pupil. I had a moment to process *that* little discovery – and to realise that Elswyth and Willow didn't have pupils, either, and my mind had just filled in the omission so I could cope with the weirdness of my current situation – before my head throbbed like a bastard and I yelped again, bending double and clutching at one ear as the doctor stepped forward and jabbed something into the other.

I went down like a sack of rocks, crumpling in a heap. Elswyth fell to her knees and wrapped her arms around me, holding me up as fire laced through my brain. It was worse than an ear infection, worse than a migraine, and I shut my eyes and let Elswyth hold me as I whimpered. The pain came in rolling waves, one after the other, each washing from my ear into my head and down my neck.

Maybe this wasn't a great idea.

'It's all right. You're all right.'

The soothing voice was steady and deep, and it took me a few long moments to realise that it wasn't Elswyth. I wrenched my eyes open to see the doctor crouching near us, close enough to touch, but he didn't reach out.

He gave me an endearingly crooked smile. 'There we go,' he murmured. 'You'll have a headache for a day or so, I'm afraid, but the sharp pain should fade.'

His mouth made a series of movements that didn't look anything like the words I'd just heard, and my mouth dropped open in shock. 'It's working,' I blurted out.

'Indeed.' He graced me with another smile, his teeth white and even, and my stomach performed a series of small flips. His eyes flickered upward; I stared at them openly, still coming to terms with their missing pupil. 'The Captain is on her way. Would you prefer to stand?'

That sounded serious, so I shifted to stand upright, swaying a little when I got there. Elswyth came with me, leaving her arm around my waist. I didn't know whether it was for support or another reason entirely, but I didn't care; it felt nice, and she could leave it there as long as she wanted, as far as I was concerned. I glanced down at her; her expression was tight, and she shook her hair around her face as if to hide behind it. Ashton stepped up to stand at her other side, his hands held loosely at his sides, his jaw darkening from my punch in a spread of deep green.

I blinked.

No pupil. Green blood?

'Elswyth!'

A voice rang across the hangar; every Tirian worker who hadn't already been watching our drama straightened at the sound of it and stopped what they were doing.

Elswyth took an audible breath then forced her shoulders straight, lifting her chin and fixing her eyes on the female storming towards us.

She was lovely, with jet black hair and eyes of a deep forest green. Like Ashton, she wore the tiny triangular plates over her cheekbones, but she also had a ridge of them over each eyebrow and along the line of her jaw. When her hair shifted with her movement, I saw that the shell of her ears was lined, too, making them pointed at the top.

When she rubbed her jaw in irritation, I realised something else.

They weren't piercings, or decorations, or anything cosmetic, as I'd thought. When I glanced across at Ashton's cheekbones, and then down at Elswyth's ears, visible through the curtain of her hair and *pointed*, I realised that the tiny plates moved when their skin moved, shifting with expressions and as they spoke.

They were *thorns*. Not plates. *Thorns.*

What. The. Fuck.

'What do you think you were doing?' the black-haired female shouted at Elswyth. 'And where did you learn to dismantle the Pod's tracker? We didn't know where you *were*, didn't know if you were *safe*, didn't know –'

'I'm back now,' Elswyth interjected.

'The Forest has already started to wilt, Elswyth.'

Elswyth winced. 'I'm not a prisoner,' she said hotly. 'And I'm not one of your crew. I left –'

'You left without notice and returned with an unauthorised alien,' the Captain snapped. 'And no, you're not a prisoner, *Lady*, but you're on *my* ship and under *my* protection. Did you tell the Forest you were going? Did you tell the *bees*? No one's been able to get in there for –'

'Hi,' I interrupted, using my brightest voice, which also happened to be noticeably fake. 'I'm Maeve.'

The Captain's eyes flicked to me, then she turned her glare to Willow. '*You gave the alien a translator?*'

It was Willow's turn to wince. 'I –'

'I asked him to,' Elswyth said fiercely. 'This isn't anything to do with Willow.'

The Captain raised her eyes to the roof. 'Green gods grant me patience,' she muttered. 'Daughter –'

'So now I'm *daughter*, because it's too much trouble to argue with the Hamadryad?' Elswyth demanded. 'Fine, *mother*. Listen to me. Yes, I did the wrong thing. I made an unauthorised trip to a Category-3 planet, and I disabled the Pod's tracker to do so. But *a human was taken*, Captain. From Earth.'

The Captain's – Elswyth's *mother's* – eyes flickered to me. Now that I knew to look, there *were* similarities between them: the changeable forest-green of their eyes, the sharp planes of their face.

'Not *this* one,' Elswyth added hurriedly. 'She agreed to come.'

'She did, did she?' the Captain muttered. She studied me for a moment, then snapped: 'Well? What have you got to say?'

I bit my lip to hide a smile. I liked her. 'My friend Tessa has gone missing. She was last seen about a month ago at the bar I work at, in the company of a man with black hair. Elswyth showed me a photo –'

'A still,' Elswyth interjected.

'– of my friend on a ship with some, um, *aliens*, apparently. And it seems their ship is on course for the place you're headed, um –'

'Natare,' Elswyth supplied.

'– yep, *Natare*, for a … a *peace summit*.' I straightened my shoulders, ignoring my throbbing head. 'I claim political asylum in order to attend the summit.'

'*Diplomatic immunity*,' Elswyth said hurriedly. 'She claims *diplomatic immunity* in order to attend the cross-Sector Peace Summit, as a member of a species with a vested interest in the Summit's outcome.'

The Captain snorted. 'Does she now,' she said dryly. 'And exactly *how*, Elswyth, did a being from a Category-3 planet *learn* about the cross-Sector Peace Summit in the first place?'

Elswyth swallowed.

'I thought so.' The Captain studied me for a moment, tapping her fingers against her thigh. She wore the same outfit as Elswyth and Ashton, as did most of the Tirians in the hangar; I wondered if it was a uniform. 'You said your friend was in the company of … aliens. Which species?'

'A starling, a cyborg, and a cephalopod,' Elswyth answered at once. 'The starling was presenting as humanoid and male; I believe the cephalopod was Enterocti.'

The Captain blinked. 'Isn't it the Enterocti Prince who has a starling consort?'

'That's correct,' Ashton said gruffly. I jumped at the sound of his voice; it was low, with a pleasant husky grate that sent a shiver over my skin.

The Captain pursed her lips. 'Then this is far above my clearance level.' Her eyes fell to Elswyth's arm, still secure around my waist. 'No.'

'*No*?' Elswyth echoed incredulously.

'I am concerned about the human female and will report it to the Admiral immediately. I am also interested in the presence of a cyborg on that ship; they do not often leave their planet, and it's possible they left unwillingly. The Tirian Grove will take appropriate action – or not – depending on the information they gather.' She tilted her head, looking unnervingly like Elswyth when she did. 'The human will be returned to Earth immediately, and you, daughter, will return to the Forest before you endanger the entire ship and the thousands of souls aboard it.'

Fuck. Disappointment churned in my stomach. This was my only lead to Tessa. What if the Tirian Grove – whatever the fuck *that* was – decided not to do anything?

Is this how I lose Tessa forever?

Elswyth exhaled slowly, then turned to me. 'I didn't want to do this,' she said apologetically, lowering her voice until I could barely hear her. 'Please believe that. But you want to find your friend, don't you?'

'Yes,' I answered immediately.

She squeezed my waist. 'Well, then. Play along.' She turned back to her mother. 'Maeve can't go back to Earth, Captain,' she said. 'She offered me food and drink, then covered me in the warmth of her body.'

I frowned at the odd choice of words.

The Captain blinked. 'I ...' She trailed off, her eyes widening.

Ashton turned; his face rippled with an expression of shock, then, so brief I might have imagined it, *hurt*, before it settled back into a scowl.

'You're *bonded*?'

ELSWYTH

THE HUMAN FEMALE WENT rigid beside me.

It was a different word in her language – *married* – but I didn't have time to ponder the difference. 'Yes,' I said with a calm I did not feel. 'I am her bonded.'

'Elswyth,' my mother said desperately, 'those customs are outdated. They came from a time when we fought over the Hamadryad, when they were stolen and imprisoned and forced into bondships. They are no longer our way, no longer recognised by the Grove's laws. You don't have to –'

I looked her straight in the eye. 'I *want to*, Captain. And you want your Hamadryad happy, do you not?'

My mother's nostrils flared. It was a rhetorical question. An unhappy Hamadryad meant an unhappy Forest, which meant a *sick* Forest, a possibly *dying* Forest – which meant a dying *ship*.

The Forests were the heart of my home planet, Tir – large, tree-filled territories inhabited by Tirian families who formed allegiances within the boundaries of their land. When my kind began building ships and travelling larger distances through space, we'd realised swiftly that the Forests were more important than we'd thought; without them, we succumbed quickly to illness and space madness – and worse.

So my kind had found a way to take their Forests *with* them.

It had failed, at first. For hundreds of years, it failed over and over again, the Forests on board the ships wilting and dying during cross-Sector travel, the Tirian sailors following not long after. Eventually, some clever soul thought: *the Hamadryad. The spirits of the Forests. Put them on board and see what happens.*

It was a success, of course, because the Hamadryad were linked to their Forests in an inextricable and fundamental way, by *elya* and biology and something even more mysterious again. They couldn't help but keep their Forest alive, and, in turn, the Forest did its best to make its Hamadryad happy. The result was a fleet of huge ships that were essentially small cities moving at speed through space, all built around a central Forest and its resident Hamadryad.

The Hamadryad also experienced an unintended benefit: we went from being – as my mother had eloquently put it, skirting over what it truly meant – *stolen and imprisoned and forced into bondships* by Tirians who wanted control of a Forest and its territory and resources, to being *free*. Well, relatively speaking. Suddenly, we *couldn't* be forced into a bond, because our anguish threatened the on-board Forest with death. We *couldn't* be imprisoned, because that made us unhappy, which in turn made the Forest wilt. We *couldn't* be forced into families, forced into bed, forced to breed in the hope we would birth another Hamadryad daughter, because if we were, we would let the on-board Forest die – along with all other souls on board our ship.

It had given us power, while simultaneously keeping us chained, only now we were chained to *ships* instead of power-hungry partners. I, for one, was grateful for it; while I might still be bound to a captain's whim, at least I got to see the universe. *And* my captain was my mother, so I was, at least, familiar with my tyrant.

My mother was not a Hamadryad. There were none in our line, as far back as anyone could remember. I was the rarest of the rare, not just a Hamadryad, but one sent by the green gods – or so the Priestesses told us. I didn't *feel* very godly, especially not with the beautiful human on one side of me, my hand tight on her waist, and Ashton on the other. My skin felt too tight, my core was hot, and I kept tripping over my own tongue.

I felt very organic, indeed.

'Elswyth,' my mother said softly. 'This is not what I wanted for you.'

My mother hadn't wanted me on board the ship, either. She wanted me safe at home on Tir, growing a large and lush Forest and becoming just as large and lush myself. She wanted my heartree to grow deep roots and long branches, and for suitors to fight for the privilege of my notice.

I lifted my chin. I'd promised to help Maeve, so I would, and this was how I *could*. I'd never asked for anything before, and I decided that it was time I did; I was *not* going to back down. 'This is what *I* want, Captain.'

She ground her teeth in frustration, but she couldn't refuse, and she knew it – not in front of the engineers and guards, and not when I'd made my wishes – and threat – clear. I'd outplayed her.

Unfortunately, this was my *mother*, the youngest captain in the entire Tirian fleet, and she always had a trick or seven up her branches.

'Fine,' she snapped. She turned and gestured to an engineer, who had been watching the entire thing unfold with wide eyes, her fingers flicking over her personal screen, no doubt relaying every moment to her parents and friends. The news would already have spread through the ship like fire-moss: there were no secrets in a place like this. 'Go and ready a family room for the Hamadryad and the human. They are newly bonded and will need privacy.'

Despite the task not being even remotely close to the engineer's job description, she gave a low bow and fled to obey my mother's instruction.

'If you want a bondship, Lady,' my mother said, studying me, daring me to say otherwise, 'then a bondship you shall have.'

I kept my face blank, but Maeve didn't; her dismay was obvious. Something like hurt twisted in my stomach. Surely I wasn't *that* repulsive. But then again, I knew almost nothing about humans; perhaps I wasn't the kind of being she would have considered.

It's not real, I reminded myself. *She's not really your bonded.*

'You will visit the Forest – and the bees – on your way to your new room,' my mother went on, her tone brooking no argument.

'Captain,' Willow said in his deep, soft voice. 'We should follow the decontamination procedure.'

My mother inclined her head, her frustration with Willow overshadowed by her need to keep her ship safe. 'As you say, Doctor. And Ashton,' she said, turning to the First Guard, who paled, 'we should discuss how this could *possibly* have happened.'

I bit my bottom lip, guilt churning through me; I hoped my mother's fury wouldn't be too bad. There wasn't supposed to be a thing I did without Ashton's knowledge, but he'd been with me so long I knew exactly how to bend his boughs; all I'd had to do was say I was feeling poorly and ask for some berry tea to settle my stomach. He'd left at once to make it for me, and I'd slipped away, making for the hangar. The hardest part of my temporary escape was dismantling the Pod tracker so no one could follow me, but I'd followed a step-by-step cast on my screen from the on-board library, and it was done.

I tried to hold onto the heady sense of freedom I'd felt as I'd piloted the Pod down to Maeve's planet. I didn't think I'd feel it again in my lifetime – not if my mother had anything to do with it, anyway.

'Lady,' Willow said respectfully, inclining his head to me. 'Will you join us? Or will you wait for your bonded outside?'

I glanced at Maeve, who was looking at anything but me. 'Maeve? What do you wish?'

She swallowed audibly. 'I'd prefer it if you came with me.'

I tried not to be too pleased. We followed Willow through the hangar; I glanced across at Maeve, but she was determinedly looking straight ahead, ignoring the stares of the engineers and the cleaning rotation. I all but bared my teeth when one engineer flashed Maeve a flirtatious smile; it was not unusual for Tirians to bond outside our kind, and Maeve's humanoid form was close enough to our own that a being would have to look hard to notice the difference. It wasn't just the similarity, though; Maeve was objectively lovely, with shining chestnut hair pulled back from her oval-shaped face, striking blue eyes made arresting by dark cosmetic on her lids and lashes, and wide, full lips that softened the fierceness of her expression – when they weren't twisted into a savage scowl, anyway. She was beautiful, and I could hardly fault the others for staring.

But that didn't mean I was willing to share her. The human was *my* adventure, the one thing I'd done for myself in my twenty-six years. The others could keep their roots in their own soil – unless Maeve decided otherwise.

Willow's clinic was to one side of the hangar. It had to be close to the dock, because he managed the decontamination for all souls boarding the ship – whether they were crew or prisoners or visiting dignitaries – but the hangar was also the place where most physical injuries occurred, so it made sense for the ship's doctor to stay close by.

The clinic door slid open, and I followed Willow inside. Maeve hung back slightly, chewing her bottom lip.

'Will this hurt?' she said gruffly. 'My head is still killing me.'

My hearts constricted at the sight of her wariness. 'It won't hurt at all. The spores work swiftly. You will need to hold your breath for half a minute. Will that be an issue?'

'I don't think so?' Maeve answered. 'Depending on how long your minutes are.'

'Less than one of yours,' Willow said, his brow creasing slightly. 'Possibly. You have many units of measurement, and I didn't have a lot of time to research; there's always a chance I've confused them.'

'Comforting,' Maeve muttered.

Willow gestured to a small, partitioned room. 'You'll need to undress. Your traditional garments will be returned to you once they've been decontaminated and some testing samples taken.'

Maeve looked down at the odd clothing she was wearing, a short-sleeved black shirt and some kind of skin-tight pants. There must have been another layer of clothing beneath her shirt, one so thin I couldn't see the seams, for her toned arms were covered in drawings – mostly of flowers. 'My trad ... Oh. No, really, you can keep the shirt, as long as I get my boots and jeans back. I don't really like this band anymore.'

Willow inclined his head and moved to his monitoring station, though he couldn't have understood that comment any more than I did.

I carefully pulled off the outer garment Maeve had offered me, then gave the vines of my armour a gentle stroke until they began to unlace themselves. I blinked in surprise at the cluster of arcadia blossoms on my shoulder; I hadn't noticed them bloom, but arcadia always had a mind of their own. I pulled the vine out gently. Willow would need to test them, too, but he'd be careful and if there were no problems, I could replant them in the Forest later, somewhere close to my heartree so I could see them. Once all the vines had unwound, my breastplate slid to the ground. I bent to gather it up, and placed it against the wall, nestling the arcadia blossoms on top, making a soft trill sound to comfort them as they budded tight in protest.

I looked up to see Maeve staring at me, her lips parted and her cheeks flushed.

'Are you all right?'

She shook herself. 'Fine. It's just ... My clothes don't sew themselves.'

'Oh,' I said, and frowned. 'Do you need some help undressing?'

'Nope,' she answered hastily. 'I'm good.'

She pulled her shirt over her head, and it was my turn to stare.

She loosened her rich chestnut hair until it spilled down her back in soft waves. The hair colours I'd seen on humans in the bar had varied wildly, from white to purple to brown to black, but I liked Maeve's best of all; it reminded me of the dappled light in the undergrowth of the Forest. The loose waves meant it rippled as she moved; my fingers twitched with the need to touch it, but I kept my hands by my sides.

Even more extraordinary than Maeve's beautiful hair was the realisation that the drawings I'd taken for another layer of garment were on her *skin*. She was wearing some kind of black strap around her breasts, but the rest of her torso, along with her arms and shoulders, were covered in stylised floral designs. Some were black, and some had colour; some were vibrant, and others were comfortably faded. I could have spent hours studying them, following the curving lines of vines and leaves and petals across her body.

I felt green blossom across my cheeks. I'd seen plenty of naked Tirians – sometimes they forgot that the Forest was more than just trees and used it for trysts with their bonded – but I'd never seen one that looked like that. And by *that* I meant all slender muscle and hard curves, so wholly delicious that my hearts beat out of time.

Don't stare, Elswyth.

I turned away to hide my face, then coaxed the vines in my boots to unravel, smiling when they tried to wind them-selves around my wrists instead. I settled them next to the arcadias and stripped off my leathers and undergarments.

Maeve coughed. I turned back, concerned, and forgot my no staring rule immediately. She'd removed her boots and pants and her breast binding, and my breath caught in my throat. Her breasts were small and tipped with pink, her thighs all graceful lines of muscle.

The air went taut between us as we stared – Maeve at me, and me at Maeve.

'You don't have a belly button,' she blurted, one hand on her stomach.

'You don't have thorns,' I answered, stroking the line of sharp points decorating my collarbone and ears.

She gave a bark of laughter. 'Fair enough.'

There was a rustle of movement behind me. 'You'll need to remove everything, I'm afraid,' Willow said apologetically, his voice rather thicker than usual.

I eyed him sideways. The doctor wasn't part of a family, but it wasn't from a lack of others trying; I knew he'd turned down several potential bonds. The gossips on the ship loved to discuss him, mostly because he was impeccably courteous and perpetually self-controlled; no one had ever seen him angry, ever seen him distressed, ever seen him green-cheeked over another Tirian. No matter how hard they'd tried to uncover something salacious, the gossips were forced to concede that Doctor Willow Unclaimed was just as he seemed – respectful and measured to a super-Tirian degree.

But his eyes were heavy as he took in the patterns on Maeve's skin, and I wondered whether there *was* a being who could break his famous self-control.

'Ink,' Willow said wonderingly, studying his hand-scanner. 'Your skin allows its absorption?'

'You pierce the skin with tiny needles and deposit the ink beneath it.' Maeve frowned. 'You don't have tattoos?'

Willow shook his head. 'We have too much arboreal DNA. Our skin knits immediately after any injury, leaving no trace of scarring. Our bodies would reject the ink and push it straight back out.' He glanced at the lilies growing up her side almost wistfully. 'They are lovely.'

'Lovely,' I echoed, my eyes on a bloom very like an arcadia covering her hip, some of its petals disappearing under the black material circling her waist.

She snorted, and, without ceremony, pulled down the flimsy garment. Willow coughed, turning away; I swallowed and pressed my thighs together.

'Choose a unit,' Willow said, busying himself at the control screen. I gestured to a unit, waiting until Maeve entered and the door slid shut before escaping into one myself, trying to will my arousal away.

Not yours. She's not yours.

Willow's voice came over the intercom. 'The sequence will begin in ten seconds. Take a deep breath and hold it ... *Now.*'

I closed my eyes and held my breath as the light microbial mist swirled around me, dancing over my skin in swift, ticklish eddies. I held my arms out and reluctantly spread my ankles, knowing that Willow would be able to detect my arousal in the monitoring tests, but not knowing what else to do.

'And three ... two ... one. Done,' Willow said. 'Breathe easy.'

I took a gulp of air and opened my eyes again.

The unit door slid aside, and Willow handed me a pile of regulation casuals in my size. Our eyes met; I lifted my chin, trying not to flush.

He gazed back calmly, then inclined his head. 'Congratulations, Hamadryad,' he said softly. 'May your love grow as wide and deep as the Forest.'

'Thank you, Doctor,' I answered, guilt twisting in my stomach once more. *Not yours. She's not yours.*

Maeve was glowing after the spore bath, her chestnut hair shining, the dark cosmetic around her eyes gone, her skin lit from within. Mine was the same, but it was lit with the green of our sap-like blood, not Maeve's pink.

She stared at me. 'That's some decontamination,' she muttered. She turned to Willow. 'I want my boots.'

'They'll take a little longer to go through the decontamination process,' Willow said evenly, 'but you will get them back, I promise.' His moss-green eyes flickered to me. 'I imagine Ashton may be some time. Will you allow me to escort you to your new room, Hamadryad?'

'Okay, someone really has to tell me what that means,' Maeve said. 'It sounds familiar, but I can't quite remember ...' She shook her head in frustration, then winced. 'Urgh. I hate this. My brain feels like it's made of cotton wool. Cotton wool that's been set on fire and poked with something sharp.'

'Tir – our home planet – is largely covered in plant life,' I said softly. 'It's divided into territories, which we call Forests. Every Forest has a heartree – the mother tree, the oldest tree in a territory, with the deepest roots and widest branches. The Forest grows around it, and it protects the saplings in a thousand different ways as they grow, helping to direct water and balance soil and deterring pests and predators. All the other trees take their cues from the heartree. A strong heartree means a strong Forest.'

'And where does the Hamadryad – do *you* – come into that?' Maeve said warily.

'Well ...' I trailed off and looked across at Willow, who gazed steadily back, keeping pace with me as I stepped from the clinic and into one of the ship's labyrinthine corridors. 'I *am* the heartree. Sort of.'

'You're a *tree*?'

I waved a hand. 'I'm its spirit. Its consciousness, outside its usual arboreal awareness. I am linked to it in such a way that I both *am* and am *not*, in that I can both exist as part of it, and apart *from* it. Do you follow?'

'Not even a bit,' Maeve muttered.

I reached out and tentatively patted her arm. 'Not to worry. Most beings don't. Just imagine ... If you were split in two, and became two distinct halves, with distinct forms and distinct needs, but you could reform at will and become one again ... That's almost what it's like.'

Maeve glanced sideways at me. 'Does that mean you were born a tree?'

'Green gods, no. I was born a twiglet like everyone else. But when I was older, I wandered away from my fathers, straight into a budding Forest, and found a sapling that sang to me. When I touched it, I *became* it.' I gave a half-shrug. 'That's when they knew I wasn't entirely Tirian.'

'What happens to your body when you ... *become*?'

I caught a lock of silver hair and twined it between my fingers. It had been dark brown when I was born, according to my mother; it had turned silver the first time I'd lost my Tirian form. 'We are all made of *elya*, but I am made of more than most. My *elya* goes into my tree, and reforms when I wish to walk on Tirian legs.'

Maeve appeared to think this through. 'I never thought I'd meet a tree, but then I never thought I'd have a *wife*, either. One's not really that much stranger than the other.' She studied my profile; I flushed under her gaze, keeping my eyes on the end of the corridor. 'Can I see it? Your tree?'

I turned to blink at her. 'You want to see my heartree?'

A tiny line appeared between her brows. 'Yes?' she answered, like a question, almost as if she was asking herself.

Willow and I exchanged a glance over her head. *She needs to sleep*, he mouthed.

'I'll take you tomorrow,' I said. 'I'm tired, and my mother will be ... unhappy ... if I push her any further tonight.'

'Your mum's hardcore.'

I had no idea what that meant, though I could probably guess. 'She is used to being in charge,' I said in agreement.

Willow's wrist screen gave a tiny click. 'Section five, room seven,' he said, his eyes widening slightly.

'Thank the green gods,' I said, meaning it.

Maeve frowned at me.

'It's the section of the ship the biologists and bioengineers and botanists live in,' I explained. 'It's closest to the Forest.'

'Your room opens *into* the Forest, in fact,' Willow said, bringing up a blueprint on his hand screen.

I made a happy *humming* noise. We could leave the room open, and I wouldn't feel like I did everywhere else – like there was a wall between me and the Forest, like I had to listen hard to hear it sing, had to concentrate to feel its whispers. I'd have the beautiful human, and the Forest close enough to touch.

I tensed. *Not yours*, I reminded myself. *She's not yours.*

'This way,' Willow said, and gestured down a hallway.

I had a room of my own, but I didn't use it very often, preferring to spend most of my time in the Forest. I could make clothes with *elya*, and I washed in the stream by my heartree whenever the fancy took me. When it came to organic comforts, I really didn't need much. Food, sometimes. Water, on the odd occasion. I could go without air for far longer than most beings, if needed. We – the Hamadryad – kept those facts secret, though. We were already different enough.

'This one,' Willow said, stopping outside a nondescript door.

I stepped forward and breathed onto the sensor. The door beeped and slid open.

'After you,' I said to Maeve. The room would be used mostly by her, so it made sense for her to see it first, to explore, to rearrange things if they didn't suit.

She gave me a wary glance and stalked into the room.

I followed her, watching as she looked around. The engineer had given me special treatment – that, or this was simply the only family room left close to the Forest. It had one main room, with a sunken bed large enough for six taking pride of place, and two additional bedrooms off the side, separated by a main bathroom. It was one of the best rooms on the ship, spacious – relatively, at least – and equipped with every luxury: an ice maker, a meal generator, a bathroom with water pipes in place of a spore shower.

But best of all – better than all of that – was the internal wall, which was not a *wall* at all, but rather glass, looking right into the heart of the Forest. A small door would give us direct access; I sighed happily as I spied my heartree through the green.

'Fucking hell,' Maeve muttered. 'I thought it would be a bunk and a sink.'

'On most ships, it would be,' Willow said. He was standing in the doorway; it would be the height of rudeness to enter a family room without invitation, so he hovered on the threshold. 'But peacekeeping vessels are built in space and never break orbit, so it doesn't matter how large or luxurious they are, as long as something can get them moving – and keep them that way.'

'You use the Pods to move between places,' Maeve said, her eyes widening with understanding. 'So this is what – like a space station?'

I didn't know what that was, but Willow nodded. 'Exactly,' he said, sounding pleased. 'Only for travel.'

'It doesn't seem like much of a battleship, though.' Maeve touched the glass wall wonderingly, then jumped back when it opaqued, blocking the view and most of the light.

'That's because it isn't,' I said, waving my hand near the glass so it went transparent once more. 'The aim of a peacekeeping vessel is to *avoid* conflict, provide a neutral place where warring parties may come aboard for negotiation. Our captains might be commanders, but my mother trained in negotiation for as long as she did military strategy. If we see conflict, it's the armed Pods and the gunships that fly into battle.' Maeve leaned on the glass, looking rather pale. 'You're safe on board,' I added, frowning.

'I just –' she said, and stumbled. 'I just –'

The whites of her eyes flashed as she crumpled to the floor.

'Oh, green gods,' I gasped, rushing to her side. 'Willow! We broke the human!'

WILLOW

WHEN I COULDN'T FIND the pulse along the sides of Maeve's spines, I realised that I was out of my depth.

She moaned softly; relief coursed through me at the sound. If she was in pain, she was alive. I manoeuvred her gently onto her back, brushing her hair from her face and ignoring the thrill running over my skin at every tiny touch. 'Apparently, the human body is mostly water,' I said to the Hamadryad. 'Perhaps that is what she needs. Would you get some, Lady?'

Elswyth wrinkled her nose at her title, but rushed to the ice machine for a cup as I unstrapped my emergency kit from my thigh and found my hand scanner and my screen. We were still close enough to Earth to easily access its systems, and I'd managed to find quite a lot of medical knowledge in the swift search I'd done. Against Tirian parameters, Maeve needed nourishment; as I took a tiny sample of blood – my eyebrows rising when I saw it was *red*, not green – and compared it to ideal human levels, it seemed that her *blood sugar* was low, amounting to the same thing.

I looked up at Elswyth. 'What do humans eat?'

She stared at me, the cup tipping dangerously. 'Oh, green gods,' she muttered. 'I've made a mess of this, haven't I? I don't even know how to feed her.' She inhaled, closing her eyes. 'Maeve offered me food when I found her. She didn't say what it was, but it smelled like white tubers when they're fried in berry-nut oil.'

'Right.' I nodded at the food generator. 'We'll start there. Can you get her some, Lady?'

'Only if you stop calling me that,' she grumbled.

I gathered the stirring human in my arms, taking the cup of water and holding it to her lips. 'I'll think about it.'

Elswyth's lips twitched before she turned away, hitting some buttons on the generator.

There was no way in the worlds I'd stop calling her that.

My mother had been an Illisae healer, but my fathers were all Tirian, and they'd raised me with a healthy respect for the Hamadryad. Simply being in Elswyth's presence made all their lessons flood back. *The Hamadryad are the green gods' chosen. The Hamadryad are the heart of our species. The Hamadryad are to be revered, respected.*

And should one choose you, Willow, never, ever give her a reason to let you go.

The last piece of advice had never seemed likely, so I'd settled with remembering the others. Elswyth had never needed me professionally, though I'd studied what little information was available about the Hamadryad before applying for a post in the peacekeeping fleet. This was the longest I'd ever been in her presence, even if I felt I knew her from another source entirely.

I stretched my fingers out to stop them trembling.

'Smells good,' Maeve croaked.

I exhaled, trying to ignore the silky drape of her hair over my arm. 'Can you sit by yourself?'

Maeve pushed herself from my arms with surprising speed. Humans – or this human, at least – were more resilient than I'd expected.

'Fuck,' she said, wincing. 'What was that?'

'You fainted,' I said, forcing down the disappointment at the distance now between us. It was a biological response; I was peak Tirian bonding age, and my hormones were craving the multiple bonds that formed a Tirian family. Maeve might not have been Tirian, but she'd certainly made my instincts sit up and take notice; my body began to ache with interest. Coupled with the presence of the Hamadryad, being in the room was a heady experience.

I gritted my teeth and tried not to think about it.

Maeve snorted. 'I don't faint. I've *never* fainted. The last time I passed out was when I discovered tequila.'

'You've never met another species and travelled through space before today, either,' Elswyth pointed out reasonably. 'Do you know what usually happens to humans in that situation?'

Maeve blinked at her, then bared her teeth in a grin. 'Touché.'

Elswyth handed her a bowl of thinly-sliced white tuber, cooked in oil and flavoured with wisdom leaf and wild spice. 'If Willow can do some research on human foods, we can program the generator to make something more suitable for you. But this is the closest thing I could think of to what you offered me on Earth.'

Maeve took the bowl and sniffed. 'That smells ... pretty close, actually. And pretty good.' She flicked me a glance. 'Are you staying, in case this turns out to be poisonous to humans?'

I bit back a smile. 'Yes. I'll stay.'

If the tubers were poisonous to humans, it was slow-acting; I excused myself an hour later as Maeve began to yawn.

I hoped she'd sleep, but I wouldn't. I had a whole lot of human knowledge to download before we left the Sector and access to their systems became more difficult.

The hangar was quieter at night. Someone had opened the viewing platform and there was a small group of engineers drinking nectar together on the balcony, looking straight out into space. They beckoned to me, but I waved them off with a smile. 'Not tonight,' I called, just as I did every time they asked.

I had a small room in the service quarter of the ship; comfortable, but nothing like the Hamadryad's family room. I rarely slept there, though. I preferred to be in the clinic, with the background noise of the hangar during the day, and the quiet hum of the spore systems at night. It was too quiet in my room, and too far from where I was needed. Though I'd programmed the spore systems to run effectively without my interference and had added several automatic safeguards, I liked to double – sometimes triple – check my work.

The ship's Second Doctor, Cedar, had left the lab just as I preferred it – spotlessly clean. They'd taken Maeve and Elswyth's clothing for decontamination and had changed the linen in the lab's four small sickrooms. On top of all of that, they'd left me a covered bowl of wild rice and night berry stew, knowing I wouldn't eat otherwise.

I uncovered the meal, then switched on my screen.

'Will?'

I looked up. 'Ash? What are you doing here? You don't finish until ...' My voice trailed off as I caught sight of the time. My food lay untouched next to my elbow, but I'd downloaded several of Earth's academic journals, along with outlines and *textbooks* – whatever they were – from several medical teaching programs. I'd found specialised information pertaining to human females, and had hacked into one country-wide database used by medical practitioners for recording patient data. The database intrigued me most of all, showing a very different way of thinking about healing – a piecemeal, reactive approach, the opposite to Tirian preventative and holistic care – and giving me a sense of common human ailments and their treatments.

'Why haven't you eaten?'

Ashton's gravelly tones rippled down my spines. I picked up a spoonful of rice and shoved it in my mouth, knowing it wasn't worth the argument, and studied his face out of long habit.

He looked haggard. He'd been furious when he'd realised what Elswyth had done; inconsolable when no one could trace her. He'd been ready to launch a Pod and search for her blind, but the Captain herself had stopped him, reasoning that Elswyth would never abandon her Forest and that she'd be back sooner rather than later. While Elswyth was gone, the Captain and her First Guard had been a team, focused on making sure their wayward Hamadryad returned; the moment she did, Ashton became culpable for her actions, and the Captain would not have held back in her dressing-down.

I swallowed the mouthful of rice. 'How bad was it?'

He lifted one shoulder in a half-shrug. 'Not as bad as I deserved. *Eat*, Willow.'

'Ash,' I scolded, before taking another mouthful. 'Elswyth is responsible for her own choices. How could you possibly know she'd do something so reckless?'

He didn't answer, watching me with an intensity that made my stomach clench.

'Who is guarding her now?'

His brow darkened. 'The Captain suggested Adair and Poppy stayed outside her rooms tonight. To *give the Hamadryad space,* the Captain said.'

That explained the intensity. Not that Ash wasn't always intense; this was just ... more. He hated Adair – the spoiled son of another ship's captain – almost as much as he hated being away from Elswyth.

Luckily, I knew how to distract him. I turned my face so my words wouldn't be recorded by the security feed. 'Am I turning off the cameras tonight, Ash?'

His lovely eyes flickered gold. Without speaking, he nodded.

A few moments later, I flicked off the cameras in the main lab, as I did whenever I saw a patient. 'What do you need?'

There was no hesitation in his response. 'You, Willow. Just you.'

I closed my eyes, willing my hearts to calm down. Ashton wasn't one for needless chatter; when he spoke, he meant every word. And when he said things like *that*, I was helpless.

'Come here, then,' I said quietly.

The thud as the tallest, strongest, most beautiful soldier on the ship fell to kneel before me still gave me a thrill, even a hundred – a *thousand* – times later. Ash was second in command only to the Captain, but here, in my lab with me, he was nothing but himself. When we were together, we shut the world out – well, the world apart from the Hamadryad, who was a universe unto herself. Elswyth was always in Ash's thoughts, as constant as the never-ending black outside the ship.

I didn't mind. Had it been another Tirian, I might have been jealous, but I felt lucky, instead. Knowing that the male I loved served the green gods' chosen made it seem as if I were one step removed from the divine.

An image of Maeve's hair draped over my arm flickered in my mind; I reached out to cup Ashton's cheek as he coaxed the vines of my jumpsuit to unravel at the crotch, freeing my cock from its restraints.

He took me in his mouth immediately, as if he was as hungry for this as I was, and my mind went blank with pleasure. His lips moved down my shaft and back up, his tongue swirling around my head. He swallowed down the pre-sap gathering there with a vibrating moan that made my whole body go tight. His clever tongue moved lower, pressing on my burl in rhythmic pulses that drew a snarl from my throat.

My fingers found his hair and tightened. 'None of that,' I chided softly. 'I want this to last.'

His mouth moved up, concentrating on teasing my swollen head. I closed my eyes as he worked, my fingers gently raking through his hair. Sensation built slowly at the base of my spines, drawn out with every clever hollowing of his cheeks and swirl of his tongue, until my hips were moving of their own accord, thrusting mindlessly into the tight, wet paradise of his mouth. He groaned as my fingers tightened again, groaned as my spare hand found his shoulder, groaned as I held him in place and chased my own pleasure, pushing deeper inside until I spilled straight down his throat.

He drew back a moment later – pausing to lick me clean as I shuddered – then wiped his mouth with a smug smile. 'I thought you wanted it to last,' he rasped, teasing.

I pulled him forward and kissed him, tasting myself on his tongue. 'Who says I'm done?'

No one cared who I loved – *well*, I thought, reflecting on some of the ship's gossip vines, *some* Tirians cared a little *too* much about it – but Ash was another matter entirely. As the Hamadryad's close guard and First Guard to the ship, any potential *karia* – the dominant female and head of a Tirian family – needed to be approved by his captain *and* the elected leaders that made up the Tirian Grove. If they decided against the family Ash chose, he wouldn't just lose his loves – he'd lose his job, too, his ability to guard the precious Hamadryad called into question by his choice of a family that others judged unworthy.

I wasn't a *karia*, of course; Ash couldn't take me before our Captain and ask for her approval. It was unlikely we'd ever find one; it was a rare female who would consider welcoming an already-bonded pair into her life. It would be too likely to upset the balance in her family, the very thing she strived to maintain.

And so, what we were – what we *did* – was secret. Steeped in the fear of discovery, fear of the consequences. We were frozen like pieces on a game board, never to move backwards or forwards. Ash couldn't lose Elswyth, and I couldn't lose *him*. We both preferred to die Unclaimed together, than accept a family separately.

I tried not to care too much. I had Ash, and I loved him. But my instincts still twitched, begging me to find a *karia* fierce enough to cope with the egos of both a Head Doctor and First Guard, a family the Captain and the Grove would approve, a family who wouldn't just accept us together, but who would be strong enough to love us for it. A *karia* who would understand Ash's devotion to his Hamadryad and not feel threatened by it.

It seemed an impossible ask.

Ashton pulled away, nipping me sharply on the thigh. 'I can hear your roots growing,' he grumbled. 'What are you thinking about?'

I took his chin in my hand. 'Probably the same thing as you,' I admitted.

His eyes searched mine, the beautiful gold darkening to brown. 'The Hamadryad and the human.'

'The Lady and the alien,' I agreed. I pulled him up, giving him a hungry kiss before walking him backwards into the spare sickroom – the one that was never used for patients, and often used for *this*.

He shuddered as I began to strip off his uniform. 'What are you thinking about the Hamadryad and the human, Ash?'

He groaned as my fingers unlaced his leathers, stroking his cock through the stiff fabric. He pulled me up for another kiss, one that left us both breathless.

'Ash?' I said again, when he was naked and his eyes were gleaming in the dark, as if he were about to pounce. 'The Lady?'

He pushed me onto the bed and covered me with his body. 'I think the human is as fierce as any *karia* I've ever known,' he said into my neck, his thorns scraping deliciously against my skin. 'I don't think she'd have to be Tirian to claim us for her own.'

I gasped as he pushed my legs apart. I wrapped them around him, pulling him as close as I could, then closer, until there was no distance between us and he was moving in a way that made me see stars. 'But Ash,' I managed, before I lost my wits completely. 'She'd have to want to in the first place.'

Ashton didn't answer.

MAEVE

One bed. I am literally living the one bed trope.

I rubbed my chin, trying not to break into a fit of hysterics.

I was a true crime podcast kind of woman, but Tessa *lived* for romance novels – the smuttier and growlier, the better. I knew all her favourite tropes – including the ones she wouldn't admit liking but blushed every time she talked about – and I knew that she would absolutely lose her mind about this.

'So, do we share the bed, or ...?' I left the question hanging.

Elswyth glanced at the monstrous mattress – it looked insanely comfortable, I wasn't going to lie – and wrinkled her nose, like she hadn't thought about it. 'Oh. I see,' she said, her voice small. 'Of course we don't have to share; I'll give you space. I can go into the Forest. No one will know any different.'

'That isn't ... That isn't what I meant,' I said quickly, catching the note of hurt in her tone. *I've only been fake alien married for a couple of hours, and I'm already fucking it up.* 'I don't want to make you uncomfortable. I can sleep in the chair.'

She looked at the Tirian equivalent of an armchair – a high-backed, armless thing made of the same material as the Pod's seats, sewn with leaf patterns – and wrinkled her nose again. 'You won't make me uncomfortable. And there's no way *any* being could sleep properly in that.'

'Okay.' I inhaled slowly. 'We share the bed.'

I'd never been fake married before, but I'd never slept next to anyone before, either. Ever. At sleepovers during my teenage years, I'd stay awake all night, and in adulthood, anyone I invited into *my* bed was kicked out – usually politely – after the fun part had finished. If they stayed until morning, it wasn't because they'd been *sleeping*.

You can do this, Maeve.

I was on an alien spaceship, about to leave Earth to find my abducted best friend, and I was worried about going to sleep next to someone.

Priorities, McCarthy.

I stripped off the clothing the handsome doctor had given me, trying to ignore Elswyth, who was doing the same on the other side of the bed. Unfortunately, my libido had other ideas, and I glanced across at her just as she pulled off the Tirian equivalent of a bra – a crop-top fastened with vines, made from some kind of silicone-looking fabric – and I got an eyeful of her perfect breasts and peaked brown nipples.

For fuck's sake, Maeve. Pull yourself together.

Elswyth saw me looking, then cast her gaze to the bed, swallowing. 'I'm not like other Tirians,' she blurted out.

I dumped my clothes on the chair. 'Yeah, I got that.'

'No, I mean ...' She trailed off, chewing on her bottom lip. 'I'm different in another way, too.'

I sat on the bed in my bralette and underwear. 'Mmm?'

'Tirians ... We live in bonded groups we call families, held together by a *karia*,' she said. 'When we bond, it's permanent. Forever. Our society revolves around our families as much as it does our Forests. But the Hamadryad are outside the family structure. We're different.' Her tone took on a note of sorrow. 'We're alone. We can bond time and time again – be claimed by ten families, by a hundred different *karia*. Even if we find one that helps us grow roots, we're still not the same as other Tirians. We always know that things might change. That we might be forced apart again.'

'Um,' I said. 'What the fuck is a *karia*?'

Elswyth lifted one naked shoulder in the sexiest shrug I'd ever seen. 'The dominant female of a family. Its leader. She decides who joins the family and acts as its protector. She makes sure that her bonded have their needs met, and she maintains balance among them. Other species have different words for her, but we think of her as our centre. As our heart.'

Her voice was at once wistful and sad; I could see why. If she was already different to the rest of her kind, the prospect of never knowing the ever-lasting bond that everyone else had could lead to a yearning for it – if you were into that sort of thing.

'Have you been ... bonded ... before, Elswyth?'

She shook her head, her flush spreading.

'And bonding is ... sex?'

She coughed. 'It's a lasting emotional tie. Some scientists think that the bonds alter Tirian biochemistry in such a per-manent way that separation from their loved ones is impossible. They think that's where the Hamadryad differ – no such alternation takes place within us. If we are allowed to bond for life, it's because we choose it.' She bit her lip. 'But bonding can be triggered by sex, yes.'

I spread my hands over the blanket. It was unbelievably soft, made from some kind of synthetic material.

Probably as soft as Elswyth's skin.

Don't do it, Maeve.

'Thank you for letting me know,' I said. I stood, and pulled back the covers, then slipped into the bed. 'Do you think we could talk about this again tomorrow? It's been a long day.'

Her face fell. 'Of course,' she said, and waved her hand near a panel on the wall, throwing the room into immediate darkness. I barely felt the jostle as she climbed into the bed; she took a few moments to get comfortable, then was still. 'Sweet dreams, Maeve.'

I started in surprise at the familiar saying. 'Sweet dreams, Elswyth.'

We both lay in silence; I peered into the dark, not knowing what I was looking for. When the quiet became unbearable, I turned on my side. 'Elswyth?'

'Maeve?' she answered at once, rustling as she moved.

I licked my lips. 'I've never gone to sleep with anyone before.'

There was a moment as she digested my confession. 'Ah,' she said at last. 'How can I help?'

I felt a rush of gratitude. Apparently, my fake wife wasn't one for meaningless platitudes. 'I'm not sure you can. I just wanted you to know.'

There was another rustle of the blanket as she moved; a moment later, I felt her cool fingers lacing through mine. I tightened mine in response, and we lay there in the dark, hands entwined.

I woke hours later. Elswyth had moved closer in the night – or maybe I'd rolled towards her – and her hair was spread over her pillow, giving off a soft glow. In the silver light, I could see the planes and angles of her face, the way her lips were curving, like she was having a good dream. Blossoms – the same as the ones that had grown on her shoulder in the Pod – were blooming up the wall behind the bed, their petals unfurling in Elswyth's light.

Her hand was still in mine.

I went back to sleep, smiling.

When I woke again, Elswyth was nestled next to me. My arm was thrown over her waist and my hand was cupping her breast; her pert ass pressed against my crotch. I gasped into her hair before I could stop myself, then took my hand away from where her nipple was hard against my palm.

Her hand came up immediately and held me in place. '*Ilikeitthere*,' she said sleepily.

'Um,' I answered blankly.

She stretched, arching against me. My face was buried in her hair, and all I could smell was the sweet floral scent of her. She might not have been bonded before, but she was pressing every single one of my buttons as if she'd seduced a thousand partners.

'*Isleptsowell,*' she sighed, then froze. 'You slept, too!'

'Mmm,' I managed. 'I slept.'

I am very *awake now, though.*

Every nerve ending in my body was singing, my skin tingling in every place we touched. It was overwhelming, and not something I'd felt before. It wasn't just the warmth of arousal, but the warmth of *comfort*, and my body was loving it.

She turned in my arms, and I was confronted with her face, too close to my own, so close that her breath was fanning my cheek and I could see every perfect eyelash and the colour shift in her pupil-less irises – green to hazel, hazel to green. My arm was still around her waist, and my hand stroked her back without me telling it to.

'Good morning, Maeve,' she breathed.

'Elswyth,' I whispered.

She held my gaze and, very slowly, moved forward and brushed her lips over mine.

Heat shot through my body as my chest constricted.

My fake wife is kissing me.

When I didn't move away, she pressed her lips down more firmly in a tentative, nuzzling caress.

My fake wife is kissing me – and I like it.

Her hand came up and cupped my cheek.

Don't do it, Maeve, I thought, even as my fingers wound themselves through her hair.

Take a step back, McCarthy, I told myself, but my lips were moving and I was kissing her back, deeply.

She tasted sweet, so sweet I moaned, wanting more. I rolled so she was draped over me and her hair was curtaining my face. She gasped when I sucked gently at her bottom lip, her tongue darting out to touch my own, her fingers stroking my cheek before moving to trace the shell of my ear.

This is mad, Maeve.

'Wait,' I gasped. 'Wait, Elswyth. We shouldn't do this. You should wait. Wait for a Tirian. Wait for your ... your family.'

She sat up, hooking her knee across my body, straddling me. The image of her like that – her thighs spread wide, her core pressed to my stomach, her hair glowing in the low light – was doing all kinds of delicious things to me. My hands found her hips of their own accord; my gaze lingered on her thorn-lined collarbone before sweeping up to meet her ever-changing eyes.

'Why?' she said fiercely. 'Why should I wait for a family who might only want me because of my *elya*? Who might only want me to gain power, to put me and my heartree on their ship and make their Forest grow? Why should I wait for a *karia* who might want me only as something to hang from their arm like a trinket? Why should I wait to be *grateful* that someone might want me, even if it's not really *me* they want?' She traced my cheek with a trembling finger. 'At least I know that if *you* want me, it's for *me*. Not because I'm a Hamadryad. Not because of the power I can give you. Just ... for me. Whatever happens, it's real.'

I swallowed.

Wasn't that what I'd always told Tessa? That she deserved love – worship, even – entirely for her own sake? That she deserved someone who saw – and who *craved* – exactly what she was, without her trying to bend herself into the shape of what they thought they wanted? That she didn't have to change a thing about herself to be worthy of that love, of that devotion?

'I do want you,' I said honestly, because I *did*, and had done since that first glimpse of her at Advena. But it was more complicated now; I knew some of the details of her life, of what she wanted, of what she *felt*. 'But Elswyth ... I'm here to find Tessa. And when I find her, I'm taking her home. I can't promise you anything more than that. Hell's bells, I can't promise you anything at all.'

She smiled, her hair glowing as it fell in a sheen over her shoulders. Blossoms were growing along the bedhead above us, filling the air with their delicate perfume. 'I don't want promises. I want someone who sees *me*. Just once.'

Without thinking, I reached up and brushed her hair back, my fingers lingering in the silken strands before tracing over the thorns on her collarbone. I barely recognised myself in that soft touch; I didn't touch like that, so gently, so *reverently*. Her thorns were hard beneath my fingertips, and sharp enough to pinch.

'What are you?' I breathed.

She grinned. 'I'm your bonded, Maeve McCarthy, even if it's only for a little while. Even if it's fake.'

My heart skipped a beat.

'I see you,' I told her. 'I see you, Elswyth. And you're so fucking beautiful it hurts.' I took her waist and flipped our places, listening to her gasp as I spread her out on the bed. I kissed her again, softly and thoroughly, as my hand found her breast. 'Tell me to stop.'

'Green gods, why would I do *that*?' she said breathlessly.

I bit my lip. 'If there's anything you don't like, or you don't want, or something that makes you uncomfortable, you need to tell me. I'll stop immediately. Okay?'

'Yes,' she agreed. 'But Maeve ... If you don't kiss me again, I think I might scream.'

I laughed softly, but I kissed her, because I felt the same. Her mouth moved against mine in a tentative exploration, like she was trying to find every slide of lips or touch of tongues I liked, and my core was melting as her hands stroked up and down my back. I cupped her, stroking the soft flesh of her breast before rolling her hard nipple between my thumb and finger. She squeaked, arching into my hand, so I did it again, then dipped my head down to take her in my mouth instead.

'Oh, gods,' she panted. 'Oh, *gods*. Maeve.'

I chuckled. 'I guess we're not so different in this way, at least,' I murmured against her, moving to the other breast. She cried out as my tongue flicked over her peaked nipple. 'Should I see if we're the same elsewhere?'

I slid my hand down, across the soft roundness of her stomach, until my fingers found her short-like underwear. I mapped the curves and dips of her, feeling wetness on my fingertips when I touched between her legs. She felt ... pretty much like a human woman would.

'Can I touch you?' I said, my voice thick. 'Can I touch your skin?'

'Please,' she answered. 'Yes. Please, Maeve.'

I slipped my hand beneath her shorts. Her skin was smooth, and I cupped her gently, feeling her wetness on my palm. My fingers slid up, searching, and encountered something that felt pretty similar to a clit. I rubbed it gently, biting my lip as her hips pressed up and she cried out.

Human-Tirian similarity number two. 'If I keep doing that, will you come?'

'Come?'

'Climax. Orgasm.'

'Oh. We call it *blooming*,' she panted. 'And yes. That's one way.'

'One way, huh?' I worked her in small circles until she was moaning, then slid my fingers back down, searching for something else. She huffed in disappointment – I bit back a laugh – then she arched as my finger found her entrance and slid inside with no resistance.

'Human-Tirian similarity three,' I murmured. She wasn't as soft as a human woman, nor as hot, but she was just as wet. I added a second finger as she gave a desperate pant that sent heat through my body, then bucked her hips, trying to take my fingers deeper inside.

I went still. 'That's ... fucking hell, Elswyth. You're *ribbed*.'

'Mating grooves,' she gasped. 'And –'

I pushed further, seeking something else, and she wailed, her hands clutching at my hips.

'And?' I said breathlessly. 'I'm assuming that's a good sound.'

'Good,' she managed. 'Very – *very* – good.'

I caressed the small divot inside her. I'd been searching for a g-spot, and I'd found something new instead. 'Are you going to explain? Or am I going to find out what this does for myself?'

'Maeve – green gods, *Maeve* – oh,' she moaned, as my fingers worked. 'It's – a notch. Males have – a *burl* – a kind of – knot – and it –'

'You fit together,' I said thickly. 'I get it. Tessa loves those knotting books. Is this what makes you feel the best?'

'That – and my – bud.'

I pulled my fingers from her, listening to her squeak again as I slid her underwear down, then pushed her knees apart and settled between her legs. She didn't look much different to a human woman, so I lowered my head and licked.

She bowed off the bed, whimpering. I slung an arm across her hips to hold her in place, then did it again.

'Maeve,' she gasped.

'Tell me what you want. What you need.'

'That,' she moaned. '*You*.'

My heart skipped another beat.

I dipped my tongue inside her, more for my sake than hers. 'Fuck. You taste like sugar,' I breathed. I licked her all over, before narrowing in on her clit – her *bud* – and flattening my tongue, my fingers questing back inside her to find her notch.

Either I was better than I thought, or Tirian bodies were more receptive than humans were, because it took all of twenty seconds for her body to tense and clamp down around my soaked fingers.

'*Maeve*,' she shrieked; I licked her until her thighs started to tremble. It was mostly for my benefit; I couldn't get enough of her taste.

'I want to eat you for fucking breakfast,' I murmured.

'Maeve,' she said again, wonderingly. I toyed with her bud for a moment, lingering until she started to shake, then dragged myself up her body, stopping to suck her peaked nipples before seizing her mouth with mine. I lowered my weight carefully, then tentatively pressed myself against her.

She threw her head back, panting.

'Is this okay?' I ground out.

'Green gods, yes,' she hissed. 'More.'

I wasn't going to argue.

I rolled my hips, panting as her hands came up and skirted over my ass. The touch sent a fresh wave of heat through my body and I came a few moments later, gasping for air as bliss rippled through my core. She pulled me down and held me tight, sighing into my neck. I shifted onto my side so I wouldn't crush her; she ran a hand over my stomach and let it rest on my thigh.

'That was ...' she began dreamily, but she trailed off before she specified.

'Are you all right?'

She blinked heavily, then fixed her eyes on mine. 'I don't think I've ever been better.'

Unaccountably, I felt my cheeks go hot. I searched desperately for something to say, for something safer, something that didn't make my chest constrict in a way I didn't want to think about. 'What will you do today?'

She rolled over; I swallowed down disappointment as she stood, then bit back satisfaction as her trembling legs stumbled. She looked down in surprise at her unsteady feet, then shot me a wide, glowing grin.

My heart decided to forego skipping, and tried to launch itself into my throat, instead.

Don't do it, Maeve. You're here to save Tessa.

'I'll take my bonded to see my heartree,' Elswyth said.

ASHTON

'Report,' I growled.

Adair smirked. 'Something wrong, First Guard?'

Poppy ignored both Adair and my foul manners. 'Ewan is waiting in the Forest, sir,' she said in her soft voice. 'The Hamadryad and the human were planning on seeing the heartree this morning.'

I gave a curt nod. Ewan was a good choice. 'And during the night?'

Poppy hesitated, but Adair didn't. 'All quiet until this morning, sir,' he said smugly.

I fixed him with my best cold stare. 'And what happened this morning, Third Guard?'

He smirked again, holding my gaze. 'She was loud, sir.'

My hearts went still. 'Loud? Was she ill? *Hurt?*'

'No, sir,' Adair answered. Poppy opened her mouth and then snapped it shut, casting him a ferocious glare. 'She was well,'

Adair went on, his tone caressing. 'Very, *very* well. *Loudly well*, if you get my meaning.'

I kept my face expressionless, though I felt anything but. 'I get your meaning, Third Guard.' I turned my shoulder to him deliberately, cutting him out of my line of sight and addressing Poppy alone. 'Any concerns, Second Guard?'

'No concerns, First Guard,' Poppy said evenly. 'The Hamadryad looked ... Well, she looked *happy*, sir.'

I stared at her. Elswyth didn't really do *happy*. Content, sometimes. The occasional joy in small moments, always in the Forest. Slight, sad smiles when arcadias bloomed near her heartree. Dutiful pleasure at spending time with her mother. The occasional shocked laugh when I managed to coax forth mirth, always swiftly stifled.

But not *happy*.

I gave another nod, mostly because Poppy and Adair were staring at me, and I had to do *something*. 'May her bonding be long and fruitful,' I recited woodenly.

Adair tried to catch my gaze as they filed out of the training room, no doubt to smirk again. Poppy shot me a mournful look that I pretended not to see.

The moment the door slid closed behind them, I slammed my fist into the seed pod hanging from the roof.

I punched wildly, until I was panting. 'You're her guard, not her bonded,' I told myself. 'She's yours to protect. Nothing more.'

I loved Willow with every fibre of my being. I'd noticed him the moment he'd stepped on board, noticed his lovely jaw and his beautiful eyes and his careful steadiness, and I'd wanted him – wanted to know what lay beneath that calm demeanour, wanted to know the male beneath the measured façade. Wanted to know what he liked and what he didn't, wanted to know what made him gasp, what made him shake, what made him come apart. I'd known what I was doing – what I was risking – when I'd stopped him in a corridor, when I'd brushed my fingers over his shoulder, when I'd bent my head to whisper in his ear and trailed my lips over the line of thorns. He knew it, too. *Are you sure?* he'd asked, before he'd pulled me into a storeroom, before he kissed me, before I fell to my knees and took him in my mouth the first time. We'd known what we were doing, and we'd done it willingly, fully aware of what the consequences of our unsanctioned bonding might be.

He was mine and I was his, forever.

But Elswyth had always been in my heart, and she stubbornly refused to leave, no matter how hard I tried to push her from it.

I knew that Willow dreamed of finding a strong, fierce *karia* who would be brave enough – or foolish enough, perhaps – to take us both into her family, someone who would challenge him and tame me. He talked about it sometimes, always in the dark, as if he couldn't quite voice the hope in the light.

I didn't dream of that, though I had to admit it sounded nice. I dreamed of my Hamadryad, with her changeable eyes and hair made of magic, growing arcadias in her Forest. I dreamed of Willow caring for her body and her soul in the way he did mine, of him cherishing her the way he did me. Sometimes I even dreamed of wrapping her in my arms, holding her tight, keeping her safe. I never let myself imagine anything more; it seemed blasphemous, too dangerous, and my mind skittered away from deeper desires, from those hungers. Elswyth was divine; her body was not for me to dream of.

It seemed that the human female had no such reservations.

I pummelled the seed pod again, so hard that the skin on my knuckles split. I watched it knit back together dispassionately, the wound gone before the green blood had dried on my fingers. I wiped my hand on my leathers and made for the door, pausing only to pick up my ash staff, its smooth surface like a balm.

One of my fathers had carved it before I'd left Tir. It had been far too big for me then – I was only fourteen years old – but I'd grown into it with time. One of my mothers – the one who'd birthed me – had charred a tiny leaf into one side and embossed it with rose gold; I ran my thumb over her design. They'd been reluctant to let me go so young, but they knew what I wanted – to guard the tiny Hamadryad with the glowing silver hair.

She had always been my destiny.

I found her in the middle of the Forest, standing before her heartree. It was magnificent, strong and tall and healthy with wide-spreading boughs and lush, graceful leaves. Unlike a normal tree, it was perpetually in full bloom, its branches laden with shy flowers the deep pink of the human female's cheeks.

'*This* is your tree?' the human female was saying, her bright blue eyes wide. 'It's *beautiful*, Elswyth.'

Elswyth flushed, the lovely green reaching all the way down her neck and to the points of her delicate ears. 'Really?'

'I've never seen anything like it.' The human gazed up at the heartree, craning her neck to look as far as she could. 'It seems a lot like an Earth oak tree. Could Tirians have visited Earth before?'

'Yes,' I answered, before I could stop myself. Their faces turned to me as one; Elswyth's happiness fled, and the human's expression settled into wariness. 'It's possible. Probable, even. Our species have been travelling the stars for millennia, and the laws haven't always been so strict. Though some historians account for similarities through convergent evolution, others believe that there have been thousands of years of unrecorded contact between species.' I looked up at the heartree, ignoring the glance they shared. 'Willow has been researching plant life on Earth. He was sceptical regarding prior contact before, but he now believes that the plant life on Earth is similar enough to plant life on Tir that a compelling case could be made in support of the theory.'

'Maybe that's why our bodies are similar, too,' the human murmured to Elswyth, so softly I was sure it wasn't meant for my ears.

I took a deep, slow breath, trying to ignore the hot stab of jealousy through my gut.

'Oh, look, Maeve!' Elswyth cried in delight.

I looked to where she was pointing; arcadia vines were twining around the exposed roots of the heartree and twisting up its trunk, blossoming in shades of white and black and blue – the same shade as the human's odd, tri-colour eyes.

'They won't hurt the tree, will they?' the human said, a hint of anxiety in her tone.

'Arcadias? No, not at all. They're made of *elya*, like me.' Elswyth bent down and touched a bloom; it fell into her hand. She smiled, straightening, then tucked it behind the human female's ear.

'And *elya* is like ... magic?'

'If you like. It's a force most beings can't see, but they know it's there, like gravity. But only some can interact with it. The Hamadryad on Tir. The Priestesses on Kjid. The Mages from Ilis. The Edge Order on the Allied Planets in Sector Four. And probably a bunch of other species we haven't met yet.'

'We believe *elya* is what bonds our family members together,' I added. 'Though Willow would tell you it is something far less magical and far more tangible.'

'Like biology,' the human said. She touched the blossom behind her ear. 'So, if a Tirian's last name is *Unclaimed*, that means they haven't found a *karia*? They're not part of a ... family?'

Elswyth nodded.

'But *karia* are all female, right? What if two males fall in love?'

My hearts stopped beating as one.

'If a Tirian doesn't desire females – and many don't – their *karia* takes that into the balance of her family,' Elswyth answered. 'The Tirian in question might have an emotional bond with her, and a ... more physical ... bond with another member of the family, or perhaps a series of emotional bonds and no physical bonds at all. Every Tirian is taken care of within the family structure, depending on their needs and wants.'

'What if someone doesn't *want* to be part of a family? If they don't want any bonds at all?'

'It does happen,' Elswyth said. 'Usually, they will negotiate their own small territory with the other families in their Forest, and live there on their own terms.'

Maeve nodded, frowning. 'And what if one member of a family falls in love with someone from outside it?'

This was safer ground, so I answered. 'If they are Unclaimed, the family's *karia* would consider taking them as a new member. She would assess the feelings of her existing bonded, and how the new member might fit in. She would examine each individual relationship, and how she herself felt, and make a decision based on whether the balance of her family would be maintained or strengthened.'

'So the *karia* is running the show in terms of family expansion,' Maeve said. 'She gets the loves she wants, and she's the glue holding it all together. It really *is* like Tessa's books. Can a family have two *karia*?'

Elswyth and I exchanged a glance. 'No,' she answered. 'There is only ever one. Her bonded always know – even if, in the beginning, she herself does not.'

'Okay,' the human said slowly. 'So your families are a mix of biological impulses and specific bonds, a chosen leader, and changing circumstances – and some think there's a bit of divine magic thrown in there for good measure. Sounds like some families on Earth, when you put it like that.'

'What is your family like?' I blurted, before I could stop myself.

The human looked at me, startled. 'Small,' she said, after a long moment of silence. 'I don't ... I've never had a romantic partner, not a long-term one, anyway, so I don't have a family in the way you mean it. It's just me and my mum. I've never met my father. He and mum had a fling on a dig when she was an Honours student – she's an archaeologist. I know his name and what he publishes on and the university he works at, and he sent us his medical records and family history and stuff, but he never really made much of an effort. When mum asked whether I wanted more contact, I kinda already thought he was a dick for fucking a student – not to mention one so much younger than he was – and didn't see the poi – *shitballs*,' she said, tipping her head back to stare at the glassed dome of the Forest and out at the black of space. '*My mum*. She's with her team in Vietnam at the moment, but she finishes up in a month and she'll know something's wrong when I don't email.'

I glanced at Elswyth; her brow had crumpled in concern, though I hadn't understood more than half of what Maeve had said. 'I'm sure the engineers can work out a way for you to contact your mother,' I said slowly. 'But you can't tell her anything, I'm afraid; it would break intergalactic law even more than it's already been broken. Will that be a problem?'

The human shook her head. 'No. She's flying straight to America once the dig finishes for a post-doc fellowship. She'll be gone for two years; we already said our goodbyes. If I can email her, I can pretend everything's normal.'

'That's a long time to be without your mother,' Elswyth said carefully. 'Do you miss her?'

Maeve blinked. 'I mean, yeah, sure. But this is not outside the norm for us. She's always been passionate about her academic career, and it's not like there's a huge call for archaeological digs in the middle of the city, so I'm used to being on my own, even when she's in the same country. It wasn't as if she had me and left; she put everything on hold until I was eighteen to give me the best upbringing she could, and even then it was *me* pushing her to go back to academia the moment I was legal. It wasn't her fault some dickhead professor knocked her up at the age of twenty-two. I know that she loves me, and I've had a fuck tonne of therapy, so I'm pretty confident that all my issues are my own and nothing to do with mum.' She bit her lip; I fixed on it, entranced, as she worried at the plump pink flesh. 'But if the engineers could hack some kind of comms channel to her, I'd be grateful. I should email Anna, and my boss, too.' She pursed her lips and gave a bright, forced smile. 'Enough boring stuff. What happens when you're the hearttree, El?'

El?

Elswyth gave her a wide, bright smile, so uncharacteristically unguarded that shock rippled through my entire body. 'It's not very interesting,' she said apologetically. She took a deep breath, then began to glow.

'Um,' the human said, and took a half-step back.

'*Elya*,' I said gruffly. 'What you're seeing is *elya*.'

'Right,' Maeve answered, then shrieked wordlessly when Elswyth disappeared. '*Um. The fuck?*'

'Watch the heartree.'

She obediently turned her face to the heartree, which rippled as Elswyth took her place within it. Its trunk and branches glowed silver before its leaves gave a rustling shiver; one bough reached out to trail blossoms over Maeve's hair.

The human gave a shocked, delighted laugh. 'Holy *shit*,' she breathed. She laughed again, a little wildly. 'I have a wife, and my wife is a tree.'

'Not *a* tree,' I said. '*The* tree.'

She cast me an unimpressed glance. 'Can she hear us?'

I shrugged. 'Sometimes. It depends on how deep she's gone.'

Maeve took a step towards me. 'Right. I'll only say this once. I see the way you look at her, elf-boy.'

I stared at her. 'I – *what*?'

'Are we good?'

I shut my mouth with a snap as my stomach began to churn.

Maeve flicked her hair over one shoulder. 'Because my arrival doesn't mean *you* can't tell her that she makes the sun rise or whatever Tirians write in their love poetry. You're welcome to tell her that *any time*. Are we clear?'

'But –'

'Because, in my experience, reluctance often becomes resentment, and I won't watch that happen,' she continued, studying me closely, taking another step forward. 'If you never gird your loins enough to be vulnerable, that's not *my* problem, and it's definitely not Elswyth's. No one is standing in your way. You can tell her how you feel about her *whenever you want*. Do you understand me?'

Somehow, she'd ended up less than an arm's length away. I could see the steel in her glare, smell the tantalising musk of her scent. She was tall, almost as tall as Willow, but I liked that she still had to tip her head back to meet my gaze.

I took a step forward of my own, deliberately crowding her. 'I understand what you think you know, human. But I'm not a being you want on your bad side. Do *you* understand *me*?'

She held my gaze for a moment, then gave a wide, satisfied grin. 'Buckle up, elf-boy. This is going to be *fun*.'

WILLOW

'Your species evolved from *what*?'

'Apes,' Maeve repeated. 'Primates.' She pulled her tight pants – *jeans*, she called them – over her thighs and buttoned them, then grinned at her boots with undisguised glee. She picked up the small electronic device I'd decontaminated with the rest of her belongings – a *smartphone* – and held it out. 'If you can charge this, I can show you. I went on a date to the zoo a few months ago. The date did not go well, but I have a tonne of pictures.'

I took her phone, shivering as her fingertips brushed mine. I turned away to hide it. 'And your species is how old?'

'*Homo sapiens*, the subset of primate we belong to, emerged around three hundred thousand years ago. We were hunter-gatherers for an extremely long time, before agriculture and permanent settlement developed around thirteen thousand years ago. Though I have no idea how many Tirian years there are to an Earth year, so that might not mean much.'

I turned back to stare at her; the answers had come smoothly, with no pause at all. Most Tirians would be hard-pressed to recite the names of their grand-families, let alone describe the origins of their species. 'This is common knowledge on your planet?'

She flushed slightly, her cheeks turning a lovely deep pink. She lifted herself up effortlessly to sit on the bench. 'No-o,' she said, drawing out the sound. 'My mum drilled that stuff into me while most kids were still reading picture books. She specialises in bioarchaeology, but she has a passion for prehistoric archaeology and anthropology. I think she hoped I'd follow her into a similar field, but ...' She trailed off.

'But?' I prompted.

She looked away. 'I didn't do well at school. It wasn't the knowledge I didn't like; it was the sitting still. I prefer to learn by *doing*, and the fancy academy my dad paid for didn't really love that approach. They liked high marks on long essays and girls with the right length skirt who spoke at charity functions, not someone who wore too much eyeliner and spent her weekends at punk shows.' She shrugged. 'I did go on some digs with my mum when I was younger. She took me to Italy, and to Greece, and into the middle of Australia. I even went on one pretty close to home. We were uncovering the weirdest thing – practise trenches from the first world war. Who digs *practise* trenches? It was so odd. Odd and horrific, when you consider that the men – *boys* – practising in those depressing holes probably went on to die in the real thing. I'll never forget what it was like.'

'I see,' I murmured, though I hadn't understood much of what she'd said. I turned again – feeling as if she was leading me on a head-spinning dance as she shoved her feet in her boots – and looked blankly at my screen. 'And how does your species differ from others on your planet? Humans are dominant, yes?'

'We have larger brains relative to our bodies. We developed the ability to control fire, and to use tools. We have sophisticated languages, long memories, and we can problem solve.' On my screen, her reflection shrugged. 'Well. Most of us can.'

'Any natural predators?'

'Before we invented guns? Sure. Big cats, wolves, types of wild dogs, bears, even. Snakes, I suppose, in some parts of the world. But after guns? Mostly ourselves.'

'And how do you live?'

I watched her reflection as she answered, taking in her expressions, the way her mouth moved, the way she gestured. I tapped on my screen, pretending half-heartedly to take notes; I was recording the session, so I'd have to transcribe it and do more of my own research later. I couldn't concentrate, not when she was so close.

'I see,' I said again when she paused, not having heard a word of it. 'And humans spread across your entire planet?'

'Almost every sorry inch of it.' She paused. 'Where is your planet? Tir, is it?'

I nodded and brought up a map on my screen. 'Creating maps of the universe isn't exact; it's difficult to locate everything accurately, unless it's an immersive projection. Which I can show you, but I'd have to take you to a simulation room. But Tir is in Sector Seven, here.' I pointed. 'It's about fourteen standard units from Earth. Around eight of your sun years. Standard units don't equate to your light years, or to Tirian years, for that matter.'

'Time is relative,' she muttered. 'Does that mean you've been travelling here for literal years?'

'Oh, no.' I closed the map, wary of what the Captain had said: *don't tell her too much.* 'We mastered elevated unit travel some time ago, though only the peacekeeping ships are built to do it. It's the way the ship usually travels; it only took a month or so for us to get to Earth, and we've been travelling that way since we left Earth's orbit. This journey is part of a routine sweep of your galaxy; the Intergalactic Council is aware of human development and likes a representative to fly by on a regular basis. We were the lucky ones this time.'

I realised that I was still holding her phone, and I placed it on my portable charger, flushing again at my absentmindedness. The charger beeped as it tried to recognise the device; after a few moments, it seemed to settle on something similar enough – our wrist screens – and its charging light flashed.

'I have no idea how long that will take,' I said truthfully.

'That's all right,' she said. 'I'm with you for the day, aren't I? That was what elf-boy said, anyway.'

My lips twitched. 'Elf-boy?'

'Elves are mythological creatures on Earth,' she explained. 'They've been around in one form or another for thousands of years, but there were elves in a popular movie franchise when I was growing up, and you all look a bit like them. I thought El was cosplaying when I first saw her.'

'Cosplaying?'

'Costume play,' she said. 'People dress up as fictional characters they like. It's a whole thing. I thought her bark armour was fake, and your thorns were some kind of piercing.' She looked at my cheekbones thoughtfully; I self-consciously touched the row of thorns there, glancing at her smooth cheeks. 'If you can't have tattoos, does that mean no piercings, either?'

I glanced at her rounded ears, the lobes and shells studded with metal and glittering stones. 'No piercings.'

'Poor Tirian females,' she said, her lips curving. She swung her legs back and forth over the side of the examination bench. 'I know you want information about humans and Earth. Can I ask why? Am I helping pave the way for a Tirian invasion?'

I coughed. 'If you ever see Tir, you'll understand why that would be impossible,' I said dryly. I'd seen pictures of Earth's forests, and even the largest, wildest example had nothing on my lush home planet. 'No invasion, I promise.' I tapped on my desk screen, bringing up the multiple infostreams I'd put together about Earth. 'We have all these facts. We can access and assess them without assistance from you. But given what you've told me about your mother, perhaps you, more than most beings, would know that facts are nothing without context. Our understanding would never be whole without a human to help translate it.' I pointed to one infostream, a flow of Earth numbers rendered into Tirian hieroglyphs. 'This tells me the average temperature for the city you live in, divided by season, month, and day, for the last fifty of your Earth years. But it doesn't tell me what it *feels* like to live in those temperatures. How your behavioural patterns change to adapt. The different food you eat, the clothing you wear, the habits you shift. I could access other sources and try to piece it together myself, but my understanding might never be accurate. Instead, I can ask *you* about what it's like to be human.'

'I get it.' She kicked her feet again. 'Why do you want to know so much about humans, though?'

'There are multiple precedents for intervention,' I answered slowly. 'When a culture reaches a certain complexity, the Intergalactic Council may make ... overtures. Usually, the measure is space travel. Humans are no strangers to space, though you are yet to travel long distances. That next step may not be far off for your kind. As Tirians are humanoid, we may be well suited for making the overture on behalf of the Council in a few generations' time. We should know as much as we can to facilitate that.'

'Overtures?' she repeated. 'So, this is about first contact? About Earth being invited to join the super-secret intergalactic cool person club?'

I blinked at her. 'Ah, yes?'

She laughed. The sound sent a bolt of sensation through me, starting at my fingertips and ending with my cock stirring with interest. *No*, I told it sternly. *She's a patient.*

It didn't help with the next thing I had to say. I cleared my throat awkwardly. 'Along with whatever information you're willing to share, the Captain has asked me to broach the possibility of taking some samples from you. Skin scrapes, blood, saliva, hair. Other things, if you're willing. You can refuse.'

Her expression turned serious; her feet stilled. 'What will it be used for?'

I let the scientific part of myself take over. 'The Captain is interested in genetic compatibility. In how close our species are. She wants me to compare your DNA and body matter to Tirian samples. She's interested in the theory that our species may have met before, and whether there is biological evidence to prove that. We're clearly quite close in some respects –' I gestured vaguely at my humanoid form '– and different in others.' I tapped next to my eye, which lacked the black, ever-changing *pupil* her own boasted.

'Can I think about it?'

I nodded again. 'For as long as you wish. But I should check your translator. The Hamadryad messaged to say that it seemed to make you uncomfortable last night. She was worried.'

'I had a slight headache – hang on,' she said, and held up her hand. '*Genetic compatibility*. Um. Does that mean what I think it means?'

I gave her a frank look. 'Very probably.'

She snorted. 'I don't know what kind of magic *your* females are, but Earth women can't get pregnant with other Earth women.'

I turned back to my screen, my cheeks spreading with green. 'I think the Captain was more concerned with what happens should you extend your family.'

Her reflection gaped at me. 'Extend my … The Captain thinks I'll take more partners?'

'Our *karia* usually do. Four is considered a small family. A pair is very unusual.'

'*Karia*?' she repeated, her voice considerably higher than usual. 'I'm not a *karia*, Willow! I'm human!'

I studied her face. 'Does being human matter? From the research I've done so far, I know that humans are largely monogamous, but you have a word close to what Tirians are. Polyamorous. If you have a word for it, I believe that means it exists, yes? Which means some humans must practise it?'

She opened her mouth to say something, then promptly snapped it shut and looked away. 'Fuck nuggets,' she said, matter-of-factly. She jumped down from the bench. 'I think I've had enough of your clinic for today, doctor.'

I inclined my head, trying to push down my disappointment.

'But will you show me the other parts of the ship?' she went on. 'Elswyth was very excited about the Forest – for obvious reasons – but, if it's allowed, I'd like to see the rest of it.'

I pressed a button, stopping my recording. 'Of course. I'll show you everything I can.'

Maeve was curious, and showing her the main parts of the ship – the parts the Captain had approved, anyway – took long enough for Ashton to finish his morning shift and join us. She looked around with interest at the main dining hall; she choked out an incredulous laugh at the central screen library; her mouth fell open at the simulation rooms; her eyes lit with fire at the guards' gym and training rooms. She met the fascinated stares of the other Tirians with stares of her own. Being looked at didn't cow her; she simply looked back. Ashton shadowed us both, his glower enough to deter anyone who might have desired more than *looking* at the alien female.

There wasn't a soul on board – other than the Captain herself – who would test their will against his.

Except Maeve, of course, who seemed not to care at all that Ashton was a head and shoulders taller than she was, and twice as wide. When she veered deliberately down a restricted hallway and he bared his teeth at her, she *laughed*.

And I had to push aside some very vivid fantasies about Ash's growl and Maeve's laugh combining in a variety of different ways.

'It really is just like a world of its own,' Maeve murmured, as I led her onto a viewing platform that looked over the control bridge on one side, the Forest on the other, and straight out into space at the end.

'As you know, we can be on the ship for years. The effects of long-term travel in low gravity aren't just physical; there can be severe emotional and psychological repercussions. Designing ships that function as small cities has been shown to minimise those reactions across multiple cultures. The effects will never be entirely overcome – there is still a sense of isolation, of disconnection from home and from loved ones, and we are still susceptible to deep-space madness – but the complexity and the size helps. And the Forest, of course. None of this would be possible without the Hamadryad and her Forest.'

She shook her head. 'We've barely been to our moon, and you're doing this.'

'Your species has had other things to think about,' I said. 'Tir has never had a world war, for instance.'

'Yes, except those *helped* us forward, technologically speaking,' Maeve said, pursing her lips disapprovingly. 'Our knowledge took huge leaps because people were desperate to come up with new ways to kill each other.'

'Maybe you'll make time for new things now. Something less violent, perhaps.'

'Perhaps,' she said, but she didn't sound confident.

Ashton was on the opposite side of the platform, looking out into the black. It was something I tried to avoid thinking about wherever possible – logically, I knew that the universe stretched forever, but it was another thing to try to *comprehend* what that really meant, and the notion tended to make me nervous – but Ash *liked* it. Evidently, Maeve didn't mind so much, either, crossing the small space to stand beside the ship's First Guard and stare out at the stars.

Ashton gestured at the small screen between them. 'This is for mapping and close viewing,' he murmured, his voice taking on the deeper tones he usually saved for me and the privacy of my clinic. 'You can look, if you like.'

Maeve worked out how to use it swiftly, despite the instructions being in a script she couldn't read, and she spent some time enlarging stars and galaxy clusters, exclaiming at their colours and shapes. Ashton and I exchanged a glance over her head; Ash's eyes were unusually heavy, his grip on his staff tight enough to make his knuckles green.

She wouldn't have to be Tirian to claim us for her own.

He gave me a slight nod, as if he knew what I was thinking. 'If you need something to do,' he said slowly, his gravelly tone sweeping down my spines, 'I could spar with you later.'

Maeve looked up instantly, not bothering to hide her interest, her eyes bright. 'Spar? In the gym?'

Ashton nodded, then trailed his fingers over his cheek, where the bruise left by Maeve's fist had long faded. 'Judging by the day we met, you're well-schooled.'

Maeve grinned. 'My trainer will be glad to hear it.' She studied him closely. 'I'd be happy to get sweaty with you later, elf-boy.'

I inhaled before I could stop myself, a vision of them twisted together swimming in my mind's eye. *They'd be so beautiful*, I thought, imagining Maeve's strong thighs tight around Ash's hips, his hands gripping her waist.

Ash gave a soft growl, noticing as my spines went straight. 'I won't go easy on you,' he warned.

Maeve's grin widened. 'Good,' she crooned. 'That's the way I like it.'

Green gods. I turned away before I could betray myself.

A low alarm began to blare over the ship's communications system.

I turned back. 'What –'

'Fuck,' Ashton swore. 'That's not the drill tone.' He grabbed Maeve by the waist, then gestured at me with his free hand. '*Go*, Will.'

We ran from the viewing platform and down the ramp as one. Maeve had pushed Ashton away and was easily keeping pace with his longer legs. 'What does it mean?' she shouted over the noise.

'It's the proximity alarm.' I paused at the bottom of the ramp and turned to the left.

'*No you don't*,' Ashton growled, and pulled me to the right.

'I have to be in the clinic, Ash,' I protested.

'You're coming with me.'

'You're breaking protocol, Ashton Unclaimed.'

'Don't start that fuckery, Will. *Run*, or I will *carry* you.'

I decided not to argue, and followed Ashton down the hall, panting.

The corridors were chaotic as every soul on the ship sprinted to their allocated room, or to their designated emergency point. I should have been in the clinic, and Ashton should have been on the bridge, but we were both running towards Maeve and the Hamadryad's room, instead.

Ashton and Maeve pulled up, neither one panting like I was, and Maeve breathed on the scanner. 'El?' she called immediately, as soon as the door slid open.

Elswyth was nowhere to be seen. 'She stays with the heartree during an emergency,' I said, meaning to be comforting.

Maeve's face creased in concern.

'Help me with the blockers, Ashton,' I said to him. I crossed to activate the protective shutters, dimming the light from the Forest.

Ashton stopped short, staring at Maeve. 'Your body can't pull water from the atmosphere like ours can,' he said, almost to himself. 'If the systems go down and the doors lock ...'

'The Hamadryad's watering jugs,' I said, spying them next to the food generator. 'Empty them, rinse them, fill them with fresh water. She will understand.'

The alarm changed.

'Okay, even *I* know that's worse,' Maeve said tightly, blinking at the high-pitched blare. 'What does it mean?'

'It means Roth,' Ashton said grimly, and caught my eye. We stared at each other for a few heartbeats, then he shook his head and went to the tiny bench to refill the jugs.

I went into the bedrooms and shuttered the other windows, concentrating on breathing.

Maeve had followed me. 'What are *Roth*?' she said.

'They're the main reason our fleet is necessary.' The last shutter fell, plunging us into darkness. 'A warrior species bent on expansion by non-peaceful means.'

'I knew there had to be baddies,' Maeve said. 'There always are, somehow.'

I shook my head. 'I don't believe in *baddies*. But I do believe in the intergenerational grooming of violent behaviour and the control of information to result in beliefs of planetary or species superiority.'

We heard the door to the rooms slide open. 'Elswyth!' Ashton said hoarsely.

'Maeve – where's Maeve?' the Hamadryad called, her voice stricken.

A moment later, Elswyth appeared in the bedroom doorway. There was a moment of tense silence as she and Maeve stared at one another. The air between them went taut and heavy, and the Hamadryad's lips parted just as Maeve's cheeks flushed a hectic pink. Before either could speak, they were moving towards one another, a sun and her orbiting planet colliding. I couldn't tell which one kissed the other, and neither could I tear my eyes away as their mouths moved together in the dimness, fierce and soft all at once; Maeve's hand came up to cup Elswyth's nape, her fingers tangling in the silver strands of the Lady's hair. A moment – a lifetime – later, Maeve pulled away, looking surprised at herself.

'Thank you,' the Hamadryad said breathlessly, glancing back to fix her eyes on Ashton. 'Thank you for getting her here safely.'

'It's nothing, Lady,' Ashton said gruffly.

Elswyth smiled, a heartbreakingly full, beautiful smile that made my stomach flip and blood rush downwards.

It was the last thing I saw before the world went white.

ELSWYTH

I shrieked in pain, my eyes instinctively shuttering. Tirians had a second eyelid to manage the swiftly-changing light conditions of the Forest – its dark depths, its bright edges – and I blinked through the viscous tears that came with it, healing whatever damage the light had done.

The light faded after half a minute or so, leaving me with a white ring around my vision and a fierce headache. Maeve's head was in her hands and she sank backwards onto the bed, moaning. Ashton and Willow were doing the same thing as me, blinking swiftly as the after-effects of the light pulse faded.

'Green gods, we'll use up our blackbark supplies after that,' Willow muttered, pressing his fingertips to his temple. 'So much for the blockers.'

'What *was* that?' I said, reaching out to rub Maeve's shoulder tentatively. Our fierce kiss had been utterly unexpected – *had Maeve been* worried *about me?* – but I would take anything she gave me, and I'd give her anything she'd take in return. Even if that thing was a shoulder rub while she was in obvious pain.

'That,' Ashton said grimly, 'was a *starling*.'

'A *starling*?' Willow repeated, startled. 'What makes you think so?'

'Because I've seen it before. Another peacekeeping ship had one in custody for inter-galaxy embezzlement. The starling pulled that move –' Ashton nodded out at the Forest, where the light had come through the dome's glass '– to escape. I saw the screencasts, both from inside and outside the ship, and watched the little fucker go supernova. It's extremely difficult to hold them, if they don't want to be held.'

'Do you think the Roth had a starling prisoner, then?' Willow said softly.

Ashton shrugged. 'I couldn't say. Maybe they had one imprisoned; maybe one was working with them. Starlings don't really pick sides. The one on the peacekeeping ship was some kind of dignitary's spawn – the guard who sent me the casts thought they'd turned to embezzlement out of *boredom*.' Ashton shook his head. 'Fucking sapling.'

Maeve grabbed my hand. I rubbed my thumb over hers, soothing. 'It's all right, Maeve, you can open your eyes now,' I coaxed. 'It's gone.'

'I couldn't tell either way,' she said, her voice strangled.

I blinked. 'What?'

She tilted her head up, her face drained of colour, her eyes struggling to flutter open. 'Elswyth, I can't *see*.'

For a moment, I didn't understand the words. *Elswyth, I can't see*. I could see – even if the light was still fading – and Willow was frowning at Maeve, and Ashton was poking at his wrist screen, so we should have been fine.

Except Maeve's eyes weren't like ours.

'*Willow*!' I shrieked, but he was already at Maeve's side, tipping her chin back and gently lifting her eyelid with the tip of his finger. Ashton strode to the door and snarled wordlessly when it didn't open.

Willow moved his hand in front of Maeve's open eyes; there was no reaction. 'Light blindness,' he confirmed grimly. 'I've read about this. It can affect species who fly too close to a star during a flare.' He glanced at Ashton. 'I need to take her to the clinic, Ash. I wasn't on duty, so I don't have my emergency kit. I can't do anything from here.'

Maeve hung her head and moaned in pain. 'God, my head is fucking *killing* me.'

'Bridge, read me,' Ashton growled into his wrist screen.

There was a pause. 'First Guard, sir?'

'The human female has been injured by the light flare. She needs medical attention. Open her door, *now*.'

Another pause. 'The Captain says no, sir.'

'The Captain says *what*, sapling?'

An audible swallow came over the audio. 'She says is the human female bleeding, sir? She says is she about to perish?'

Ashton took a deep breath. 'She is not bleeding, sapling. But she has lost her sight.'

'The Captain says you must stay, sir. Until the threat has been cleared. She says ...' Another swallow. 'She says that she is interested to know why you are not on the bridge, and why Doctor Willow Unclaimed is not currently in his clinic. Sir.'

Ashton shut off the communication with another wordless snarl. 'Will. *Do something*.'

'Do you have any blackbark, Lady?' Willow said to me.

I ran into the bathroom and grabbed the regulation box of medical supplies, dumped it on the bed next to Maeve, then ran back and found a glass and filled it with water. Willow took it from me without comment, then measured out a tiny dosage of blackbark powder for Maeve.

'That isn't enough,' Ashton growled.

Willow shot him a glare; I blinked, startled. I'd never seen the doctor *glare* before. 'We have no idea what this might do to Maeve's system,' he snapped. 'As the Captain said, she isn't dying. Yes, she's in pain, but pain is preferable to un-thinkingly administering what might be a *poison* to her, First Guard. I do wish you'd believe that I know what I'm doing.' He mixed the black powder into the water. 'Maeve, I need you to sip this. We're going to have a few small mouthfuls, wait for thirty minutes, then have a few more.'

'Tell me what I'm putting in my body,' Maeve said tightly, pressing on her eyes.

'It's the powdered bark of a tree native to Tir,' I answered, going down on my knees before her and taking her hands. 'It has pain-killing and calming qualities. It also encourages muscle repair by stimulating certain proteins.' I looked up at Willow. 'It's the gentlest of all our painkillers. You can give it to Tirian children. Willow has chosen this one because it is absorbed slowly into our systems and can be purged swiftly through vomiting and fluid intake.'

'Do you trust him, Elswyth?' Maeve said slowly.

I met Willow's gaze. 'I trust him.'

Maeve nodded, then winced. 'All right then.'

I took the glass from Willow and held it close to Maeve's lips, so close it brushed her skin. She sipped at it cautiously.

'That's enough,' Willow said, when she'd taken half a mouthful. 'We need to do this slowly.' He ran his hands through his hair. 'Green gods, I'd give my entire clinic for my scanner. Maeve, may I feel your pulse?'

She nodded, and Willow placed his fingertips beneath her throat. I watched, fascinated. Tirians didn't possess a pulse point there; ours were along the many branches of our spines. There was something intimate about watching Willow touch her like that, so gently and so seriously, and he wasn't immune to it, his pale cheeks flushing a deep green as he sucked his bottom lip between his teeth.

I glanced across at Ashton. He was watching closely, his arms folded, every muscle in his body tense.

I sat back, giving Willow room to examine Maeve's eyes again. I hadn't thought much about why they were here – in my room, in *Maeve's* room – rather than where they should be – in the clinic and on the bridge respectively – but now I didn't have to. They were watching her so closely; too closely, almost. The hot stir of jealousy bit at my stomach; around me, the plants around the room shrank back, the arcadias over the bed giving an almost audible whimper.

I looked down at my hands. If Maeve was Tirian, she'd build a family with multiple partners; my mother had already mentioned it – gently, as if she were warning me.

I mulled over how I would feel if Maeve claimed another Tirian. The jealousy stirred, but curiosity did, too. What would it feel like to be part of a family like everyone else? What would it feel like to share a life with Tirians I could *trust*?

I knew – somewhere deep down inside, somewhere that was made of instinct and *elya* – that Maeve would never welcome a being who would make me uncomfortable, a being who could harm me. She'd care about my opinions, my feelings, my *safety*.

She'd care about my desires, too. About Tirians who could make my body sing the way she did.

I stretched out my fingers, watching my skin glow slightly at the thought. Perhaps I'd help her along. I could let her know which Tirians I liked, and which ones I didn't. I could make a list.

It isn't real. She's here for Tessa. She's not really your bonded, not your karia.

The thought was like a sudden downpour of icy rain. I clenched my fingers into fists, swallowing the false hope, pushing it back down where it belonged, down to the most secret depths of my being.

Maeve giggled.

I blinked at her.

'You didn't tell me your painkillers got you high, Els-wyth,' she said thickly, drawing out the sound of my name.

'High?'

'Y'know. Wasted. Ripped. Blasted. Juiced.'

Willow frowned. 'Maeve –'

'*Intoxicated*,' she said with exaggerated care. 'That's the one I was searching for.'

'They don't,' I said, exchanging a glance with Willow.

'Oh, beautiful,' Maeve said, laughing. 'If I could see where I was going, I'd be fucking flying right now.' She paused. 'I think I'm flying anyway.'

'Well, this is going fantastically,' Ashton growled. 'We've drugged her.'

'It's all right, elf-boy,' Maeve said condescendingly. 'I'm not that sad about it. If there was music right now, I'd be dancing.' She paused. 'Do you have music?'

'Of course we have music,' Ashton answered tersely.

I shuddered, remembering the awful racket at the club where I'd met Maeve. 'I don't think it's the same.'

Maeve laughed. 'I bet you listen to trees.'

Willow and I exchanged a glance.

'Oh my God, you *do*,' Maeve said into the silence. 'You listen to *tree music*.' She laughed again, uproariously, and put an arm across her face.

'Try not to grind your teeth, Maeve,' Willow said softly, watching her closely. He looked up. 'Ash ...'

'I know,' Ashton muttered. He tapped his wrist screen. 'Bridge, read me. The human needs *urgent* medical attention.'

I felt a hand hit my leg. 'El, beautiful,' Maeve whispered, her fingers creeping up my thigh. 'Come fly with me.'

I flushed, glancing sideways at Willow. He cleared his throat and hastily stepped away from Maeve, studying the room's food generator with sudden intensity.

Maeve sat and nuzzled at my stomach. 'Maeve,' I whispered to her. 'Ashton and Willow are here.'

She gave a deep chuckle. 'As if either of them would care. I know I wouldn't.'

I stared down at her, the false hope stirring briefly once more. *Perhaps I* will *give her a list.*

'Bridge, *read me*,' Ashton growled. '*Now.*'

'The Captain said she'll let you take the human to the clinic, but that she will expect you and the doctor to report immediately after she is settled, First Guard, sir,' the voice over Ashton's wrist screen said tremulously.

My guard gave a wordless snarl; it ripped through the quiet and made me shiver.

Maeve just laughed. 'Poor little elf-boy,' she said mockingly. 'Did something make you cranky?'

Ashton glared at her. My door hissed open and he turned on his heel and headed directly for the bed; I stepped out of the way, startled. He scooped Maeve up like she weighed nothing at all and held her close to his chest.

'Come on,' he growled at me.

I exchanged a startled glance with Willow, and we followed him out of the room.

It took Willow all of five minutes to give Maeve a tincture that reversed the effects of the blackbark and use one of his healing wands to rebuild the damaged tissue in her eyes. Maeve blinked swiftly afterwards, swearing she could see better than before, but bemoaning the loss of her short high.

'What will happen to them?' she said, when Willow and Ashton left to present themselves to my mother on the bridge.

I bit my lip; my stomach churned. I couldn't tell if it was jealousy again, or whether it was something else entirely.

'I don't know,' I whispered.

ASHTON

THE CAPTAIN WAS CALM, which was somehow worse than anger.

'Just so I have this right,' she said. 'In an emergency situation – one clearly indicated by the ship's alarms, which you have heard during more training sessions than I could count – my First Guard and the ship's Head Doctor spent their time not at their designated posts – *posts they are entirely aware of, and have evacuated to during the aforementioned training and throughout countless ship's drills* – but in the quarters of *my daughter* and her *alien bonded*, ignoring their *duties* and their *vows to this ship* and their *loyalty to Tir*. It does *not* escape my notice,' she went on, cutting Willow off when he opened his mouth to respond, 'that the ship's Hamadryad *also* left her post to check on the wellbeing of her alien bonded, and nor does it escape my notice that *at no point* did either of you suggest the Lady *return* to her heartree, thus leaving the ship in danger of not only attack, but vulnerable to Forest wilt *and everything that could come with it.*' She raised one dark brow. 'Is that the full canopy, or am I standing in the shadows?'

Willow swallowed audibly.

I'd been in the Captain's service long enough to know that any attempt to minimise harm would be met with a more extreme punishment. We wouldn't get away unscathed, but if we were honest, we might not lose our jobs and be dumped at the next space station to wait for a ride home.

'I take full responsibility, Captain,' I said, keeping my eyes on the floor. 'Doctor Willow Unclaimed was heading back to his lab. I stopped him from going. I allowed my worry for the Hamadryad and the human to interfere with duty. There is no excuse.'

'I've seen the security cast,' the Captain snapped. 'The doctor didn't need much convincing.'

Willow's jaw clenched. 'That is true,' he said levelly. 'I admit that my primary concern was for the Lady and Maeve.'

The Captain exhaled through flared nostrils. 'Do you think I was not concerned for *my daughter*, or for my own family? And yet *I* went to the bridge – *as is my duty and my honour.*'

'Yes, Captain,' I answered.

She gave a wordless growl. 'I am at a loss for what to do with you both,' she bit off. 'I *should* stand you both down and send you home. I would be within my rights to do so, and it's no less than you deserve.' She turned her back on us and flicked on her wall screen. 'Unfortunately ...'

I stared at the screen. 'Oh, green *gods*.'

'Precisely,' the Captain snapped. 'Precisely *that*, First Guard.'

Willow frowned. 'What am I looking at?'

I supposed that all he would see on the Captain's screen would be a radar image full of noise – the glow of a star, the hard light of planets and moons, and four moving blips.

The thing was, there should have only been *one* moving blip – us. No other craft was registered to be in this quadrant. The smaller blip I knew to be the ship we were trailing at a distance – the ship we'd used elevated unit travel to catch up with, the ship belonging to the cephalopod prince. The ship that we thought Maeve's friend might be aboard.

One of the others, I supposed, would have been the Roth ship that set off our alarms. Its trajectory showed that it had been close to the cephalopod's ship; it was now veering further and further away, presumably after the starling's light show. The proximity between the two ships suggested it was the cephalopod's starling consort – the one that had taken Maeve's friend from the club – that had gone supernova, rather than a Roth prisoner; it could have been a defensive action. If so, it was an effective one; Roth eyes possessed a pupil like Maeve's – if shaped differently – and I guessed that there wouldn't be too many beings on the Roth ship still able to pilot.

I didn't feel bad for them.

But there was one more ship, entirely unexplained, coming up fast behind us.

'Do we have visuals?' I said abruptly.

The Captain met my gaze. 'You're not going to like them.'

'Ah,' I managed.

'*Ah*?' Willow repeated. 'What –'

'Another one,' I said grimly. 'Another Roth ship.'

Willow stared at me, then raked his hands through his hair. 'I didn't think they came this far out!'

'They don't.' The Captain switched off her screen. 'Hence the reason I will not send you back to Tir in disgrace. But by the green gods, Ashton, you are *this close* to being demoted and having Adair take your place.'

'Adair is a fool, Captain,' I growled.

'Adair was *at his post* during the *emergency*, Ashton Un-claimed, not mooning after an alien,' the Captain snarled. 'I'm trying not to think about what else might be going on here. You know the rules of a First Guard. I'd wager you know them better than I do, Ash. Any family wishing to claim you for their own needs my *express approval* before I even *consider* taking the proposal to the Tirian Grove. As you are yet to seek this, you seem to be dancing on the point of a *fatal* breach of duty. This is not to mention that this involves *my daughter*, and if *any being* touches her without her *express invitation and ongoing consent*, I will remove multiple parts of their bodies *with my teeth*.' She loosed a growl. 'Given the circumstances – and given that I believe the human would have torn bark from you if did anything to upset Elswyth – I will cover for you this time. Next time, I'll toss you out the airlock.' She took a step forward. 'Not only that, I will strip you of your title, your commendations, and ruin your reputation in every Forest on Tir before I do so. Are we clear?'

I dropped my eyes. 'Yes, Captain.'

'Get out of my sight,' she said. 'But out of my sight and *to your posts*. That is a *direct order*.'

I gave her a swift bow and strode towards the door.

'Ashton?' she called after me. 'I am ready to consider a pro-posal *any time*. And I will consider with an open mind. But if you break the rules, you will *not* find me understanding.'

'You're doing that thing,' Willow said, when we were far enough from the Captain's quarters that we could both breathe again.

'What thing?'

'The thing where you and the Captain have a conversation – one that I can understand – on one level, and another conversation – one that is perfectly indecipherable to me – on a second.'

'We don't –' I started, but stopped when Willow's fingers brushed my elbow.

'Ash,' he said softly. 'What's going on?'

There was a storeroom ahead to my right; when we got there, I swiped my fingers over the sensor and swept Willow inside as if we were looking for something. The moment the door slid closed behind us, I pushed him up against the shelf and kissed him hungrily.

He sucked my bottom lip, groaning as I pushed my thigh between his. 'I know this move,' he grumbled. 'You're trying to distract me.'

'Is it working?' I kissed across the line of his jaw and down his neck.

'It always works,' he said crossly. '*Ash*. Tell me.'

I rested my forehead against his, taking a handful of his waving hair and letting it trail through my fingers. I loved his hair; it was strong and smooth and it caught the sun like the pale petals of seaside daffodils.

'Ashton,' he said warningly.

'You didn't miss that much,' I admitted. 'You know those ships shouldn't be here. So *why*? Why have *two* of them appeared? It can't be a coincidence.'

'One called the other here?' Willow said slowly, his hands tightening on my hips.

'Perhaps. If that's the case, what are they after?'

Willow was the smartest soul on the ship; he caught on within a heartbeat. 'The cephalopod ship – or *us*?'

'Exactly. And either way, we need to work out whether they could be a danger to the Peace Summit and Natare, too.'

'What can we do?'

This was the hard part. I dipped my lips to his and kissed him slowly, thoroughly. 'I love you.'

'I love you too, but you're avoiding the question.'

I slid a hand between his legs and squeezed his half-hard cock. 'Can't I just distract you instead?'

He went still. 'It's bad, then.'

'Representatives from every known Sector will be at that summit. We can't let the Roth get close, Will.'

'Ah,' he said. 'Our ship will be the first line of defence.'

'The edge of the Forest protects the heart.'

He bit his lip. 'Then we need to get Maeve and the Hamadryad off the ship.'

'Yes.'

'How?'

I ran my fingers up the length of him and cupped his swelling head through his pants. 'I haven't figured it out yet.'

'But you will,' he said, with enough certainty that I swallowed. Willow had faith in me that I didn't feel myself.

'I'll try,' I said, my voice hoarse. *How do I get Elswyth off board without her heartree?*

Willow reached behind me and locked the door, then dropped to his knees.

'Will?' I said thickly.

His fingers went to the waistband of my leathers. 'You were right, Ash. Distract me.'

MAEVE

It had taken a few weeks of wandering for me to get a handle on the massive ship. Its corridors were labyrinthine, but it was almost impossible to get lost; in one way or another, every path led to the Forest. That didn't mean I always knew where I was; I'd accidentally stumbled into places I clearly shouldn't have been numerous times. It was easy to tell when I'd crossed some kind of silent line; when I was heading for somewhere I didn't have clearance for, Ashton or Willow – whichever one drew the short straw of keeping an eye on me that day – would silently put their hand under my arm and gently escort me elsewhere.

I wasn't usually into that kind of touch; it was the sort of gesture I'd usually answer with a raised eyebrow and a less polite *kindly fuck right off*. As it turned out, though, there were a lot of things I didn't mind when it came to those two males, including the way Ashton scowled at any being who got within arm's length. He'd drawn the short straw that morning, and had been *particularly* grumpy; in answer, I went out of my way to get under his skin, smiling flirtatiously whenever someone gave me the look over. When a pretty male favoured me with a wide smile, I answered it, then followed up with a wink.

Ashton growled deep in his throat – like a fucking *lion* – and his hand closed over my wrist. A moment later, I was being dragged bodily away.

I laughed with absolutely zero restraint, which made the pretty male frown in confusion and Ashton growl even louder. I kept it up – until Ashton dragged me into a training room.

Its purpose was immediately recognisable. Most of the room was empty, its floor not the stone-like white that lined the ship's corridors, but a springy green moss that felt like the Pod's pliable chairs. There was no equipment, just objects that looked like weights to one side, and a wall of hanging bags that seemed suspiciously like giant seed pods.

The ship's Third Guard, Adair, was pummelling one with strapped fists; he stopped when we walked in, his face taking on its habitual smirk.

'Come to teach the human her place?' he sneered, somehow managing to both leer at me and dismiss me in one impressive expression.

Adair was, as we would say on Earth, a dick.

Ashton ignored him. 'Do you want to spar with me, or with a simulation?'

I was immediately curious about their training simulations, but answered truthfully. 'You.'

He gave a sharp nod. 'Here, then.'

He gestured to an inset on the moss-covered wall which held an array of fibrous bandages and some pots of salve. There was no protective gear – no headgear, no guards, no vests, and not a mouthguard in sight – but this seemed to be normal to Ashton, who wasted no time stroking the vines of his armour until the bark chest plate fell to the floor.

I swallowed.

Ashton was cut. Breathtakingly, intimidatingly cut. The kind of cut that would take a human man years of his life and several interesting – and possibly illegal – supplements to achieve. His white shirt didn't hide much, clinging to every ridge and line of muscle in a way that had my throat closing over and my mouth growing dry.

Among other reactions my body was having.

The massive guard seemed to have zero awareness of the lust currently coursing through me; he strapped his hands with a determined expression, one he might wear into battle. When he was done, he turned to me, a bandage in hand.

'Here,' he said gruffly.

'I can do it.'

He raised an eyebrow. 'I know you can,' he answered, and waited.

The temptation to let him touch me was too great; I held out a hand.

At the first brush of his fingertips, the shock ran through me again; I bit my lip so hard I tasted blood. It was as if my body had been asleep before it stepped aboard this ship and was finally waking up. I watched silently as he strapped my hand; I had to concentrate on staying upright when his fingertips brushed my wrist.

My wrist. Not anything *fun*. My fucking *wrist*.

When he finished one hand, he checked his work, trailing his fingers over my palm before taking up the other hand. I tried to steady my breathing as I prepared for a second round of torture.

'Is all well?' he asked innocently.

I bared my teeth. 'Perfectly fine.'

'Probably nerves,' Adair said.

We both ignored him.

My fingers were curled, and Ashton straightened them gently. Like Elswyth, his skin was cooler than a human's, but I liked it; I was much too hot, standing with the giant male in my personal space. He was surprisingly careful, his every touch soft and considered, as if I were made of something breakable.

Usually, I'd feel belittled by someone thinking I needed such a soft touch. But Ashton's gentleness as he wrapped my hand didn't feel like condescension.

It felt like respect.

'How does that feel?'

I stared at him for a moment, wondering if Tirians could read minds, before I realised he meant the bandage. I cleared my throat and curled my fingers into loose fists. 'Good.'

A slight green flush spread down from his thorn-lined cheekbones. He gave his signature terse nod. 'Good,' he repeated, and stepped back.

Adair leaned against a wall, his arms crossed, his face set in a sneer.

I had a sudden wish that it was him I was about to throw punches at.

'I can tell him to leave,' Ashton said, watching me carefully.

Not making the choice for me; noting my agitation and offering help.

I pulled my hair over my shoulder and braided it into a rough plait, then tucked the tail under my shirt so it wouldn't get in the way. 'Tell who to leave?'

Ashton's lips curled up at the corners. 'Well then,' he said, stepping back and taking his place in the middle of the room, holding his arms loosely by his sides as he rolled his massive shoulders. 'Show me what you've got, human.'

I stepped forward to meet him. The world began to slow as adrenaline surged; I raised my hands, one before my face and one shielding my neck, ready to fight.

Though I wouldn't have been opposed to a fuck.

I waited for him to throw a punch, but he didn't, holding his relaxed pose, his expression one of pleasant blankness. Against the wall, Adair snorted.

I smiled, and struck straight at Ashton's face.

He'd evidently been off his game the first time I met him; his arm came up before my fist got anywhere near him and blocked the blow. He didn't return it, resuming his pleasant expression and relaxed stance.

I struck again, this time aiming for his stomach. He wove out of the way with surprising grace.

'Good,' he said approvingly. 'You're more likely to do damage there.'

'Except you wear armour,' I muttered.

'We do. But our armour is more likely to crack than our bone, so it's a better choice than a strike to the face, no matter how satisfying *that* might be.'

I struck again, dancing around to aim at his side. He blocked the blow, and returned one of his own, aiming for my cheek. I ducked it just in time, managing to land a punch under his upper arm.

'Good,' he said again. 'But this time mean it, Maeve.'

I laughed and danced forward, delivering a number of strikes to his torso. He blocked several punches then caught my wrist, spinning me around and pinning me against his body, just as he had when I'd first boarded the ship. I tried my usual moves to escape, but he hooked a foot around my leg and I found myself face down on the floor with what felt like a thousand kilos of muscle pinning me down, his hands around my wrists.

He shifted slightly, holding his weight off me. His breath shivered over my ear. 'You let me do this.'

'What makes you say that?'

He chuckled. 'You're not struggling.'

'Maybe I'm conserving my energy,' I said archly.

'For what?'

I yanked a leg up and pushed an arm outright with all my strength, throwing him momentarily off balance. I used my slight advantage to push his bulk off me, then was on my feet a moment later, landing a solid kick to what – in a human – might have been a kidney.

He gave a soft grunt and was back on his feet before I could do any further damage. I'd expected frustration, anger even, but instead his eyes were lit gold with challenge and his lips were carved into a smile.

'Again,' he said.

We sparred for what felt like hours and no time at all. At some point, Adair left, and other guards arrived to watch instead, but I didn't notice who because they didn't matter. Nothing mattered but the massive male in front of me who moved around the training room as if he was as much a dancer as a soldier. Nothing mattered but the moments his skin slid over mine, the moments his weight pinned me down on the floor, the moments his eyes glowed when I fought back with all my skill and all my strength.

Nothing mattered but his soft words when we were a sweating, panting mess and he judged we'd done enough, before he pushed me to the door with his hand on the small of my back so I could take a shower.

'You're good, human.'

I didn't know what was wrong with me. There were *thousands* of Tirians aboard the ship, and a good portion of those used *Unclaimed* as a kind of last name, which meant they were available – for flirting, at least, given their rules about bonding and families. I didn't care, though; even when I saw a particularly attractive example of the species – to my human-skewed lens, anyway; I got the feeling that Tirian beauty standards were different – I felt no compulsion to offer my usual *well, hello* smile. I just ... didn't want to.

Not with the rest of the ship, anyway. There were three Tirians who were a different matter. An entirely too seductive, *delicious* matter that I wanted to break open and lose myself in.

I wouldn't. I *couldn't.*

You're here for Tessa, I reminded myself each day, with increasing desperation.

This isn't real, I reminded myself, when I shared a sleepy kiss with Elswyth each morning.

You're going back home, I reminded myself, when Elswyth sent a list of names to the hand screen I'd been given – one column of Tirians she liked, and one she didn't – with an addendum beneath: *Just in case.*

You're not Tirian, I reminded myself, when I studied the list, and my heart skipped a beat at two names in the *yes* column.

But the further we flew from Earth, the harder it was to hold on to those reminders. The longer I spent on the ship, the more its white corridors and beautiful Forest began to feel comfortable, feel normal – to feel like *home*.

And the more time I spent with Willow in his clinic, listening to him talk, or the more often I walked through the ship with Ashton, teasing him and being teased cautiously in return, and the more time I spent with my body wrapped around Elswyth, listening to the musical cries she gave as I pushed her to the brink over and over, the more the unfamiliar warmth would spread through my chest, making me ache for something I'd never imagined before.

I spent most of my mornings with Elswyth in the Forest – Tirians always said the word reverently, with a pronounced capital *F*, and so I did, too – but I inevitably got twitchy sitting still after an hour or so. Ashton had started teaching me the Tirian hieroglyphic language – the magic of the translator didn't extend to *visual* translation, unfortunately for me – and we spent a good deal of time sitting nestled in the roots of Elswyth's heartree. I'd periodically reach up and touch her trunk, just in case she could feel it.

Ashton watched me do it every time, but he never touched the heartree himself.

'I know that you need the Forest psychologically, but is that the only purpose it serves?' I asked him one morning, as I lounged on a bed of moss beneath Elswyth's reaching boughs.

He eyed me sideways. 'Thinking of stealing our secrets, human?' he said, in the deadpan way he had when he was teasing.

I snorted. 'Yes, undercover intelligence mastermind over here, desperate to get back to her home planet with all the information she can about the space tree-elf aliens,' I drawled. 'I just realised that the Forest must be a huge energy suck for the ship, actually, but I'm sure that your engineers are a million times smarter than I am and have done something about that.'

He leaned back, considering. Ashton always sat painfully straight; it made me want to rumple him up, to see him curled up on a couch with corn-chip crumbs on the front of his hoodie while he watched something excruciatingly trashy on a streaming service.

Tessa, I reminded myself desperately. *I'm here for Tessa.*

'I suppose it is an energy ... suck,' he said slowly. They were starting to get used to Earth slang, but it was still hilarious to watch them try to work out what I was saying. 'But at the same time, the Forest is assisting in oxygen production, and purifying the air. We don't need as much oxygen as you seem to – the air on Tir has larger quantities of other elements – but it's still necessary for our survival. The Forest's roots are part of the water filtration process, too. The water is chemically treated, but the roots assist in its cleaning as it cycles through the ship. And I think ...' He trailed off, tilting his head back and staring up into the canopy. He looked like a statue – the handsome-as-fuck, overly-muscled kind, the sort you'd stare at and wish would come to life. 'You shouldn't underestimate how much we *need* it. The landmasses of Tir are almost completely covered in forest, and it grounds us. Balances us. Calms us.' He dropped his eyes back to me. 'We don't function without it. We need it like oxygen, need it like water, need it like food. Have you ever felt something like that?'

I met his intense stare, his irises flickering between brown and gold, as my cheeks flushed. I swallowed, and, without thinking, reached out to touch Elswyth's trunk again. Her leaves shivered, whispering in a non-existent breeze. I jerked my hand back.

'No,' I said, trying to convince myself. 'No, I haven't. But I'm sure I can imagine.'

He looked away.

I cleared my throat and willed my cheeks to cool, desperately searching for a safer topic. 'Willow said you had arboreal DNA. How the heck did that happen?'

Ashton shrugged, studying the black of space past the glass dome. 'There are several theories. Our kind is very old, and we started keeping written records only recently, so we might never know for sure. Some say that the trees on Tir developed sentience. Some say that both the Forests and the Tirians are evolutionary branches stemming from a creature we have no knowledge of.' A smile tugged at the corners of his mouth. 'Some say that our ancestors were just *really* fond of trees.'

I snorted. 'I suppose that's not unheard of on Earth, either. We have myths about half-human, half-tree beings, and women who transformed into trees to escape men. Anna told me about a famous poet who seemed overly fond of trees, too.'

Ashton grinned at me, a full, unreserved, overwhelming grin. He was always handsome – even with the pupil-less eyes – but when he smiled like that, my heart thumped hard against my ribs. 'Each to their own,' he said, 'but imagine the bark burn.'

I tried not to.

The screen at his wrist beeped and he stood straight. 'Speaking of injuries, the doctor can see you now,' he said. 'Come on, human.'

I waved to Elswyth – well, to Elswyth-heartree – and led the way to Willow's clinic, mostly to prove that I could. The ship was fairly quiet, and had been since the light flare. I could tell that the Tirians were on edge, though I wasn't sure why. I could guess, especially given the new daily drills we had to run through: drop what we were doing, make our way to our evacuation points, wait. Ashton had told me to carry around a bottle of water, just in case; Tirian skin could, apparently, take water molecules from air when it really needed to, which I very definitely could not. I didn't mention that I'd die of oxygen deprivation far more quickly than thirst; it seemed rude, especially when the First Guard was so careful to make sure the bottle was always filled to the brim.

My evacuation point was with Elswyth, in the hangar next to one of the tiny Pod ships. We didn't practise the next bit, which was to get inside and – in Ashton's words – *fly like fucking wind demons, as far away as possible.*

I didn't know what wind demons were, but I got the gist.

He and Willow wouldn't evacuate; they'd stay with the Tirian ship no matter what, like the Captain of the Titanic. I frowned at the thought, reaching up to feel the tiny furrow between my brows.

Willow was running a spore cleaning cycle in his clinic when we arrived, so we waited outside for it to finish. The spores were magical; we didn't have an exact equivalent on Earth, but I gathered from Willow's explanations that they were close to a type of microbe. Though organic in nature, the ship's maintenance staff could program spore mixes to target different things. The ones in the showers were gentle, leaving the good skin bacteria and eating up the bad; the spores used for cleaning were harsher, consuming everything in a matter of seconds. The Forest had its own special mix to ensure that rot and mould were eliminated; and there were spores that swept through the ship every night at the same time, leaving everything shiny and clean for the morning.

Every single part of the process had been designed by Willow, while he was the Tirian equivalent of an undergraduate student.

There's a reason he's the Head Doctor, Ashton had said wryly. *His brain is bigger than almost anyone else's on Tir.*

The clinic door slid open. 'All done,' Willow called from inside. 'Come in.'

I went in alone; Ashton used the time I was with Willow to report to the Captain, then go back to Elswyth. I knew he was telling the Captain every tiny detail he could about me, but I didn't really mind; when you were an open book, you had no secrets to protect.

It occurred to me that what I was doing was possibly traitorous – treasonous, even – but I didn't know what options I had. I could lie or obscure the information, I supposed, but given that Elswyth had been able to access the internet before I'd even come on board, it was all information that the Tirians would have found eventually anyway.

I was just happy I'd been able to email my mum, though she hadn't even noticed I'd gone. She spent her return email complaining at length about her university accommodation and the onboarding process – she wasn't great with administrative IT – and I answered with a medium level of sympathy and an off-the-cuff comment that I'd taken a spur-of-the-moment trip north and might not answer emails straight away.

I'd also contacted Advena's owner, Jessa, and told her I was taking some time off. She was yet to email me back, but given she'd been pressing me to take leave since Tessa's disappearance, I assumed she wouldn't be too pissed about it.

I'd emailed Anna, too, but received no response. I let her know that I was safe, and asked her to do the same, but with every day that passed with nothing back from her I was getting more and more worried. Anna didn't exactly have the best home life, and I knew all too well that she didn't have many people looking out for her. I'd gathered from the lack of media when I searched online for my name – and the lack of panic from my mum – that Anna hadn't called the police; I supposed it was probably better in the long run, but if she didn't get back to me soon, I considered trying to contact them myself.

'You look pensive,' Willow said softly.

I lifted myself up onto his bench. 'I left home for one friend, but now I'm wondering if I've abandoned another.'

He glanced across at me, his fingers stilling on his screen. 'Are they in danger?'

I bit my lip. 'I don't know. That's the problem.'

Willow nodded. 'How can I help?'

Tirians didn't go in for meaningless platitudes, nor emotional displays. I liked that about them. Instead of saying *I'm sure she's fine* or *it's natural to worry*, Willow asked a practical, useful question. He *would* help, too, if he could; it wasn't an empty offer.

'I'm not sure you can,' I said. 'But thank you anyway.'

He gave me a tight smile. 'Let me know if you figure it out.' He held up some tiny jars. 'Are you comfortable with me taking some more samples today?'

I decided that I was, then proceeded to hold my breath as Willow took a tiny scrape of skin and a few errant hairs. Where Ashton smelled like freshly-baked cookies and Elswyth like an edible bouquet, Willow was something spicier, like raisin toast – which meant that I wanted to slather him in butter and gorge myself, metaphorically speaking. His closeness did delicious things to my body; my nipples strained against my top – I'd thrown my bra down the first available garbage shoot and was yet to regret it – and I squeezed my thighs together to ease the ache growing between them.

Keep it together, McCarthy, I told myself.

After the hair and skin, he took some blood; it wasn't anything like having a blood test. Instead of a needle, Willow had a tiny stamp. It snuck under my skin so swiftly I barely felt the pinch, drawing the tiny amount of fluid he needed for the sophisticated Tirian systems, which could run multiple tests on just one drop. He took some swabs from my cheeks and tongue and ran a scanner over my face to build a digital image of my bone structure. All the while, he spoke, easily and softly, telling me what he was doing and why.

'There's something else the Captain has requested, but you can refuse,' he said, flushing slightly, his cheeks green.

'Mmm?'

'A scan.'

'You've already scanned me. My respiratory system, my skeleton, my digestive tract, my eyes, my heart. What else is left?'

'Your reproductive system,' he said, pretending to type on his screen.

I knew his real typing by now, and I knew that he *pretended* to type when he was trying to stay professional. 'Does that mean you'll probe me?' I teased.

'No!' he protested. I'd made him read a few short sci-fi stories about probing and he hadn't been into them at all. *She didn't consent!* he'd growled during one of them, outraged.

Turns out, my aliens were pretty feminist. I was here for it.

'The scan is entirely external,' he went on. 'But ... I will need to be close.'

I shivered. 'How close?'

'It's like one of your pregnancy ultrasounds. The scanner needs to touch your skin.'

I was momentarily glad it wasn't an internal scan, because if he gave me one of those, Willow would immediately realise how much I didn't care about him touching my skin.

'Fine,' I said brusquely. 'What do I need to do?'

'Lie down,' he instructed. 'Lift your shirt when you're ready.'

I settled down on the bench. It was made of the same material as the seats in Elswyth's pod, and it moulded to my body, comfortable as a bed. I shimmied my shirt up to my ribs.

'Are you comfortable?'

I nodded.

'May I begin?'

'Yes, doctor,' I answered. 'You may.'

'Let me know if this is too cold,' Willow said softly.

I jumped when the scanner touched my skin, and he pulled back and warmed it between his hands before trying again. He was looking across at his screen, not at me, so I took the opportunity to study his face, drinking in the moss-green eyes, the square line of his jaw, the arch of his fair brows. Willow's features were slightly different to the other Tirians; his eyes were larger, his cheekbones sharper, his jaw wider. His birth mother had been from a different species, he'd said; when he'd spoken about it, his voice had been so sad that I hadn't pressed any further. Regardless of his parentage, he was handsome as fuck; the lack of pupil was no longer a shock, and nor were the sharp thorns lining his cheekbones and ears. In fact, every time I looked in a mirror, I was surprised to see the black circles in my irises and my thornless skin.

He set the scanner down on my stomach again; I managed to stay still the second time. 'I've been doing some research about what goes where,' he said, 'but you might have to help me.'

'Why does the Captain want this? Is she planning a breeding program?' I half-joked.

'She doesn't care about other humans,' he answered, frowning distractedly as he moved the scanner over my stomach. 'She cares about you. If you were to get pregnant, she wants to know what the baseline should look like, so we could help if something went wrong.'

I was touched; from what I understood of other women's experiences – I had heard some *stuff* at Advena; people will tell you all kinds of things when you work behind a bar – the doctors on Earth didn't even give that much of a shit about human women.

Not that I had *any* intention of getting pregnant, ever. Babies had never been my thing.

'There it is!' Willow said triumphantly. 'Your left ovary.'

'Congratulations,' I told him.

He flashed me a rare, wide smile. 'Now to find the other one. Humans are surprisingly complex.'

The scanner moved across my stomach; his free hand settled next to it, keeping my skin taut.

I sucked in a breath.

'Maeve?' he said immediately, concerned.

'All good,' I choked, trying not to imagine what his hand would feel like elsewhere.

He shot me a slight frown, then looked back at his screen. 'There,' he said. 'The right ovary.' He frowned again. 'There's something on this one.'

'A cyst, maybe.' I'd had cysts before, along with the pain, bloating, and nausea they could cause, but had been lucky enough to avoid needing surgery. I'd had so many of these scans I could almost have done it myself.

I'd never had them done by a doctor I wanted to touch so badly, though.

'I'll look it up later,' he muttered, making a note; I bit my lip to keep from smiling.

He moved the scanner down, closer to my waistband. I hooked my fingers underneath and tugged it down slightly, letting him search for my uterus. His free hand brushed over my skin and came to rest just below my hip. Heat flared between my legs.

'Is it weird?' I said, mostly to distract myself. 'Looking inside people?'

'I don't think so,' he said, adjusting the scanner slightly. 'I feel like I know you better.' His fingers shifted absently over my hip.

'You can do that without the scanner,' I teased.

He was silent for a moment, as if weighing up his response. 'I hope I will,' he said at last, meeting my eyes.

I couldn't stop my lips curving up at that.

He moved the scanner slightly lower. My mouth went dry as he brushed over some of the short curls there.

'Uterus,' he murmured.

'Mmm,' I managed.

'Done.'

I knew I shouldn't have been disappointed when he took the scanner away, but my lips twisted and the flesh between my legs throbbed.

And then I realised his hand was still on my hip.

He didn't say anything, and neither did I. We both watched as his finger drew an idle circle around the sharp rise of bone, then observed the goosebumps form on my skin.

We both watched as he drew a line across my stomach and his fingers circled my other hip. Though his fingertip was cool, heat spread through me at the touch. A moment later, his eyes widened as he realised what he was doing; he snatched his hand away.

'Sorry,' he said hoarsely. 'I don't ... I'm so sorry, Maeve. There's no excuse. You should go.'

'Should I?'

'You're my patient. That was beyond inappropriate. I can't ... I *won't* betray your trust.'

'The scanning is done,' I pointed out.

'I'll find someone else to update my notes,' he said, not looking at me. 'You like Cedar, don't you? They can take over.'

'They'll have a hard time doing that if I refuse to see them.'

'Maeve –'

'Willow, I get it, I really do. Believe me, if I thought you were taking advantage of me, your balls would be hanging from my earrings right now.' I reached out and touched his hand. He inhaled at the contact. 'If you don't want to touch me, then *of course* don't touch me. But don't keep your distance on my account.' I placed his hand back on my hip, back where it made my entire body hot and shivery all at once.

'I –' His lovely brow crumpled. He swept his thumb back and forth over my skin, sending delicious waves of heat across my stomach and an answering echo between my legs. He groaned, fanning out his fingers as if he couldn't stop himself, as if touching me was as inevitable as the dawn. Despite my craving for Elswyth, all I wanted in that moment was to hook my legs around Willow's hips and feel him thrust into my body until he lost his measured control.

His body dipped until his beautiful face – his beautiful *lips* – were an inch from mine. My breath was uneven, shaky, and I sucked my bottom lip between my teeth and bit down. He watched me do it, his moss-green eyes glowing as they fixed on my mouth.

He took a deep, shuddering breath. 'The Hamadryad,' he said, and straightened, tearing his hand away.

I snorted. 'Half the ship seems to think I'll find more partners, Willow. If you think we haven't already had a conversation about this, then you are severely underestimating both of us.'

He blinked at me. 'She knows?'

'She gave me a list of Tirians she wasn't comfortable with, and another of ones she liked. Take a guess which list you were on, Willow.'

He swallowed, closing his eyes for a moment. 'That's … That's extremely flattering. But I think …' He opened his eyes and gave me a look full of resignation. 'I think this means something different to me than it does to you.'

'What does it mean to you?' I said softly.

'It would be the beginning of something that I would never want to end, Maeve.'

The warmth spread through my chest at the admission, chased by sorrow. Because there *would* be an end. When I found Tessa, all of this – whatever I had with Elswyth, whatever I started with Willow – would just … stop. They'd become nothing more than memories – memories that would make me ache in a way I didn't want to understand.

Even though I knew that – even though I *knew* I was being unfair – I couldn't leave it there.

'How would you want it to begin, Willow?'

He shot me a look of such naked desire that my breath caught. 'I'd begin with a kiss,' he said, his gaze falling to my mouth again. 'Slow and gentle, until I learned every curve of your lips. Until I could memorise the taste of you.' He reached out and took up a lock of my hair, sliding it through his fingers. 'I'd bury my hands in this, until I knew how it felt against my fingertips, against my skin.' I took a shuddering breath. 'Then, when you were ready, I'd touch you.' His hand slid around and cupped my cheek. 'It would be innocent – at first. I'd stroke your face, your lovely ears, your neck.' His hand slid down to rest on my collarbone. 'Here. I'd learn the shape of your arms, what made you shiver. What made you *writhe*.'

I gave a needy pant as his voice roughened.

'Then I'd touch other places.' His hand slid down, cupping my breast through my shirt. I arched without thinking, pressing my hardening nipple against his palm. 'Here, until you were whimpering.' His thumb ran over my nipple, back and forth, sending bolts of sensation straight between my legs. He leaned down; his breath caressed my ear. 'Until you were *begging*.' His hand moved down to grasp my hip; a disappointed whine escaped my throat before I could stop it. 'Because I want to touch you until I know every single thing that you like, and every single thing that you love. I want to touch you until you fall to pieces, Maeve, so thoroughly and so completely that only I can put you back together again.' He grasped my hip more firmly. 'And after that – if you wanted it, though I hope you would *need* it – I'd want to bury myself so deeply inside you that we couldn't tell where you started and I ended.'

I stared at him, my heart beating wildly. 'Holy heck, Willow,' I said. 'That sounds pretty fucking good to me.'

His jaw clenched; he took his hand away. 'That isn't all I'd want from you, Maeve.'

I swallowed. 'Guess we're at an impasse, then.' I shifted on his bench, hot and needy and all kinds of uncomfortable.

For a moment, I let myself imagine what it might be like. To have something more than just one night of sex. To have someone who cared for me, who supported me, someone who I whispered to at night. Someone who made my life better by simply existing.

I inhaled as the realisation hit me. I already *had* that. Elswyth gave me all those things – and more.

Willow was watching me carefully, his expression unreadable. He reached out and trailed a feather-light touch over my cheek. 'I used to think green was the most beautiful colour,' he murmured. 'But I find myself liking pink more by the day.'

We stared at each other; the world stilled around me.

Maybe there were others – two others, in particular – who *also* made my life better. Maybe the Tirians were right about their whole *family* thing.

And maybe I could give *them* the things that they gave me. Maybe I'd make *their* lives better, too.

'Fuck it,' I snarled.

'I think I've changed my mind,' he said at the same time.

We reached for each other as one, his hands cupping my face, mine fisting in his hair as our lips met. It wasn't anything like the gentle caress he'd described; his kiss was hot, demanding, *hard*. Our lips fought a fierce battle until mine parted and his tongue pushed between them, dancing until he took control and used it to fuck my mouth until I moaned.

He pulled back, his eyes darkening. 'Make that sound again,' he demanded.

I managed to conjure a smug smile. 'Earn it.'

He smiled back, just as smugly, and a moment later I was flat on my back and his mouth was on my neck, licking and sucking and scraping his teeth over the sensitive skin. I forgot myself and moaned again as his hand found the swell of my breast, his thumb brushing my nipple through my shirt.

'You've done this before,' I said breathlessly.

'This?' he said, circling my aching peak. 'No. Not this, I haven't.' He pinched me and I cried out; his eyes were fixed to my face, taking in my every reaction. He swallowed, his hand moving down to rest on the bare skin of my stomach, beneath where my shirt had bunched over my ribs. 'I want to see you.'

'Thank the fucking stars,' I muttered, and dragged my shirt unceremoniously over my head.

A growl ripped from his throat as he stared at me, naked to the waist. 'You are temptation personified,' he grated out. He circled my nipple again, watching it pebble beneath his fingertip.

I arched my back shamelessly, pushing into the touch. 'If you want to keep kissing, there are a number of fun places I can suggest you try.'

'Here being one of them?'

'It's especially fun with tongue,' I told him.

He gave a wicked grin, so different to his usual calm that it set my heart pounding. 'Most things are.'

He took me in his mouth, sucking until I cried out. He worked one breast and then the other, holding me still when I squirmed beneath him, my hips rocking up, desperately seeking friction. His rough tongue flicked my aching flesh, my inner walls fluttering as arousal built. Without warning, he sucked again – hard – and I whined at the delicious shock, my back arching at the sensation, trying to draw him closer.

'Green gods, Maeve,' he murmured, his mouth travelling downwards as I continued to squirm beneath him. 'You could make a stone catch alight.'

My body interpreted that as a compliment; my cheeks flushed as the warm feeling spread through my chest again. I tried to ignore it, pressing my thighs together desperately. He noticed the movement; a moment later, his hand slid down and he cupped me through my jeans, giving me the pressure I was craving. I moved shamelessly against him, chasing my own pleasure until sensation began to flood my core.

'Fuck, Willow,' I choked.

'So beautiful, Maeve,' he murmured. He took a shuddering breath. 'Gods, the things I want to do with you.' He pulled back, pressing the heel of his hand down harder, just where I needed it.

I cried out. His free hand found a breast and his thumb brushed over my nipple, back and forth, back and forth, until the pleasure turned sharp and I cried out again, panting as my climax began to build.

His fingers came together and tugged; every thought fled my mind as the pleasure broke and I came, crying out wordlessly as the waves crashed through me. Willow made a satisfied sound, one so entirely male I almost laughed, his fingers absently caressing my breast as my body calmed.

He helped me sit when I was done, my core so utterly wrecked by the strength of my response that my legs were shaking. I ran my fingers over his jaw, watching as his lips parted and his eyes flared. I traced the thorns over his cheekbones before moving down, skirting his strong shoulders and chest before descending over his hard stomach and lower.

He caught my hand before I could touch anything interesting. 'I don't expect reciprocation, Maeve.'

I shivered, because they were words that I had literally never heard from a human male's mouth. 'I'm not doing it because you expect it. I'm doing it because I want to touch you, Willow.'

He searched my face, his eyes flaring a glowing green. 'Are you sure?'

I raised an eyebrow at him. 'Yes, Willow, I'm sure.'

He let go of my wrist; I seized the opportunity and cupped his cock through his leathers. He was rock-hard, though the nature of the leathers made it difficult to discern much else. I stroked the vines over his seam and watched them slowly unravel, then sucked in a breath as his leathers parted and he was bared to me.

His basic shape was familiar enough – a deliciously long, thick shaft, with a swollen head – but *luminescent* white pre-cum was leaking from the *two* slits on his crown, and his shaft was marked by ridges reaching from his base to his tip. The biggest difference of all was a swelling on the underside of his shaft, about halfway up; it was the size of a small coin and looked very much like the *burl* to Elswyth's *notch*.

I took him in hand without preamble, wanting nothing more than to climb on his lap and sink down. I had a feeling that his burl would press exactly where I liked it – on my g-spot – and would drag over it in the most delicious way as I moved.

No, Maeve, I told myself.

Not this time, anyway.

I wrapped my fingers around his base instead, watching his face. He tipped his head back, his lips parting; the light caught the thorns on his cheekbones. The warmth in my chest flared and spread; I shook my head against the feeling, unsettled by the strength of it, and moved my hand up Willow's cock, skirting over the unfamiliar burl.

He groaned as I touched it, his entire body tensing. Like Elswyth, he seemed to be hyper-sensitive, my every movement causing his muscles to cord and his body to bow. I sucked my lip between my teeth, watching as a few slight movements of my hand unravelled the self-controlled doctor. I liked the feeling of him in my hand, liked that my fingers couldn't meet around him. His cock was heavy and slightly harder than a human's, a pleasure to touch. His head glimmered enticingly, wet with glowing pre cum; my mouth watered as I watched it dampen my fingers.

'Maeve,' he groaned.

Those lips. I could imagine those lips doing all manner of things, but mostly I just wanted them pressed on my own. Watching them moan my name wasn't exactly the worst, though. I tightened my grip so he'd do it again, leaning to brush a kiss across his mouth.

He shuddered, his hips moving instinctively, thrusting up into my hand. I almost moaned myself as I felt him swell under my fingers, his burl pressing into the top of my palm.

'*Maeve,*' he hissed, and came.

I bit down hard on my lip as I watched. I'd never seen the doctor *messy*, and the glowing cum painting his stomach was all kinds of lovely. His sculpted chest was heaving, his beautiful forearms corded, and his strong fingers scored into the chair beneath him.

He was *glorious*.

I stroked him through the aftermath, until I felt like I'd milked every last drop from his body. I had the urge to leave my hand exactly where it was, so I did, waiting for him to soften.

He didn't.

I blinked at him. 'Um. Do Tirians ...'

'Do Tirians what?' he said, his voice low.

'Human men, uh, go soft. After they come, I mean.'

He looked down at my hand on his still-hard cock, a slow smile blooming on his face. 'We go soft,' he said, his eyes heavy. 'After five or so times.'

'After –' I sucked on my lip again. 'Well, *that* is a definite evolutionary perk.'

He laughed, a deep sound that made my toes curl. 'I'll be sure to put it in my notes,' he teased.

I studied his face. 'You're good,' I said bluntly. '*Very* good. Especially for someone who hasn't done that before.'

His face shuttered; he looked away.

My hand flexed around him; an unfamiliar spike of jealousy shot through my stomach. 'Ah. You *have* done that before. My mistake.'

His eyes flickered back to me. He sat up, took a blanket from the pile next to the examination bench, and spread it over his lap. I let go of his cock reluctantly, making an embarrassing squeaking sound a moment later when he pulled me into his arms.

He pressed his face into my neck. I tried to steady my breath; this was *nice*, as nice as being held by Elswyth, as nice as anything I'd ever felt. Warmth spread in my chest again; I tried to deny it, but I knew what it was.

Feelings.

'I've done that before,' he murmured eventually, his lips moving against my skin. 'A hundred times. A thousand times.'

I froze. 'Does that mean you're bonded? But you can't be bonded. Your name is *Unclaimed.*'

'I am unclaimed,' he said quietly, his breath whispering over my hair. 'I don't have a family. I don't have a *karia.*'

'Oh,' I said. '*Oh.* You bonded a male? Or –'

'I bonded a male.'

Some strong feeling flooded my chest as I turned that fact over in my mind; it might have been anger – or disappointment, maybe. I pushed myself off his lap. 'So what the fuck was this then, Willow?'

He blinked, startled. 'What do you mean?'

'You're bonded. Like, *forever* bonded. So what the fuck are you doing here with *me*?'

'I *want* to be here with you,' he said sharply. 'Which he is fully aware – and supportive – of.' He met my gaze calmly, seeming to weigh up his next words. 'We've been waiting. Waiting for the right family. Waiting for a *karia* to claim us *both.*'

My breath caught at his tone. 'You're joking,' I said flatly. 'You can't mean *me*, Willow.'

He gave me a look that confirmed he did, indeed, mean *me*.

I backed away from him. 'I know how your families work. I can't be your *karia*. I'm *human*. How could I possibly be what you need?' A thought struck me – not just a thought, but a *suspicion*. 'Do I know him? Your bonded?'

He studied me a moment, then silently inclined his head.

'Who is he, Willow?'

He swallowed.

'*Who*, Willow?'

He cleared his throat. 'Ashton Unclaimed.'

My heart beat hard in my ears. I didn't give a shit about the nature of their relationship. If I'd been on Earth, I wouldn't have even blinked – I'd be the worst kind of hypocrite if I did – but we weren't playing by Earth rules.

'Ashton's not allowed to bond without permission, though, is he?' I said slowly, *furiously*. 'And it's not just that – he's in love with Elswyth, so obviously that it's fucking painful.' My hands clenched into fists. 'The Captain didn't say shit about Elswyth bonding me, so there's a good chance she'd approve me for Ashton, too, isn't there? I solve all your fucking problems, don't I?'

'Maeve, that isn't –'

'Fuck you,' I said furiously. I turned and pulled on my shirt, the fastest I'd gotten dressed in my entire life. 'You fucking *cowards*. I get not coming out – I really do – but using me as a cover? *Fuck you*, Willow.' I turned back to face him. A dull ache was spreading through my chest, my stomach churning with a hurt so fierce it almost took my breath away. 'You don't really want me at all, do you? Either of you.' My breath caught. 'I'm just a means to a perfect end. You get Ashton and he gets Elswyth, and no one gets in trouble for breaking the rules. One big, happy *family*, with a human *karia* too stupid to see what was going on, to see that she was never really part of it.' I rubbed my chest; it did nothing to ease the pain. 'Serves me right.'

He went utterly still. 'Maeve, please –'

'No,' I said, shaking my head. 'Absolutely not. You're right, doctor. Someone else can take your fucking *notes* from now on.'

With that, I turned and stormed from the clinic.

WILLOW

'WILLOW?' ASHTON'S VOICE WAS sharp.

'I ...' I trailed off, staring blankly at my wrist screen.

'Will? What's wrong?'

I swallowed. 'I fucked up, Ash,' I whispered. 'I fucked up. Really, really badly.'

Maeve's scent was all over me, the deep, heady musk causing my hearts to pound and my skin to tighten. I wanted her here, wanted her back on my lap, in my arms, wanted my hands – my *mouth* – on her smooth skin. I wanted it so badly I could barely think straight.

'What did you fuck up, Will?'

I took a shuddering breath. 'Everything,' I said flatly. 'I fucked up everything, Ash. For both of us.'

There was a pause. 'Stay where you are,' he said. 'I'm coming.'

'You're on duty –' I managed, before the comm cut off.

I paced my clinic, raking my hands through my hair. Without realising, I'd slung the blanket around my shoulders; I grabbed a handful of the *iriis* wool and breathed in, deeply. Maeve had been on it – *half-naked* – and it held her scent better than my skin did.

The clinic door hissed open. 'Willow?' Ashton said softly, his brow creased. I waved my hand over the controls, locking the door behind him.

He stared at me warily. 'Will? What's going on?'

'Who is with the Hamadryad?'

He looked away. 'I had to leave her with Adair.'

'But you *never* leave her alone with him!'

His mouth twisted. 'I had to make a choice. Poppy is on her way to the Forest. She'll get there before Adair has any chance to open his mouth and ... well, be *Adair*. And if he does, it might finally be the excuse I need to send him back to his father's blighted ship. But you're deflecting, Willow.'

'Maeve was here,' I said.

'I know that, Will. I can smell it.' His hazel eyes burned as he took a step forward. 'And I can smell what you were doing, too.'

I searched his face, but there was no trace of hurt there – some jealousy, perhaps, and a spark of arousal as he breathed in, but no hurt. He reached up and stroked my cheek.

'It was glorious, Ash,' I said softly.

'Then what happened, love?' he murmured.

I let him draw me into his arms, let myself rest on his strength. 'She thinks that we're using her. That I'm using her to be with you, and you're using her to get to Elswyth. That all we want is someone to solve our problem.' I closed my eyes. 'When she said it, I was so surprised that I couldn't find the words to respond. And we *were* planning it, Ash. We talked about it. I couldn't lie and say that we hadn't. But I didn't get the chance to explain that wasn't all there was.'

He tipped my chin up so I couldn't look away. 'And?'

'She stormed out. She was angry, Ash. And *hurt*.'

He studied my face. 'Good.'

I blinked. 'What? Ash, she –'

'Stormed out, hurt and angry. Would she do that if she didn't care?'

My lips parted; he swooped down and stole a kiss. I let him kiss me, then pushed him away. 'You don't understand, Ash, she was –'

'Terrifying?' he supplied. 'Filled with rage?'

I nodded.

'Good,' he said again. He saw the look on my face. 'Will, love, if Maeve didn't care, she would have walked out with a laugh. There wouldn't have been any rage, because that female only picks fights when she cares about something. She's protecting herself. I'd wager it's probably one of the first times.'

'Protecting herself?'

He gave a wry smile. 'You're the smartest being I know, Willow, but sometimes you're thicker than heartwood. Maeve is clever and quick and funny and beautiful. So why hasn't she ever had a ... What do humans call them? *Partner*?'

I licked my lips. 'Because she didn't want one.'

'Exactly. She didn't *want* one. But now she's met Elswyth, and now she's met *you*, and she's changing her mind. Even if it's slow. Even if she hasn't realised it yet.'

'What do we do?'

He kissed my forehead. 'We let her be angry. I've been watching her for weeks, love. The trick with Maeve is knowing when to push forward and when to retreat. She'll be angry for a while, but while she's angry, she'll think about *why*. So we give her space to do that.' He ran his hands over my shoulders. 'I like you like this.'

I forced a laugh. 'When I'm worried that I've ruined everything?'

'Dishevelled and sated and covered in her scent,' he murmured, his voice going deep. He took a handful of my hair and tugged my head back so he could press kisses to the lines of thorns on my cheekbones. 'She told me an Earth story the other day. Something about a type of ancient Earth guard rescuing a royal female from a creature called a dragon.'

'A dragon?'

'It sounded like a cloud-lizard from Sector Three. All scales and claws and a long tail. The Earth ones breathe fire, apparently. Its name was George.' Ashton thought for a moment. 'Or maybe that was the guard. There were trees involved, with some kind of fruit. But the point is,' he went on, 'that at the end, Maeve said *if I was in the story, I wouldn't kill the dragon. I'd probably kiss it, instead.*'

I blinked. 'She'd kiss the creature?'

Ashton laughed; my chest constricted at the sound. 'Will, love, in this metaphor, *we* are the dragons. We're not human, not like her in many ways. And we're putting her in danger. Not her body – we're a danger to her hearts.' He blinked. 'Well, her *heart*. I don't understand how humans get by with just one.'

I licked my lips. 'You don't think it's a disaster? You don't think I've ruined everything?'

He tucked a lock of hair behind my ear, grazing the thorns there as he did. 'I have no doubt it feels like it. And I have no doubt that things will be rocky for the next little while. But no,

Will. I don't think this is a disaster.' He brushed his lips over mine. 'It's the next chapter in the story.'

'*The Human and the Hamadryad*,' I murmured.

'Exactly.' He adjusted the blanket around my shoulders, his nostrils flaring slightly as he inhaled Maeve's scent. 'We were never going to do this the same way as every other Tirian. We were never going to settle for the first family that came along. We knew we'd wait, wait for a *karia* perfect for both of us, wait for her to find us. And she has.' He took another deep breath. 'Green gods, that *scent*. I can barely think straight with it on you.' He shook his head. 'She's ours, Willow, and we're hers. We just need to wait for her to realise it.'

'I hope you're ready for a fight, Ash,' I answered. 'Because I think that realisation might be most of the battle.'

Ashton grinned, the full, wicked grin that set my body alight and my hearts pounding. 'I'm always ready for a fight, Will,' he purred. 'Our *karia* will lose the battle, but when she does, we'll make sure she knows her loss isn't a loss at all. We will all win this war, Will. You, me, Elswyth – *and* Maeve.'

ELSWYTH

I settled against the roots of my heartree, watching Maeve pace back and forth. The arcadia blossoms tracked her steps, turning their petals this way and that as Maeve moved. The first time it had happened, Maeve's face had lost all colour and she'd gone uncharacteristically quiet, but that was weeks ago, and now she barely noticed the way the flowers followed her as if she was their own, personal sun.

'I can't believe him,' she burst out, not for the first time. 'He didn't seem ... I didn't think ... I mean, I *trusted* him. I'm usually not so *wrong*.'

'Are you sure you're wrong now?' I asked mildly, also not for the first time.

'What other explanation is there?' She scowled at a nearby willow tree, which gave a sad, silent sigh, but bore her displeasure with understanding. She tugged on the ends of her lovely hair. 'I just ... Ah, fuck it, El. I have no idea why I'm so worked up about this.'

'Don't you?'

She turned her bright blue eyes to me and quirked an eyebrow.

I got to my feet. 'Maeve,' I said, keeping my voice gentle. 'You like him. It hurts because you *like* him.'

'I know I like him. I don't think that's –'

'No, Maeve,' I interrupted. 'You *like* him. He sings to something inside you. I can *see* it. You're scared of what that means, and you're hurt because you were starting to let yourself be vulnerable. You think he betrayed the beginnings of your trust, and that's made you angry.'

She stared at me, then ran her hands through her hair. 'By all means, Elswyth, don't hold back.'

I bit back a smile. 'My bonded is strong enough to hear anything I have to say.'

She shook her head. 'I just realised I haven't even asked how *you* feel.'

I considered it. When she'd come back with Willow's scent all over her skin, the hot jealousy had flared – then subsided. There was something about that mix of spice and musk that soothed me, made me feel safe. And it wasn't as if she hadn't told me. I'd given her a list, for the green gods' sake.

I was shocked, though, by Willow's confession that he'd already bonded – and that it was to *Ashton*. When I examined my feelings, I had to admit that some of the jealousy came from the notion that Ashton was somehow *mine*. He was *my* guard, *my* protector. He'd been by my side for sixteen years. There was a large measure of comfort in the selfish notion that he lived and breathed and fought for *me*, and it was unsettling to realise he had a life – and a love – outside my existence.

'I'm fine,' I said, because it was mostly true. 'But I think you need to work out what you want, Maeve.'

She started pacing again; the arcadias watched her in a rippling rhythm. 'I don't want anything. I *can't* want anything. It's impossible.'

My hearts skipped a beat. 'What's impossible?'

She groaned and pressed the heels of her hands into her eyes. 'I don't catch feelings, Elswyth. I don't, and I can't.'

'*Never have* isn't *never will*, Maeve,' I said softly.

'Tessa,' she said desperately. I watched as she straightened, her resolve hardening. 'I'm here to find Tessa. Not anything else.'

I rubbed my hand over my chest. I hadn't expected anything different, but it still hurt. 'What will you do if you find Tessa?'

She blinked at me, surprised. 'Take her home.'

'And if she doesn't want to go home?'

She frowned. 'Of course she'll want to go home.'

'Will she?' I challenged. 'Did she *look* like she wanted to go home in that still, Maeve? Did she look like she wanted to be rescued?'

Maeve chewed on her bottom lip.

My heartree rustled. *Careful*, the soft sound said. *Don't push too hard.*

The heartree knew Maeve, *loved* Maeve. The heartree knew what she'd grown to be to me. To *us*. But the heartree also knew that I had to push gently. To go slow. In this – in listening to her heart, instead of the rest of her body – Maeve was like a wood-kit, trembling in the Forest undergrowth, the slightest noise likely to make her bolt.

'I don't know what she looked like,' Maeve said, after a long moment of silence. 'She looked ... comfortable. But a still is just a photo, yeah? A moment in time, captured on a screen.' She studied my face. 'A lot can happen outside a moment.'

'Yes,' I said, meeting her gaze. 'It can.'

We stared at each other; our eyes locked. The air went taut between us, like it did every time. It sent a shiver over my entire body, the now-familiar ache blossoming between my legs.

How can she not feel this? I thought mournfully. *How can she not know?*

She does, the Forest whispered. *She will*.

'Those eyes,' Maeve said huskily. She brought a hand up and cupped her breast through her jumpsuit. 'Every fucking time.'

The heartree bent its boughs so that we were screened from view by a curtain of leaves, blocking out Poppy and Adair, who stood some distance away beneath a tall laurel.

My breath hitched.

Maeve stalked towards me, her face settling into the intense expression I'd come to know well – the expression that promised pleasure, lots of it, and quickly. She dropped to her knees beside me and took my chin in her hand, rubbing her thumb over my cheek. 'A lot can happen *in* a moment, too.'

'Here I was, hoping you'd make it last,' I murmured.

She laughed, her free hand stroking the vines of my suit until they unwound and it fell open to the waist. 'I'll do whatever you want, beautiful.'

Then stay with me, I thought, but I didn't say it out loud. Instead, in a smooth move she'd taught me in the gym, I swapped our places and gently pinned her on the moss between the heartree roots.

She looked up at me in surprise.

'You always give,' I told her. 'Every time. You make me ... *come*, then you make *yourself* come, and then it's over, or you make me come again. You never come first, and you never let me try to please you. You've never even told me what you like.'

She swallowed. 'El –'

I shook my head. 'Please let me try.'

For a moment, her intense expression fell, and she looked ... *uncertain*. I tried not to let my shock show, keeping my own face still.

She touched my cheek again, her expression smoothing. She relaxed back against the moss. 'Okay, beautiful. Have at it.'

Heat flooded my body. I whispered to the vines of her jumpsuit, and a moment later, it was in pieces on the Forest floor, leaving Maeve in only her underwear and boots.

I ran my hands over her arms, tracing the shape of the slender muscle beneath her smooth skin. The contrast between her softness and hardness made my hearts pound and my breath stutter; I bent and took her nipple in my mouth so she wouldn't see how much she affected me.

'Oh,' she breathed. I licked the hard peak the way that she did to me, with small, hard flicks. Her body twitched beneath me. 'Oh, like *that*.'

I switched breasts, nuzzling and licking and sucking until her hips were pressing up. I lowered my body, giving her something to press against, and realised that one of her hands was between her legs.

I pulled back. '*Maeve*.'

She flashed me a grin. 'Just helping.'

I narrowed my eyes, then flicked a glance at her jumpsuit vines. A moment later, they were winding around her wrists and around the heartree's trunk, pinning Maeve's hands against the smooth wood.

Maeve's eyes widened, her cheeks flushing a deep pink. 'I –'

'You said you'd let me try,' I said sternly. I stroked her arms. 'Is this too tight?'

She pulled gently against the vines. 'No, it's …' She bit her lip. 'Fuck, Elswyth, I've never been so wet.'

The heartree rustled smugly.

She likes it, I realised. 'I didn't know this was something you wanted.'

She cleared her throat. 'Um. Neither did I.'

I frowned. 'You haven't done this before?'

She shook her head, her hair falling over her breasts. I brushed it back; I wouldn't let her hide from me, not now.

'I, um. You need a lot of trust for something like this, and I …' She trailed off.

I ran my hand over her stomach. Maeve wasn't shy; she'd told me what her life was like on Earth. Different partners all the time, something a Tirian could only wonder at. Different partners that made Maeve skilled at knowing what others wanted, and what to give them.

But *different partners*, only ever once, whom Maeve pleased, but who never learned to please *Maeve*.

My bonded, who had spent so much time pleasuring others that she'd never had a chance to learn what they might do for *her*.

I kissed a trail over her stomach. New tendrils budded and stretched from the vines, curling around her underwear and tugging them down until she was naked beneath me. 'I'll leave your ankles free. This time.'

'This time?' she repeated thickly.

I mouthed lower, over her mound, then brushed my lips over her bud. 'This time.'

I went to work between her legs. I licked over her seam, and was rewarded with a hoarse, wordless moan. I sucked lightly on her bud, my hands pressing into her thighs as she twitched and squirmed. I licked around her entrance, then sank my tongue inside as her hips bucked. I swapped my tongue for two fingers and pushed them deep inside her, searching until I found the rough spot human females had instead of notches, pressing gently against it until she wailed.

'Elswyth,' she begged, her cheeks covered in a hectic flush, her eyes glinting a deep blue. 'Please.'

'What do you need, Maeve?'

'More,' she breathed. 'More of you. More of *everything*.'

I doubled my efforts, flattening my tongue and working in time with my fingers pressing inside her. She whimpered, straining against the vines; I flicked a thought at them to tighten. She gasped when they did, and a moment later, she was clamping around my fingers and my hand was damp with her sap. I licked until she was twitching and shuddering, then sat back, feeling uncharacteristically smug.

She watched me through heavy lids, her cheeks pink, her brow damp with sweat. 'Elswyth. Fucking *hell*.'

I stroked the vines until they released her hands, then checked her wrists. There was nothing but a slight redness where the back of her hands had rubbed on the heartree's bark; I soothed my fingers over it. 'You're incredible, Maeve.'

She swallowed, her lips pursing. 'What are you doing to me?' she whispered. 'It's like ... It's like I'm being re-made from the inside out. The things I thought impossible almost seem close enough to touch.'

I bent and kissed her, brushing my lips over hers so softly she sighed. As her arms linked around the back of my neck, my wrist screen beeped. I shifted so we could see it.

Routine assistance manoeuvre imminent, flashed over the screen. *Prepare for orbit sequence.*

'Something ... help ... now?' Maeve said, her forehead creasing as she tried to read the Tirian glyphs.

'Very close,' I said, then told her the correct meaning.

'So we're stopping to help someone?'

'We're not stopping, not really. Ships never stop when they're in flight. They can't. In deep space, there are very few opposing forces to slow them down, and if they enter a body's orbit – like a moon or a planet – they get caught up in that body's gravitational pull.' I scanned the rest of the message. 'That's what we're doing now. The Captain is directing the ship into the orbit of a small moon, which will slow us down.'

Maeve gave a heavy-eyed smile. 'I would have listened in physics class if you'd been my teacher.'

I flushed. 'I could never be a teacher.'

Maeve's smile turned to a frown. 'Of course you could be,' she said. 'You could be anything you wanted.'

I kissed her again, just because I could, shivering in the warm glow of intimacy, so new and so unfamiliar and so *wondrous.*

'So, why are we *slowing*?'

'The message said that our ship picked up a distress signal from the moon – a small, personal craft that ran out of water. It's a Darnagh ship, and they're a peaceful species, so we're slowing so the guards can take them some ice.'

Maeve laughed softly. 'Space ice. My life is so wild.'

'Do you want to watch?' I offered. 'They simulcast the official trips off the ship as training exercises.'

'The *official* ones,' she smirked, pulling her jumpsuit back on. 'But not the one *you* made.'

'My mother discourages the collection of strange aliens, as it turns out,' I said dryly. I held my hand out to her, pulling her up, breathing her in. 'Come on. It should be good to watch.'

'*Fuck*,' Maeve breathed. 'I wonder if this is how people felt watching the moon landing. All tense and breathless and full of adrenaline.'

I rested my head on her shoulder, resolutely ignoring Adair. When my heartree had drawn back its leaves, Poppy had gone, which was unusual, but Poppy's love Rosa was doing the ice run, so I supposed she'd gone to watch with the rest of her family. I didn't begrudge her – I'd want the same – but Adair was making my skin crawl even more than usual with his knowing smirks and too-long glances.

The Pods were tiny specs of white on the screen, almost lost against the endless black of space until whoever was taking the screencast narrowed in on their location. The Darnagh ship had landed on one of an unnamed, gaseous planet's many moons; the Pods crawled towards it, each weighed down with an ice net and a sizeable cube of treated ice, carefully cut to fill the specifics of the smaller ship's tank. The Darnagh captain must have been oddly careless with their water supply – or else they'd run into some kind of trouble.

I frowned at the screen. 'I wonder where they were headed. We're still so far out from the centre.'

'The universe has a centre?' Maeve said absently. 'I thought it was always expanding. Although, to be completely honest, that fact weirds me out, so I try not to dwell on it.'

'It is constantly expanding. It's not the *centre* in a topographical sense, it's the centre in a *cultural* sense. For some reason, there was an explosion of life very early in Sectors Five, Six, and Seven. The sectors comprise multiple galaxies, each boasting multiple solar systems, most with complex life forms. It doesn't take very long – in the scheme of things – to go between them, so they're like ... a bunch of your cities being close by, all with different life forms and cultures, each bringing something unique and interesting to universal development. Tir is on the edge of Sector Seven, and Natare is in the middle of Sector Six.'

'So you and the one who stole Tessa are practically neighbours,' Maeve murmured.

'Are you still so certain she was stolen?' I said gently.

Maeve shot me a frown. 'No,' she admitted. 'But I need to know for sure.'

The Pods entered the moon's orbit and began their descent to the surface. The cast zoomed in on their progress as their landing thrusters engaged and they sank gently down, landing a few minutes later in a tiny cloud of dust. It immediately settled, some of it on the Pod.

'Urgh,' I said, wrinkling my nose. 'Those Pods will need a thorough wash.'

Maeve snorted. 'You're a *tree*,' she said. 'Your heartree literally lives in soil. Scared of a little bit of moon dust?'

'Soil is *lovely*,' I argued. 'Full of things that feed my Forest. Black and thick and comforting. Moon dust is dead. It *sticks*. And it gets everywhere.'

'Like sand at the beach.'

'Exactly.' I paused. 'Except I don't know what a *beach* is.'

'Hmm,' she said, and brushed a kiss across my forehead. 'We should find one. You'd look hot as fuck in a bikini.'

On the screen, the Pods slid open, and their pilots and seconds stepped out. The screen darkened their helmets, so it was impossible to tell who was who. They worked together to unhook the ice nets, then began floating the blocks towards the Darnagh ship.

'Do all moons have low gravity?' Maeve asked curiously.

'They vary, usually depending on size. But this one is only slightly larger than your Earth moon, so the force is quite similar.'

The side of the Darnagh ship slid open, revealing its storage bay. The bay was surprisingly empty; I'd have expected travellers this far out from the centre – and Darnagh this far from their home planet – to have extensive cargo, but the bay was clear except for a few crates.

There were no Darnagh to be seen.

I frowned, then glanced across at Adair who – to his credit – had his shadow-green eyes trained on the screen, rather than me and Maeve. 'Where's their cargo?' he muttered. He met my frown with one of his own. 'Wouldn't they come out to meet the beings saving their asses?'

'Perhaps their suits are damaged?' I mused.

'Then why wouldn't they ask for replacements?' he said practically. 'This is space travel for beginners. Ice, food, comms, supplies for repairs. The most common issue during flight is hull damage from objects too small for the radar to pick up, and to make repairs you need suits. The Darnagh mastered intergalactic travel *generations* ago. This is ...'

'Odd,' I supplied when he trailed off.

Our shipmates thought so, too. They gestured at each other, clearly communicating over the suits' direct comms; after a moment, one of them gave a visible shrug. They directed the ice inside the hold, then disappeared from view, working to secure it.

Adair's wrist screen lit up. 'I don't like this,' came my mother's voice in a wide comm that would go to those working to get the ice delivered as well as the guards on board the main ship. 'I don't like this at all. Secure the ice and get out, warriors. And that is a direct order. Guards on board, stand by.'

The image on the screen stayed eerily still. I took Maeve's hand, gently squeezing her fingers.

Adair stepped closer, frowning intently at the screen. It was a mark of how tense we were that Maeve didn't snap at him, just huffed a little under her breath, squeezing my fingers. She didn't like his scent – she said it reminded her of cigars, whatever that meant – and she hated it in her space.

She hadn't had a problem with Willow's *raisin toast* or Ashton's *baking cookies*.

The second pair pulled their ice block towards the Darnagh ship. The first reappeared – Adair took a deep breath – and took the ice off them, floating it up into the ship and disappearing for a second time.

'Return to the ship,' my mother snapped through the guards' channel on Adair's wrist screen. 'Immediately.'

The second pair moved back to their Pod, retracting the ice net before climbing in and taking off.

'Come on,' Adair growled at the screen.

'Rosa Hawthorn and Bough Unclaimed, return to the ship *now*,' the Captain snarled.

My heartbeats thumped against my spines; the tiny arcadias that had bloomed on my shoulders closed. Adair's fingers brushed the holster of his stun gun; his bark armour shifted, growing another layer in response to his readiness for battle.

'Fucking hell,' Maeve muttered.

A handful of heartbeats later, the pair emerged from the storage hold; they jumped down, their boots stirring the moon dust once more. They hastened towards the ship, climbing inside.

'The ice net,' Adair hissed.

The Pod took off without them retracting it, the net trailing empty in its wake.

'That's going to be a nightmare when they dock,' I murmured.

'Saplings,' Adair agreed.

The screen followed the two Pods' journey back to the ship, blacking out as the first craft began to dock.

Adair stood, stretching slightly. He tapped his wrist screen. 'Further orders, Captain?'

'Stand by. The Darnagh aren't returning comms. I don't like this one bit.'

My lips twisted. 'They could be desperate for the ice, and starting the filtration and treatment as we speak. It will take hours, after all. Best to start now. They may not have comms from their utility rooms.'

Adair frowned. 'You think they might have said thank you.'

I fidgeted.

'Looks like it's all right now,' Maeve said soothingly, taking my hand. 'Do you want to go back to the Forest?'

I could feel it calling to me, feel the heartree's worry, an echo of my own. The Forest was picking up on the mood of the ship, and it wasn't happy. I gave Maeve a forced smile. 'Let's go back to the Forest.'

She studied my face. 'Do you want Ashton?' she said bluntly.

'I'm sure he has other things to do.'

Maeve glanced at Adair. 'Call the First Guard.'

He scowled. 'I don't –'

'The Hamadryad is anxious,' Maeve said, cutting him off, 'which means the *Forest* is anxious. Call Ashton. *Now.*' She tugged on my hand. 'Tell him to meet us under the heartree.'

'Aye,' Adair muttered sarcastically.

Maeve stared him down. 'If you were better at your job, it might be *you* the Hamadryad wanted when she felt unsafe. But it isn't, because you're not. Instead of being a dick, how about you try to be a better guard?'

Adair flushed green. He opened his mouth, evidently thought better of it, and tapped on his wrist screen. 'First Guard, your presence is requested in the Forest,' he said instead.

Maeve gave a curt nod. 'There you go.' She pulled me off the viewing podium and back down the corridor.

I bit back a smile, but didn't tell her that Ashton wasn't the only one who made me feel safe.

WILLOW

I TAPPED ON MY screen, stopping the decontamination spore shower. 'You're done,' I said, glancing at the security feed to make sure the guards hadn't reacted adversely. It was extremely uncommon, but because the decontamination spores were a higher strength than those we used in the personal showers, there was always a chance for rashes or, on a handful of memorable occasions, fainting. The fainting generally didn't have anything to do with the spores, but was more often due to guards or pilots returning exhausted or injured, so I had to stay vigilant.

Sage and Ewan hadn't spoken about their trip to the small, dusty moon, but I hadn't expected them to. They answered my questions about their wellbeing swiftly, Ewan flashing an apologetic smile. The decontamination was a formality – albeit an important one – and they were eager to get to the Captain to debrief.

The guards pulled on their clean casuals and moved out with thanks. I gathered up their suits, keeping the helmets in a separate bag, then ran the cubicle spore cleanse to make sure the tiny rooms were ready for the second pair of guards.

I opened the sliding glass door. 'Come in,' I called, dumping the clothing and helmets in a woven basket; I'd deal with them later.

Rosa and Bough stepped through the door together, still wearing their helmets.

'Well done on your mission,' I said. 'You know the drill.' I gestured to the cubicles. 'Pick whichever you'd like.' I moved to the central screen, tapping to check the spore sequence. 'Any injuries to report?'

Neither of them answered.

I frowned into the silence, watching my brow furrow on the screen. I didn't know either of them well, but I'd helped deliver Rosa's daughter, and she was usually warm, albeit quiet. 'I know you're saving the debrief for the Captain, but I need to know whether –'

Something pressed to the side of my face. In the screen's reflection, a green-gloved hand held a silver object to my temple.

'Are you a doctor?' a deep voice said.

I froze.

The silver thing – a gun, I knew – pressed harder. *It will bruise*, I thought stupidly. *Ash will be angry.* He hated seeing me hurt, which was why he refused to watch me when I had to spar during routine assessments. He poured over my every scratch, my every slight and meaningless injury, regardless of the fact it would be gone in a matter of hours, if not minutes.

'*Are you a doctor?*'

'Yes,' I said quietly. 'Yes. I'm a doctor. Do you need help?'

The being in the suit – male, I suspected, taking in the wide shoulders and defined biceps under the jumpsuit fibres; they *both* seemed male, which meant that Rosa was somewhere else entirely, and one of these beings was *wearing her suit* – gave a deep, grating growl. 'Not me,' they said. 'Someone on my ship. You will come with us.'

It wasn't a question. I took a deep breath. 'What kind of injury?'

'A bite,' the second being grated out. 'An infected bite.'

'I can give you something –'

The silver pressed harder. 'No. You will come with us. She needs ...' The hand at my temple shook slightly; in the screen reflection, my eyes widened in fear. 'It's not just the bite. She's ill.'

'And you have no doctor?'

Two vibrating snarls bounced off the lab walls. 'Not anymore,' the second suit said.

I dragged in a breath; it was more ragged than I liked. There was a reason I'd never volunteered for guard training; I was made for the clinic, not conflict. 'All right,' I said. 'What kind of life form?'

There was a short silence. 'We can't understand her,' the being with the gun said reluctantly.

I took that to mean they didn't know. 'Organic, though? What is her basic structure?'

'Organic. Warm blooded. Humanoid.'

I blinked. 'Right. I'm going to gather what I need. I won't make any sudden movements.'

I kept my visit bag ready-to-go, though it was rarely used; generally, patients came to me. I spent a few moments considering its contents: it was ready for *Tirian* patients, not an unknown humanoid species. My hand trembled as it rested on the soft bark.

What would Maeve need?

I chewed the inside of my cheek, considering. Maeve would need my hand scanner to check the extent of the damage. The healing wand, for use if the wound was clean; synthetic sutures – rather than vine fibres – if it wasn't. The blackbark and redleaf resin mix we'd cautiously perfected as a painkiller. Antibiotic spores, both for her skin and an oral dose for her blood. A dose of vitamins for injection, and a month's worth of wafers for afterwards, just in case.

I stiffened, something crossing my mind. 'The female. She is not your species. Is she a prisoner?'

The gun went back to my temple so swiftly I didn't see it move. 'Not your concern, doctor.'

I made an embarrassing strangled sound and closed my bag – but not before I pressed the emergency button under my lab screen.

I felt oddly vulnerable as I stepped into the hangar. The noise was normal – echoing bustles, chatter, the sweeping sounds as engineers cleaned and checked the moondust-coated Pods – but it fell silent in a handful of heartbeats, as if the ship was holding its breath.

The gun was pressed firmly to the back of my head.

'Stay back,' my captor called. 'We're taking the doctor, but that's all we're doing.'

My eyes darted around the hangar. There wasn't a guard in sight; they'd come for the landing and left again, probably waiting for the debriefing. There were mechanics working on some of the larger ships – they needed frequent upkeep – along with the engineers cleaning and checking the Pods.

'Doctor!'

An engineer – the same one who the Captain had demanded find Elswyth and Maeve a family room on Maeve's first day on the ship – was staring at me, screen in hand, her face a crease of concern and confusion.

'It's all right, Juniper,' I said, as calmly as I could manage.

'Stay back,' the male behind me growled.

Juniper's fingers were sliding over her screen, no doubt communicating what was happening to the entire ship. The male behind me noticed, pushing me forward with a shove that made me stumble.

'Doctor!'

'Juni, just …' I took a shuddering breath. 'Tell Ashton to stay with the Hamadryad, yes?'

Her eyes widened; she took a step forward. 'Doctor –'

'Stay *back*,' my captor snarled. He fired a warning shot into the hangar floor.

I stared at the mark it left. 'Oh, *fuck*,' I said stupidly.

A perfectly round hole, no burning around the edges. Through it, I could see a mess of wires that made up part of the comms and power systems, but I sent a silent, frenzied prayer of thanks to the green gods that the shot hadn't gone further. It wasn't a weapon of Tirian design; it was a weapon that didn't so much shoot *through* things as *consume* them. And it had been – thankfully – on its least devastating setting.

A Roth weapon.

Every Tirian in the hangar froze. Any notion they might have had of *rescue* froze with it. Another shot from that gun wouldn't just be dangerous; it could be catastrophic.

Another shot could see the entire peacekeeping vessel destroyed.

'Willow!' Juniper cried.

'Tell Maeve she's the one we'll always wait for,' I said desperately, as the male behind me pushed me into the waiting Pod. 'Tell her I'm sorry.'

'I'm sorry, too,' the male muttered, and raised his hand; everything went black before I had the chance to see it fall.

ASHTON

ELSWYTH WAS CURLED IN Maeve's arms, surrounded by a nest of the heartree's roots, which seemed to have emerged from the soil purely for the purpose of protecting their Hamadryad.

'Sorry, Ashton,' she said softly. 'I don't know what's happening. I can't seem to calm down. The Forest still thinks something is wrong, and I ...' She trailed off.

The heartree's roots flexed slightly, cradling me tighter. My arm was slung across Maeve's shoulders, my hand resting gently on the small thorns decorating Elswyth's collarbone.

I swallowed. 'There's nothing to be sorry for,' I said gruffly.

She couldn't possibly know how true those words were. Sitting with them – my back against the heartree, my arm around Maeve, my hand on Elswyth's skin – felt as if the universe and everything wonderful in it was suddenly in my reach, in my arms. An almost divine sense of rightness settled over me: I was *meant* to do this, meant to be here, meant to gather this strange, fierce human and my Hamadryad close to me to protect them – with my body, or with my very soul, if needed.

The only thing missing was Willow.

Even as my hearts ached for it, ached for my love and the completion he would bring, I knew I needed to be here. I gazed out at the Forest, taking in the very real consequence of the Forest's – of *Elswyth's* – uneasy fear.

The entire starboard side of the Forest was buzzing; the bees were agitated, aggressive. Three botanists and the Head Apiarist had been stung before they silently bowed out, leaving the bees to the Hamadryad to calm.

The bees weren't the worst of it, though.

'All good, beautiful,' Maeve whispered to Elswyth, for the hundredth time. 'It's all good.'

The heartree was *wilting*. My stomach had twisted as I walked into the Forest to see its drooping boughs and curling leaves; it was so deeply *wrong* to see the strong, beautiful heartree like that, and a shocking reminder of how important Elswyth was to the Forest and to the ship.

To *us*.

I moved my thumb, stroking lightly over her thorns. She sighed. 'Oh, that's nice.'

Maeve turned her face to raise an eyebrow at me. Her lips were mere fractions from mine; I could see lovely teal highlights in her eyes. My heartbeats sped up until I was certain they'd be able to hear the thundering inside my chest; my lips tingled with the need to lower my mouth, to capture hers, to kiss her until neither of us could think straight.

'Where do you want him to touch, beautiful?' she said. I stifled a groan; Maeve's lips curled upwards.

She knew *exactly* what she was doing to me.

'There is perfect,' Elswyth murmured. I spread my fingers and stroked her more boldly, my fingers tracing patterns on her skin; her head fell back, her lips parting. 'Mmm.'

Maeve gave a wicked grin. 'You're not just a pretty face, elf-boy.' Her eyes turned back to the curtain of leaves encasing us. 'Oh. *Look*.'

The heartree's leaves were uncurling as we watched, returning slowly to their usual healthy shape. I continued stroking Elswyth's skin, relief coursing through me as I simultaneously wished this would never end.

'First Guard! First Guard! *Ashton!*'

Elswyth straightened as the call tore through the Forest. 'Juniper?' she said in confusion.

The engineer wove through the heartree's canopy, her face flushed green, her eyes wide with distress. 'Lady – Hamadryad – I'm so sorry,' she babbled. 'But First Guard, we need – you need – sorry – *he* needs –'

'Take a breath,' Maeve said sharply. 'Take a breath, Juniper.'

Juniper paused and closed her eyes for a moment, inhaling before straightening her shoulders. 'First Guard,' she began again, her voice steadier. 'There's been an incident, sir. It seems that two unidentified beings took Rosa and Bough's uniforms during the ice drop and boarded our ship in the guise of our guards. They –' she swallowed '– they took Doctor Willow Unclaimed, sir.'

I froze. My hearts beat in my ears as I stared at her, unmoving; across the ship, the emergency siren began to blare.

Juniper stared at me, stricken. 'First Guard, sir?'

'*Ashton*.' Maeve said, and turned in my arms. '*Ash*.' I fixed my eyes on her as she searched my face. She turned back to Juniper. 'What else, Juni?'

Juniper swallowed again. 'Ah. They, um, had a Roth weapon.'

I felt her words like a blow.

I set Maeve and Elswyth carefully aside and stood, every muscle tight as stone. I would find them, find *Willow*, and when I did, I would tear those Roth into a thousand tiny pieces for *daring* to lay a hand on the male I loved. 'Then those Roth have begged for death,' I said calmly.

'He said you should stay,' Juniper blurted. She twitched when my eyes turned to her, but she didn't back down. 'Doctor Willow, I mean. He said two things.' She held out her screen, where I could see Willow being pushed through the hangar by a being dressed in Rosa's uniform. Rage darkened my vision when I saw the gun pressed to the back of my beloved's head. 'He said to tell Maeve, um, some stuff, and that he was sorry –' Juniper's eyes flickered to my human '– and he said that you should stay with the Hamadryad. Sir.'

My hands clenched into fists as I watched the Roth mutter something before striking Willow on the temple; I snarled aloud as Willow crumpled and was bundled unceremoniously into the Pod.

A soft cry cut off the harsh sound; I turned to see Elswyth clap a hand over her mouth to muffle the sound. She raised her eyes from Juniper's screen to glance at Maeve and I by turn.

'The Forest was right,' she choked. 'There *was* still something wrong.' A moment later, I blinked against a swirl of white light as she returned to her hearttree.

Soft fingers touched my hand. 'What will you do?' Maeve said quietly.

'Go after him,' I answered gruffly. 'I can't let –'

'Oh, green gods,' Juniper whispered, cutting me off. 'Oh, *no.*'

She wasn't looking at me, though; she'd turned away, and her eyes were on the Forest.

Which was slowly turning from its verdant shades of green to a dull, dead brown.

WILLOW

When I woke up, everything was black.

I groaned, tentatively stretching out my limbs. My arms and legs were fine, and other than a stiff shoulder – it was pressed uncomfortably against a hard, cold floor – my torso was unharmed.

My head, however, was not.

I sat up slowly, raising a palm to my skull. The skin was split just behind my left ear and raised with bruising, my hair caked with drying blood, but it didn't feel as if the bone had broken. It throbbed like a solar flare regardless. I probed it with my fingertips until I was sure the wound was knitting, then wiped the blood on my shirt.

'They got you good with that one,' a deep, amused voice said. 'He had to knock you out for the flight to the ship, but he didn't mean to hit you so hard. He's not so bad, the one that dragged you here, despite that pool of green you're lying in.'

I started in surprise at the voice.

'Oops. Sorry about that. You're safe, I promise. Well, you're safe, relatively speaking. You could be far less safe. Perhaps. I'm not really the best judge of these things.'

I peered into the darkness. 'Where are you?'

Two glowing golden orbs appeared a few spans away. I hissed, inching back.

'Had my eyes closed. Hang on a heartbeat.'

The glow spread, illuminating a humanoid form sitting propped against the wall. They looked male, with a slender, toned form, golden skin, and curling hair so dark it blended into the shadows. Pretty, from what I could see, his lips stretching into a wry smile.

'Ah. You *are* Tirian. I couldn't think of another green-blooded species.' He shifted slightly; one of his legs was stretched out before him, a thick band of black surrounding his ankle.

'Catonians,' I said absently. 'Riya. Seveerns. Sorry – is that a *dark matter chain*?'

'What, this old thing?' he said cheerfully, poking at the black band. 'That'd be it. It's starting to get annoyingly uncomfortable, sitting in one position for – well, a few months now, I think; I've never really had to bother with *time* before. I don't suppose that bag contains dark matter shears, by any chance? I'm not sure they exist, but I'd be deeply grateful for them if they do.'

'Why are you chained with dark matter?' I said, slowly inching further away.

'Well, I had a little misunderstanding with the Roth Prince. I wanted some of the contents of his on-board treasury, you see, but he didn't really want to give them to me. I managed two missions into his vaults before they caught me on the third.

My twin always told me I was too cocky for my own good.'
He grinned a wide, white smile. 'I prefer to think that I'm
determined.'

'But ... *dark matter.*'

'Oh! Well, I may have this odd humanoid form at the moment, but I'm a starling,' he said practically. 'You see, my twin
wears a meat costume because he dabbles in politics – among
other things – on Natare, and I may have borrowed some of
his identikit to make it through the first few layers of the Roth
Prince's security. I had to don a form that looked like his.' He
examined his hands. 'It's not perfect, but it's close enough. It
didn't fool the Prince, though; he figured out who – and what
– I was. Starlings can only be chained by dark matter, but it's
not widespread knowledge. The Prince was smarter than I'd
anticipated.'

'I –' I winced. 'I think this is making the pain worse.'

'I have no doubt; I don't do well without company, and
she's been asleep for a while now. Your bag is behind you. I'm
assuming you're some kind of healer? They're worried because
she won't wake up.'

I blinked. 'She? *She.* My patient. Where is she?'

The glow around the starling spread. We were in a bare room
with a single, tiny window set high up in the wall. Security
recorders blinked in every corner. I had been dumped next to
a screen, behind which was a universal waste disposal unit and a
light cleanser, the most basic hygiene requirements resembling
those generally found on prison ships.

Across from me was a low, hard-looking bed. Oddly enough,
it had two plump pillows covered in expensive silkworm cases,
and a pile of blankets that looked to be made of rare *ura* fibre
from a system of planets in Sector Eight.

A female was nestled in the pile, her eyes closed, her cheeks flushed, her brow and pale hair damp with sweat.

I'd expected a Kjida, or a Skalavian, perhaps – a being from a lesser-known species, as the Roth would have recognised a Darnagh or a cephalopod. This female was familiar to me, surprisingly so. 'A *human*?' I said incredulously.

'Isn't she sweet? Unfortunately, the Roth think so, too.'

He said it lightly, but he strained towards the female on the bed, his ankle pulling at the dark matter band.

I scrabbled behind me, sanitising my hands with a spore rinse before yanking my hand scanner from my bag. Its soft light swept over her; I swore when the readings stabilised. 'She's dying,' I said bluntly. 'She has sepsis. Her liver and kidneys are failing.'

The starling blinked at me; the light in the room dimmed and brightened. 'Then what are you waiting for?'

I found what I needed and crossed the room cautiously. The female was pale and fragile-looking, with delicate features and fair hair pulled back into a braid. She stirred restlessly as I confirmed her temperature – thirty-nine Earth degrees Celsius – then sighed a breathy groan as I gave her a shot of antibiotics and vitamins.

'She needs fluids,' I murmured.

'You hear that, you horned bastards?' the starling called. 'She needs fluids!'

I glanced at him, startled. 'Where is the source of the infection? The being who took me mentioned a bite?'

The light in the room swirled; the starling's eyes glowed. 'Her shoulder,' he said, his tone furious and full of caverns. 'Her right shoulder.'

She was lying on her stomach, so I gently peeled away her cocoon of blankets, realising that the light sheet wrapped around her was a silk-cotton blend from Etryia. She was lying in a cell with a criminal, dying, and yet the Roth had covered her in fabric worth more than their ship.

'This makes no sense,' I murmured.

The wound on her shoulder wasn't a bite so much as a *tear*. Her flesh was ragged and angry and all kinds of colours it shouldn't have been in the starling's golden light.

'What did this to her?' I said, getting angry myself.

The starling shifted his weight. 'The last doctor.'

'The last ...' I stared at him. 'The last doctor *bit* her?'

'I've learned quite a lot since I've been here,' the starling said evenly, 'which doesn't give me hope for my eventual release, but I digress. I've never paid much attention to the Roth before – rather obvious and distasteful, all that *taking over the universe* nonsense – but it turns out that Roth society is old-world, with a strict monarchical hierarchy and very few living females. So few females, in fact, that they capture them from elsewhere to ... use. The last doctor was trying to give her to the Roth King. For no good reasons, one might assume.'

I looked back at the unconscious human. 'Why did he tear her skin in this way?'

The starling gritted his teeth. 'Because she didn't want to be given to the Roth King, and she tried her best to get away. He bit her to keep her still while he tried to sedate her.'

My nostrils flared; rage burned inside me. 'Do I need to check for damage elsewhere?'

He shook his head. 'The Prince himself separated the doctor's body from its mushy flesh computer before anything further could occur. The doctor deserved no less.'

I gave a soft noise of assent and sprayed my spore solution over her wound, trying not to disturb her. She shivered when I dabbed at it with a wipe, removing traces of dust and sweat. The antibiotic shot was already working; her breathing had evened, and she felt slightly cooler to touch.

'I can't use the healing wand on a wound like this, and I don't think stitches will work,' I said at last, after examining her torn skin for what felt like hours; I'd only rarely seen something so raw and painful-looking. 'But I can cover it with a fibre bandage which will promote healing and keep it clean. I've got a painkilling solution which will help with both the wound and her fever, but she needs to be awake to take it. Humans react slightly differently to Tirian medicine, and I want to make sure it does what it's supposed to. I'll give her another shot of antibiotics in a few hours.'

'Will she live?'

The deep, gruff voice came from the opposite side to the starling; I turned and stifled a gasp. The wall, it turned out, was of opaque glass, which had now become clear. Behind it I could see a Roth male, complete with pale skin, jet-black eyes, black horns curving backwards from his temples, and *muscles*. A whole lot of impressive muscles, draped in the uniform of the Roth imperial forces.

I sat back on my heels. 'I don't know,' I said honestly. 'She's improved, but the damage to her organs wasn't slight.'

The Roth gave a curt nod. 'She lives, you live,' he said bluntly. 'She dies ...' He trailed off, his eyes flicking to the starling. 'She dies, and all bets are off.'

'Well then.' The starling grinned, his eyes glowing. 'That sounds fair enough, don't you think, doctor?' He drew up his legs, linking his arms around them as he studied me. I had the sudden notion that of the two other males, the one in the cell with me was by far the most dangerous. 'I'll tell you a secret,' he whispered loudly. 'If she dies, the Roth won't get the chance to kill you.' His grin widened, and my stomach dropped. '*I'll do it myself.*'

MAEVE

'YOU NEED TO SEND a rescue team for Willow,' I snapped. '*Now.*'

The Captain raised an eyebrow. 'And you need to understand who is in charge here, Maeve McCarthy, and that it is very much *not* you, even if you *are* bonded to my daughter.'

'Then what are you doing for Willow?'

'Firstly, trying to work out where he is,' she said calmly. 'Everything else is rather moot until we know that, don't you think? The Pod he was taken in has a tracker, but it's been disabled. More than that, there are no heat signals *anywhere* nearby. Wherever they've taken Willow, they're cloaked.'

'Then we need to be looking. We need to be –'

'Exactly how do you think I became captain of a peacekeeping ship, Maeve?' she drawled. She sat back in her seat, comfortable in the meticulous green and white of her meeting room, wearing her bark armour like I wore sweatpants. 'There are four reconnaissance ships out as we speak, sweeping every inch of this Sector for visuals and with radar, the kind of lower-tech searching the Roth can't cloak from. My engineers are analysing the movement of space junk to see if we can track the Pod's path, which is a mathematical process so complex it might as well be magic. You're not only insulting *me*, you're insulting my entire crew of highly-trained, highly-experienced peacekeeping soldiers. This is *literally* our job. Is it yours?'

I glowered at her. 'No, Captain.'

I liked Elswyth's mother *a lot*.

She took up a cup of the sickly-sweet tea most Tirians preferred, made from the leaves of a common tree on their home planet. It didn't do much for me – I was a coffee-as-black-as-my-heart type of woman – but they all drank it because it was chock full of minerals their bodies needed, and it helped with their inner balance, their *elya*. I loved to watch Elswyth drink it; she'd start glowing on the first sip, and there was nothing in the entire universe as beautiful as Elswyth when she glowed.

I rubbed my chest as warmth spread through me at the thought.

'There is something you can do for me.'

I blinked, shaking my head to clear it. 'What?'

She took a mouthful of her tea then set her cup back down. 'You can stay calm, Maeve,' she said gently. 'At the moment, that's even more important than trying to find Willow. I've seen the Forest. I know Elswyth won't take her Tirian form. I've tried to talk to her, but she's either not listening, or so deep inside herself that she can't hear. I know that you and my First Guard are spending every moment with her. I know you only slept two hours last night, and that Ashton hasn't slept at all. And I know that it's the two of you stopping the browning from going further. But if Elswyth picks up on your fear, it won't help her control. Willow is *one* Tirian in danger. If the Forest continues browning, *thousands* of souls on this ship might die.'

'Willow isn't *just* a single Tirian in danger. He's –' I faltered. What *was* he?

The Captain gave me a sharp look. 'I know what he is to you, whether you want to admit it or not,' she said, '*and* what he is to my First Guard.' She ran a hand through her unbound hair, sighing. 'Green gods know I'd hoped this would turn out differently. I gave Ashton so many chances to tell me.'

I looked down at my hands. 'I've been thinking about it a lot,' I admitted. 'I suspect Ashton was ashamed. He knew what he stood to lose, and he knew that he could damage Willow's reputation, too. If he loves Willow the way he loves Elswyth, then he'd die before he hurt him. I *know* he'd die rather than lose Elswyth. He probably thought the risk was too much, and not just to himself. So he said nothing at all, and when I came along, they ...' I trailed off, rubbing my chest again.

'Silly males,' the Captain said, shaking her head. 'The truth might have made their every dream come true, and instead, look where they are. Where *you* are.'

I blinked. 'Where *I* am?'

The Captain growled under her breath. 'You've been watching the stream of Willow's kidnap for days straight,' she said. 'Over and over, you play the same thing. You pause it, you study it. *Why*, Maeve? What is it you're looking at?'

I stared at her, my heart pounding. I didn't bother asking her how she knew what I'd been doing; the Forest was being monitored more closely than the crown jewels.

Tell Maeve she's the one we'll always wait for.

'I look at Willow,' I said eventually.

'And what do you *see*?'

A bowed head, I thought. *A bowed head, hunched shoulders, his beautiful long fingers clenched into fists, his knuckles green. His eyes desperate, his hair dishevelled from the gun.*

'I see his fear,' I whispered. 'I see his fear, and I –' I stopped.

The Captain sipped her tea, waiting.

'I see his fear in a way I couldn't see Tessa's,' I said abruptly. 'He didn't want to go. His whole body was tense. He was glancing around, trying to find a way out. He was desperate.'

'And Tessa wasn't,' the Captain said.

'No.' I inhaled. 'No. She wasn't.'

'And now you're afraid you've left your world, your life, everyone you love – but it was a mistake.'

'No,' I said, standing and pacing between the walls of the Captain's office. I stared at a potted plant in one corner, its leaves curling before my eyes. 'No. It wasn't a mistake.'

The Captain's mouth was tight. 'You'll still take Tessa back to Earth, then?'

What was Willow?

I rubbed my chest, something I couldn't seem to stop doing. The warm feeling warred with a worry so deep and so complete that my brain could barely comprehend it; it was a strength of feeling only understood by my heart.

I'd been told that bonding was so intense that some Tirians believed it changed them on a fundamental level, as if the very reason for their existence shifted. Afterwards, they wanted their *karia* and their family, and no other. I'd been on the ship with thousands of Tirians for weeks, and felt nothing but polite interest.

What I felt for *my* Tirians – for Elswyth and Willow and Ashton – was far more than *interest*, and it certainly wasn't polite. What I felt for them was so strong that I couldn't stay away – and nor did I *want* to. The notion of returning to Earth – returning to my normal life – and picking up where I left off was unthinkable. I didn't want to go back to my gym, back to my apartment, back to *Advena*. I didn't want to go back to Saturday nights with no-strings hookups. I didn't want to go back at all.

What was Willow?

He was mine.

And he wasn't the only one.

'If Tessa wants to go back, then I'll take her back,' I said. I squared my shoulders. 'But I won't be going with her. Elswyth chose to call me her bonded. So that's what I'll be, for as long as she wants.' I turned to the Captain. 'And I want Ashton and Willow. I want all of them. I want *everything*. I want your approval.' I swallowed. 'Please.'

The Captain's lips curled. 'Are you admitting you're their *karia*, Maeve?'

I pushed aside my stubborn pride. 'It seems I was wrong. About that one thing, mind you. Not about anything else.'

'I see,' she said, amused. She sat back in her chair, then flicked an image from her desk screen to project on the wall. It was an official-looking document, with Tirian hieroglyphs imposed over some kind of seal – a graceful oak tree growing inside a star. 'Lucky, then, that I was prepared.' She gave a smile – one of genuine happiness. 'The Tirian Grove has already approved Ashton for your family. You have both my personal and my official blessing.' She raised her chin. 'But if you hurt my daughter, Maeve, I'll compost you. Alive.'

Some strong feeling coursed through me – relief and joy and *hope*. 'Fair enough.' I spread my fingers over my chest, trying to tamp down the warmth there. 'I, um, didn't expect it to happen so quickly.'

'Time is relative,' the Captain said. 'Quick minds, quick hearts, and all that.'

'Um, yep, that is … a thing. Best go and tell Elswyth, then. And ask Ashton, I suppose. I guess it's a bit like proposing, isn't it? I mean, it is forever.'

Forever. Me, having a forever.

Oh, God.

I swallowed again.

'Maeve,' the Captain said a moment later, her lips pursed as she tried not to laugh. 'Stop delaying. Get out of my office.'

I steeled myself. 'Yep, going. Now, as it turns out.'

'Now,' the Captain agreed, and gently took my arm, steering me to the door. 'Don't make me rethink my decision. Remember the composting.'

'Going. Right now. And I won't forget the composting.'

When I got back to the Forest, it was as if I'd never left. The heartree's leaves were dull brown, its boughs heavy, and the trees around it were wilting. Ashton stood beneath its branches, his back straight, his chin lifted, but his eyes were heavy with fatigue, and he was wan from sleepless nights and constant worry.

He tensed when he heard me approaching, his hand flying to his holster.

'Just me, Ash,' I said softly.

He relaxed. 'Maeve.'

I looked up at the heartree. 'Any change?'

He shook his head. 'She's holding off further damage to the Forest,' he said, his tone proud. 'But she hasn't come back, either.'

I reached out and stroked the heartree's trunk. My fingers were trembling, so I spread them over the comforting bark. 'I need to ask you something, Ash, and I need an honest answer.'

Ashton frowned. 'Always.'

My throat narrowed; I swallowed. 'I need to know what you want. Well, *who* you want, really.' My fingers played restlessly over the heartree's trunk. 'And I hope you're listening, Elswyth, because we all need to be on the same page.'

'On the same page?' he repeated, his frown deepening. 'Maeve –'

'We need to be honest. *I* need to be honest. Because I want you,' I said in a rush, looking down at the heartree's exposed roots, suddenly unable to meet his gaze. 'I want you, Ash. And I want Willow. And if you only want Elswyth, that's fine, but I need to know before anything else happens, so that –'

He strode forward and seized my mouth with his.

The kiss was so utterly unexpected that for a moment, I simply froze. Then I came to my senses and kissed him back, my hands cupping his cheeks, my fingers caressing his thorns. He pulled me closer, his arms so tight around me that it felt as if he'd never let go. His kiss was confident, his lips sure, and when his tongue flicked against mine heat sparked the entire way down my spine.

'Elswyth, beautiful,' I gasped, leaning on the heartree's trunk for support when he broke the kiss, 'this is where I need you to speak now, or forever hold your peace. Or whatever.'

The heartree shivered behind me, its bark a delicious rasp against my back. Its boughs lowered, shielding Ashton and I from the Forest's cameras.

'I guess she approves,' I said, unable to stop my lips curling up. 'Luckily, the Captain and the Tirian Grove do, too.'

Ashton went utterly still, his eyes closing. When he opened them again, his irises were golden with hope – and something else. He shuddered, then fell to his knees.

A delicious mix of power and lust flooded my body, making me almost light-headed as warmth bloomed between my legs at the sight of him kneeling before me. I took a handful of his lovely mahogany hair and forced him to look up. My fingers were still trembling, but it was for a different reason now. 'I was looking at this all wrong. I thought it was all about Tessa,' I said softly. 'But I just realised it can be both, can't it? I can find Tessa *and* a family. I can find my friend *and* forever.'

'Forever?' Ashton growled.

'If you want me for that long.'

He leaned forward, ignoring the pull of my fingers in his hair, and rested his forehead on my stomach. 'I've wanted you since the moment you punched me in the face.' His hands came up to grip my hips. 'I prefer action to words, Maeve, but I will tell you this. It's not just want. I *need* you.'

I closed my eyes at his admission; those simple words were better than any song. I stroked the vines of my jumpsuit with my free hand, deciding that actions suited me just fine. 'Then have me, Ash.'

He gave a rumbling growl as my jumpsuit fell open, baring my breasts and stomach. He reached out and traced a feather-light touch around my belly button, blinking in surprise, but he wasn't distracted for long. His hand moved up, cupping a breast, his thumb brushing over my nipple until it ached.

'Pink,' he said wonderingly.

I grinned. 'If you're impressed by that, wait until you get between my legs.'

He groaned, his eyes on my face. 'There's no backing out, Maeve. If we bond, you'll be stuck with me – stuck with *us* – for the rest of our lives.'

'Not stuck,' I whispered. 'Blessed.'

He was still a moment, then he growled again, tearing my jumpsuit from my body until I was naked before him, one hand still in his hair to give myself the illusion of control. I wasn't in control of this, not even a little bit; I was stripped bare in every possible way. But Ashton hadn't taken advantage of my vulnerability; he was rewarding me for it, instead, trailing kisses over my stomach even as his hands skirted up my thighs.

My head tipped back against the heartree's trunk, my legs spreading of their own accord. His fingers found my centre and stroked gently, spreading my wetness over my skin. I moaned at the soft touch, my hips angling forward, begging for more, and a moment later his mouth was there, his breath warming my skin, his tongue flicking against me.

White light began to shine all around us.

'Elswyth,' I panted. 'If that's you, beautiful, come back.'

Ashton licked a line from my entrance to my clit, holding my hips as I shuddered. 'She's watching,' he said, his voice full of affection. 'She knows this time is for me and you.' He licked me again; I moaned. 'But if she ever feels differently ...' He delivered a tiny, wicked suck, just where I needed it. 'There will be two males waiting to give her anything she wants, exactly the way she wants it. We will give our *karia* and our Hamadryad every-thing they need.'

The heartree shivered behind me again, its leaves whisper-ing as the white light brightened.

'Fuck, Ashton,' I breathed, imagining him and Willow with Elswyth. 'I –'

I shrieked as he flattened his tongue and began to work me properly. I held his head in place, my hips circling, as his thumb found my entrance and slipped inside. His free hand cupped my ass, kneading the flesh until his caresses had me half out of my mind and pleasure was building deep in my core.

'Ash,' I gasped. 'Ash, I'm –'

His tongue flicked faster; he withdrew his thumb and pressed two fingers inside me.

The sudden intrusion had me clamping around him, moaning wordlessly as I came. My legs trembled as he growled again, the sound vibrating against my sensitive clit as he licked me through it, his fingers moving in and out of my body to prolong the waves of sensation. When I was done, I tugged on his hair.

'I want you inside me,' I said thickly.

'No,' he answered calmly, continuing to flick his tongue against my clit as I shuddered.

'No? What happened to giving *everything they need*?' I said tartly.

'No,' he repeated, pressing his fingers back inside me, his thumb circling my clit as if he'd been pleasuring me for years, as if he knew exactly how I liked it. 'Not until Willow is back and we're all together. But hold onto something, because we're doing that again.'

I didn't even consider arguing with *that*.

It took a little longer for him to coax a second orgasm from my over-sensitive body, but he didn't seem to mind, applying himself to the task single-mindedly while the heartree glowed around us. When I slipped to the ground, utterly boneless, I reached for the impressive bulge between his legs but he twitched out of the way, stroking my arms, my stomach, my hair, as if I was something precious.

I didn't hate it.

I *really* didn't hate it.

'Ashton,' I croaked. 'Where the *fuck* did you learn to do that?'

My guard gave a smug smile. 'Tirian males aren't stupid. We are taught about female bodies. And about gentleness, and watching carefully, and noticing signs, and that tongues aren't just for talking.' He reached down and cupped between my legs, the first possessive thing he'd done, pressing the heel of his hand just hard enough against my clit to make me squirm. 'They teach us about our role in a family, and how to best serve our *karia*.'

I took his free hand and kissed it. 'Do you trust me, Ash?'

'Yes,' he said, without hesitation.

I sat up and took his face in my hands, kissing him deeply, tasting myself on his tongue. If there was no going back, then I was going to kiss my guard every free moment of the day and night. When he groaned, I pulled back, nipping his bottom lip. 'And do you trust me to protect Elswyth?'

He went still. 'Yes,' he said, almost as swiftly as the first time.

'Then go and find Willow,' I whispered. 'Trust me to watch over Elswyth. Go and find him, and bring him back to where he should be. Bring him home to us.'

WILLOW

THE HUMAN FEMALE WOKE from her restless sleep sometime later; without a regular time sequence in the cell, it could have been hours, or it could have been days. I'd kept myself busy fashioning a fluid drip from bits and pieces I had in my bag between monitoring her heartbeat and temperature and taking frequent naps. The Roth kept up his watch, not shifting a muscle as he stood outside the cell with his arms crossed. *Ash would be impressed*, I thought.

The starling had mostly kept quiet, flashing the occasional grin at our stoic guard, as if he found the entire situation amusing. He might have, I supposed; he seemed to have an odd sense of humour. Starlings lived long, and they tended to lose their minds after a few tens of millennia; it wasn't entirely a surprise to find one that was slightly unhinged, especially if he had been in captivity. They weren't made to be kept in a cell.

'Vesper?' the human croaked, her voice cracked and quiet.

I frowned, but the starling answered, and I realised it was his name. 'Right here, little lodestar,' he said. 'Haven't moved an inch.'

'I feel ...' She trailed off, staring at me. 'You're new.'

'I'm new,' I agreed. 'Greetings. I am Willow. He.'

'Anna,' she rasped. 'I don't suppose you have any water?'

I passed her the utilitarian glass next to her cot, then carefully helped her sit so she could sip at the water inside. I'd already laced it with another dose of antibiotics and painkillers.

'I feel better,' she said, after she'd finished.

'You are far from *better*. But you have improved,' I said. 'Could you manage some food? The starling – Vesper – said that you haven't eaten for days.'

She wrinkled her nose, but eventually nibbled at a nutrient bar from my bag. When she pushed the remainder back into my hand, she glanced at the glass wall and the Roth behind it. 'Hello, tall, dark, and looming.'

His face didn't change, but his eyes were fixed on her with an intensity that almost made *me* squirm; I couldn't imagine how it might make Anna feel.

'Is he always that ... attentive?' I murmured.

'Always,' she answered. 'I hated it at first, and now I'm afraid I have Stockholm Syndrome.'

I frowned at her.

She sighed. 'A human thing. Never mind.'

'Humans have a lot of *things*,' I said solemnly.

She blinked at me. 'You know humans?'

'I know *a* human,' I corrected. 'Now I know two.'

'Did your human have a nervous breakdown when you met them?'

I smiled. 'My human walked on board our ship as if she owned it.'

'How nice for her,' Anna said grumpily. 'I wish I could have done that. Instead, I was scared, and then I got *bitten*, and then I got sick, and now ...' She trailed off, staring at the Roth, who met her gaze without blinking.

'Were you injured anywhere else?' I said carefully.

She cleared her throat. 'Only my mind and spirit, but unless you're a counsellor as well as a medical doctor, I suspect I will need to work through that myself. Or with Vesper,' she went on, shooting the starling a tentative smile. 'I don't think we will be leaving any time soon.'

'If you need help, I will find you help,' the Roth said, his voice deep and throaty.

I glanced at him, surprised.

Anna sighed again. 'I wish I could understand him.'

I frowned. 'You don't have a translator?'

A line appeared between her fair brows. 'A translator?'

Anger stirred in my stomach – anger, then relief that my translator had been updated to include human languages, because otherwise, this might have been a disaster. 'You couldn't do it?' I said to Vesper. 'I thought starlings could facilitate translation without any kind of techplant.'

He gave a half-shrug, and a wide smile. 'I am a selfish being at heart. I've been rather enjoying having her all to myself.'

I eyed him sideways, wondering whether Ashton would think it was appropriate to exchange blows with a being in chains.

'*Vesper*. Willow better not be implying what I think he's implying,' Anna chided harshly.

Vesper rolled his eyes. 'One moment.'

A scent washed through the room, wood charred by new flames, mixing with Anna's sweet, fresh scent. A moment later, Anna shook her head.

'Say something, you big lump,' Vesper said commandingly, gesturing at the Roth.

The Roth scowled in response. '*Something*,' he growled a moment later.

Anna gave a shocked laugh. 'Oh,' she breathed. 'I understood that. *Oh*. Thank you,' she rushed. 'Thank you. For the blankets and the pillows, and for ... after the doctor ... *Thank you*. And please thank the Prince as well. For the ...' She trailed off.

'Beheading?' Vesper supplied lazily.

Anna glared at him. 'For the *protection*.'

The Roth studied her expressionlessly. 'I will tell him.'

'Technically, it's his fault you're here in the first place,' Vesper said, stretching as far as his dark-matter binding would allow. 'I wouldn't be too effusive in thanks.'

'The Roth took you?' I said slowly. 'From Earth?'

Anna sank back down into her pillows, as if she'd exhausted her energy; sweat was beading on her brow, so she might well have. I gave her another sip of water. 'He took me.'

I filed that information away for if I ever got off the ship. If the Roth had taken her against her will, then he'd broken even more laws than the three beings who'd taken Maeve's friend Tessa; she, at least, had possibly gone consensually.

I closed my eyes and allowed myself a moment of despair. Getting off a Roth ship wasn't likely; staying alive was only slightly more probable. I needed to prove myself useful enough that they wouldn't kill me once Anna had recovered. If the ship had no doctor, then that was a helpful start.

The longer you're alive, the longer Ash has to find you, the hopeful part of my brain whispered.

I quashed it, then sent a quick prayer to the green gods that Ashton wouldn't be stupid enough to come.

'Willow?'

I looked down at Anna. 'Yes?'

'Will I die?'

I mustered a smile. 'Not anymore,' I told her. 'Though your recovery may be slow, unless I can fetch more supplies from the ship's medical lab.'

'Slow is better than never,' she said, sinking down into her nest of luxurious blankets with a sigh.

I stood and went to the glass. 'I have enough antibiotics, but the drip I made isn't sufficient,' I said to the Roth. 'She'll need more fluids in six hours. Can I go to your lab to get more supplies?'

He scowled at me. 'No,' he said immediately. 'You will tell me exactly what you need, and I will bring it here.'

Better than nothing. 'I need –'

An alarm blared.

The Roth's eyes widened. *'Brace,'* he snarled.

I flung myself at the bed and over Anna moments before the ship shuddered, and our ears rang with the sound of a giant *boom*.

ASHTON

'MANUAL MODE,' I GROWLED at the Pod.

The Pod's computer gave a soft *beep* as it shifted from automatic and the controls unfurled from the dash. I flicked off the engine boosters and set a course for a large arc around the two ships before me.

They were lurking in an asteroid belt around a small moon, which was how our systems had missed them. The peacekeeping ship would pick them up soon enough; the ships were trading hits back and forth in a strange, slow battle that would show on the space conditions radar as soon as our ship got close enough. It was how I'd found them; the Pod's system had registered the disturbance as a solar radiation storm, which I'd thought odd, given the distinct lack of suns nearby.

I watched as an asteroid roughly the size of our peacekeeping ship was struck by a rogue missile, breaking into a million shattered pieces. The shockwave reverberated through the belt, splitting smaller asteroids on its way. The Pod shook when it hit us, the shield system giving a high-pitched blare of warning before the Pod stabilised.

I shook my head. 'This can't be right,' I said to myself. 'This *can't* be right.'

Roth ships came in two models: the hunting craft that Maeve said looked like spiders – whatever *spiders* were – and the rarely-seen spherical ships carrying dignitaries. When Maeve had seen a picture of the spherical ships, she'd laughed until her eyes shone with tears. *I wish Hollywood could see this*, she'd choked, but never explained what she meant.

I'd seen the hunting craft rope in countless victim ships. I'd seen them land on terra and unfurl their mechanical legs, scuttling after their prey. I'd even seen a spherical dignitary ship launch an anti-matter missile at a small moon, watched as it *disappeared*. Not exploded, not imploded. Just simply and suddenly ceasing to be.

But I'd never seen two Roth dignitary ships target *each other*.

One had been on our radar; after the starling's light show, the scuttler had returned to it like an ice wolf retreating to lick its wounds. It had clearly been trailing the cephalopod prince, possibly hoping to take home a prize captive.

The other dignitary ship was entirely new, but given the readings on my screen, its path through space was similar to our own. Which meant it could have been close to Earth, for reasons I had zero knowledge of.

'What are they doing?' I muttered, bringing an image up on the navigation screen. As I watched, one ship shuddered, quaking under the blow of the other craft's weapons. A few moments later it retaliated; the opposing ship's shield glowed briefly as it absorbed the heat missile.

The Roth shields were strong, the second strongest I knew. They were made to hold out for long periods of time against a range of weapons – but not, usually, *their own*. I estimated it would take half an hour or so for one of the ship's shields to falter and those weapons to start doing real damage.

Before I'd left, Juniper had showed me how to look for residual energy patterns left by our Pods, warning that the patterns were almost impossible to spot from a distance. I was fairly certain that the stolen Pods had flown to the dignitary ship to my right, which meant that Willow was on board – somewhere. I ground my teeth as the other craft shot blow after blow against Willow's ship; though its shields were holding and the weapons had yet to do any damage, he'd feel the shock as the shield absorbed each hit, and his ears would ring with the noise.

And if the ships kept this up, and a missile got through ...

I swallowed and pushed the thought away. I refused to think about it. Willow was as essential to my life as breathing; nothing would touch him.

I wouldn't let it.

I studied the two ships as they played out their silent battle. The Pod's defences were strong, but nowhere near strong enough to join the battle alone and withstand becoming a target; when we flew the Pods into conflict, we did it as a fleet. I tapped the control panel, thinking it through.

The Roth that had stolen Willow clearly needed him. Roth ships usually had their own medical officer, so either the ship had lost their doctor, or there was a species or situation on board that the doctor couldn't handle. The chances of Willow still being alive were good because of that; they wouldn't have taken him if there wasn't a reason. They'd made no attempt to do our ship damage, nor to hurt any of the crew, which was a distinctly *un*-Roth way of approaching things; it puzzled me, but I didn't have time to mull it over properly.

I needed to make a decision.

The Roth were powerful, but we Tirians were equally so. We wouldn't be the universal peacekeepers if our tech wasn't cutting-edge, our shields the strongest, our weapons devastating. The Pod could get past either of the ships' shields; I had blueprints of the dignitary ships, letting me know where I could sneak inside.

'But which one to choose?' I murmured.

Willow was in the ship to my right, the ship that seemed to have come from Earth. I wouldn't know precisely *where* he was being held until I was inside and I could pick up his bioprint. I imagined he'd be under guard, though they'd hopefully be distracted by the battle. I could try to find him, then get us both out.

If the shields held.

If they didn't hold, the battle would start for real, and Willow would be in even greater danger. So would I, if I snuck on board to get him.

My other option was the craft to my left; the craft that had been tailing the cephalopod prince.

The Pod's weapons wouldn't take it out, but I *could* get on board. I could find its control room and sabotage it from the inside.

It would be dangerous, but if I could neutralise the ship before the shields failed, then Willow would stay safe. Well, saf*er*. If anything, it would buy us more time to conduct a rescue.

It wasn't much of a choice after I realised that.

I raised the Pod's shields and directed it forward.

The only unguarded point of entry on a Roth dignitary ship was, unfortunately, the waste chute. It was disguised well, barely discernible on the underside of the ship's rounded hull, distinguished only by the slight wearing of metal where the chute's cover slid back and forth to allow the ejection of frozen waste into space.

The Pod rode the shockwaves as I got closer to the ship. I struggled with the turbulence for a few minutes, swearing as the Pod was pushed off course by a rogue shot. The Pod was small enough that I hoped they wouldn't notice me amidst the asteroids and increasing amount of debris, but that didn't mean I was safe.

The dignitary ships were deceptively big. They weren't as large as our peacekeeping ship, as they were intended for transport rather than long-term accommodation, but they still dwarfed the Pod. My fingers flickered over the controls, getting the craft ready to land on the ship's hull.

The Pod slipped through the larger ship's shields without difficulty, buffeted by the continual shockwaves. It latched onto the Roth hull a short distance from where I needed to be. It was further away than was ideal, as I didn't like being exposed in space for longer than was strictly necessary, but I'd make it work.

'Suit,' I said gruffly.

Tirians didn't need much when it came to space. Our bark armour was enough to protect our bodies, as it regulated both temperature and pressure, and prevented damage from solar rays and moisture loss; given our arboreal ancestry we were less susceptible to low temperatures and changes in air pressure than most organic species, anyway. My armour grew down to cover my hands and feet, forming gloves and shoes that were made of a flexible, slightly sticky, leaf-like fibre. The same substance encircled my neck, allowing the close-fitting helmet descending from the Pod's roof to settle over my head and fix itself to my armour.

At the press of a final button, the Pod's roof slid open. I got out slowly, hating how unnerved I felt by open space. Looking at it was one thing; *being* in it was another entirely. I took a deep breath and deliberately ignored the black stretching behind me, narrowing in on the waste chute as the silent battle played out between the two ships. Feeling too exposed, I crouched down and elected to crawl across the hull, the sticky fibre on my hands and feet anchoring me with each slow movement.

'Willow would laugh at me,' I muttered to myself. I let myself think about how he looked on *his* knees as a distraction. Whenever he knelt, he took me all the way down his throat, an action which made stars appear behind my eyes; he would look up at me as he did it, his own eyes glowing until I splintered into a million pieces.

I wondered if Maeve got to her knees for Elswyth.

That image made me uncomfortably hard; my cock throbbed against my armour as my mouth watered at the memory of her taste. At the first touch of my tongue to her lovely pink folds, my body had shuddered through a wave of *elya* and my blood had heated as the core of my very being shifted. There was no going back; where before my hearts had held two, there was now three. I was hers. My *karia*. My human.

'We will be together. *All* of us,' I told to myself.

I allowed my mind to wander into new territory; territory that still seemed blasphemous, but was almost within reach. I imagined waking up next to Maeve, of kissing her rosy lips as Elswyth stretched out beside her and gave Willow a sleepy smile. I imagined parting my human's folds and thrusting inside while her head fell back on Willow's shoulder and his hands worked between her legs, imagined us pushing her to a climax that would make her scream. I imagined her pleasuring Elswyth as we watched, imagined Willow pressing inside me as our Hamadryad begged and whimpered beneath Maeve's touch. I imagined us sharing each other, so fluidly that it didn't matter whose fingers or tongue or cock was where, just that they *were*, until all four of us were gasping, floating messes in our shared bed.

I'd never imagined anything I wanted so badly.

'Get Willow first,' I reminded myself as I reached the chute. I reached out and traced the faint line where the cover joined the hull.

Its system would release at scheduled times, but I couldn't wait for that to happen; it could have been moments, or it could have been *hours*. I tapped the control panel on my forearm. 'Can you open the waste chute?'

The Pod's computer thought about it while it meshed with the Roth ship's outer systems. 'Negative,' it said eventually. 'Cannot override waste disposal settings until fully bonded with internal systems. Can override waste disposal security feed. Proceed?'

'Proceed,' I told it, hoping the lack of surveillance might buy me a few extra minutes.

I hadn't expected it to be easy. Roth defences were thorough. I'd have to damage the hull to open the chute, which could trigger some kind of alarm, although I was counting on the ship's guards being engaged elsewhere and assuming that the damage had come from the other ship, not a rogue Tirian breaching their defences through the spaceship equivalent of a sewer.

I flicked a switch on my armour's vambrace and got to work with the laser cutter.

As I'd hoped, when I cut through enough of the chute's cover for the ship's system to register it as damage, it opened by itself. I waited as the waste was ejected – only half-frozen, which was disgusting to see, but it iced over once it left the relative warmth of the climate-controlled ship – then inched closer to peer inside.

Down a deep, dark hole.

I sighed. 'You're lucky I love you, Willow,' I grumbled, and crawled inside.

The chute wasn't overly long, and a few minutes later I was pulling myself into a small engineer's bay. Tirian systems worked their way into other species' tech like a virus, so I inserted a small chip into the waste system control panel and let it do its work. A moment later, the Roth symbols flashing on the control screen changed to Tirian characters, and I brought up the ship's schematics. I was pleased to see that they matched the blueprints I'd already studied, meaning our intelligence was up to date, but less thrilled to see the thing I'd been dreading – that most of the beings on board were gathered in the control room, the exact place I wanted to be.

The ship shuddered with another missile blow as I considered my options. I'd hoped to reach the control room so I could activate the time delay on the ship's self-destruct sequence, which was accessible only from a separate system localised to the captain's control panel. By doing that, I'd be able to give myself enough time to escape.

However, Willow's voice said wryly in my memory.

'*However*,' I conceded aloud.

Fighting my way through the twenty-five highly trained Roth warriors currently in the control room would be brave but ultimately extremely stupid; more importantly, it would take *time*. And Willow might not *have* time.

From here, I could still do damage. I could dismantle the shields and let the opposing ship's weapons do their work, while crawling as fast as I could manage back to the Pod, praying desperately to the green gods with every awkward shuffle that no critical hit occurred during those precious minutes. If I delayed the shield commands from here, though, it gave the Roth in the control room time to override my instructions.

I sighed. Taking down a ship from its waste disposal bay might not be glamorous, but it would get the job done, and that was the point.

I tapped the control screen. 'Deactivate all sight and defensive shields,' I said.

'Deactivating,' the system agreed. 'Please wait.'

I examined my armour, counting my heartbeats. As I waited, I studied the control panel; one button blinked at me like a large red eye, reminding me of Maeve's Earth story about princesses and dragons.

I considered the control panel. 'You could be a dragon,' I said to it.

The red light flashed. 'Password required.'

I eyed the screen. 'Override.'

The system thought about it for a tense handful of moments as it dug deeper into the Roth controls. 'Overridden,' it announced. 'Shields deactivated.'

I nodded to it – it wouldn't know, but it was only polite – and, feeling as if I might have temporarily lost my mind, activated my cutter for a second time. I carefully directed the beam around the control panel, then wrenched it out of its bench as the red light flickered and died.

'This is going to be a blast,' I muttered, and I manoeuvred myself back into the waste chute, the control panel under one arm.

The trip back was fraught. I moved as quickly as I could, but the ship's shields failed before I reached the chute cover, and it began taking direct hits. Shields weren't the Roth's only protection; the hull was made of a metal mined on their home planet, Scytha, and it was impervious to almost anything, though dent after dent was appearing as the opposing ship continued its assault.

I flattened myself against the metal as one large dent appeared between me and my Pod. The hull glowed briefly at the friction, but the heat dissipated quickly in the void of space. It wouldn't be the same inside the ship; the heat would radiate and begin to cause damage to the ship's infrastructure. I moved forward in an awkward shuffle, reaching the Pod with my hearts beating hard in my ears. I hadn't been scared until this moment, but the missile had been uncomfortably close.

The Pod slid open. I tossed the control panel in the passenger seat then climbed in, trying to quiet my pulse as the Pod closed and the environment stabilised. When the pressure had settled, I pulled off my helmet and shoved it back into the small hold in the Pod roof, then activated the systems.

'Automatic pilot, back to the peacekeeping ship,' I said tersely.

The manual controls slid back inside the panel. 'Automatic mode activated. Returning to Peacekeeping Ship Number Seventeen-Hundred and Sixty-Three, Title *Forest Souls*.'

I settled into the pilot's chair. It moulded to my back and the restraining vines wrapped around my torso and shoulders, keeping me in place. The Pod detached from the Roth hull; the boosters activated, and it shot through space, dodging crumbling asteroids.

I blew out a breath.

It felt wrong to be flying *away* from Willow, but I'd need backup for a rescue. I knew where the ship was now, and I punched the coordinates into a communication back to Juniper and the peacekeeping ship. I'd insist on being part of the rescue, but if I tried to go in alone and got killed, that would be of no use at all to Willow.

Hold on, my love.

The Pod shuddered.

'What –'

'Critical damage sustained,' the Pod's system told me calmly.

'Fuck,' I answered.

There was another shudder, and the side of the Pod bent inwards.

And so did my shoulder and ribs.

Agonising spears of pain shot through my body. I heard my ribs snap and my shoulder gave a sickening *pop* as it dislocated. My head felt odd, and waves of fire pulsed through my face and down my neck.

The pain was excruciating, but I would have welcomed its continuance, because as my spines twisted, my body went numb. I watched dully as the emergency shadow-moss grew from the Pod's roof to cover the holes open to the void of space.

'Get back to Maeve,' I croaked, before I passed out.

WILLOW

'WHAT'S HAPPENING?' ANNA WHISPERED, struggling to sit up on the cot.

The Roth outside the cell was speaking into his wrist screen. His face gave nothing away, and I was again struck by the notion that Ashton would approve, but it was frustrating to get *nothing* from the male's blank expression. The window was too high for us to reach, and the shuddering seemed to be coming from the other side of the ship, anyway; I wasn't sure we'd see anything other than space if we managed to get to the window in the first place.

The Roth loosed a growl that needed no interpretation; something wasn't right. His eyes flickered to Anna. There was something going on that I didn't fully understand, but there was heat and possession in that black gaze. If the Roth had stolen Anna from Earth to be part of their infamous breeding pens, this was hardly the way to go about it; Anna was being treated as part prisoner, part princess.

'We are being attacked,' the Roth ground out. His eyes went to Vesper. 'You must protect the female.'

The starling gestured at his ankle. 'How?'

The Roth growled again. 'In any way you can.' He glared at me. 'You, too.'

'I'm a doctor, not a warrior,' I said calmly.

He snorted. 'I know Tirians,' he said. 'You are born and given spears in place of rattles.'

My lips twitched reluctantly. 'We will look after Anna as best we can.'

He nodded and disappeared; the cell's glass wall went opaque again.

I glanced at Vesper. 'Can you see anything?'

He closed his eyes; the cell went dark. I sighed and got up, groping around the wall until I found the light switch. I waved it on, but kept the lights dim, thinking it might coax Anna to go back to sleep.

Vesper frowned. 'By the stars,' he said. 'They're fighting *each other.*'

'Who is fighting each other?'

He opened his eyes; the room warmed, bathed in a golden glow. 'The Roth. The heat and light shapes are consistent with a dignitary ship – with *this* ship. There's ours and one more, and they're shooting missiles *at each other.*'

Anna squeaked. 'The Prince,' she said weakly.

'Your saviour will be just fine,' Vesper said, settling back against the wall and closing his eyes once more.

'What do we do?' Anna whispered.

I tried to smile. 'There's nothing we can do,' I said. 'Not about *that*, anyway. But you can rest, and drink some water, and try to eat something more in a few minutes.'

'I'm scared,' she said.

I took her hand and held it between mine. Her hands were different to Maeve's, her fingers so slender they were almost too thin. My human's fingers were long and graceful and capable, and I felt a rush of heat just thinking about them, and how they'd felt in my hair and against my skin. 'I'm scared too. But they clearly won't let you die, Anna. They risked their lives to steal me so I could help you. They're not going to stop protecting you now.'

She settled back in her bed, flushing. 'They stole you? For me? They shouldn't have done that.'

'They could have gone about it differently, yes. But I'm glad they did, if you are feeling better.'

Vesper made a vomiting noise.

'Hush,' she chastised him. 'Not everyone is as bitter and heartless as you, Vesper.'

The starling gave a half smile and turned his face away – but not so far that he couldn't still see her cot.

I smiled again, this time for real. *Maeve isn't the only human wrapping other beings around her little finger.*

MAEVE

'I NEVER THOUGHT I'D have to say this sentence, but El-swyth, *please* come out of your tree.'

The heartree shivered, but there was no answer.

'I know you're in there,' I grumbled, resting my forehead against the trunk. 'The Forest is green again, and I *know* you did that. The bees still sound pissed, but honestly, I'm not sure I can tell the difference.'

A barely-perceptible laugh danced on the air.

'Come on, El,' I coaxed. 'I haven't seen you in days. I'm starting to forget what you look like. There's no way you can be as beautiful as my memory makes you.'

A *humph* murmured close to my ear, but it didn't sound entirely serious.

I rubbed my cheek against the rough bark. 'Come back. For me, if nothing else. Ash has been gone for ages and no one's heard from him. I have honestly never been this worried about anything, ever.'

Arms circled my waist; I suppressed a sigh of relief. 'When was he due back?'

I pulled her hands tighter. 'He said he'd check in every hour. But he's been gone for four hours and there's been *nothing*.'

'The Pod's comms systems could have been disrupted by the asteroid field,' she pointed out sensibly.

'Or something bad could have happened.'

She tugged my waist until I turned in her arms. Something inside me eased as I drank in her lovely face, her changeable eyes, her rippling silver hair.

'We have a saying,' she murmured. 'Bad feelings only grow in tilled soil.'

I touched her cheek. 'Is that like ... you only think bad things if you *let* yourself think them?'

She smiled. 'Something like that.' She pushed my hair back from my face. 'I'm worried, too. But Ashton is a warrior. He's strong and capable and smart. He'll come back. He has to. I could see what he was doing with his tongue and I think maybe ...' She flushed green. 'I think I want him to do that to me.'

'You don't mind?' I whispered, watching her carefully. 'You don't mind being part of a family?'

She snorted. 'Maeve, it's everything I've ever wanted and never thought I'd get to have. *You* are everything I've ever wanted. You arrived here, and somehow made all my dreams come true.' She studied me. 'Will it make you feel better if we waited in the hangar?'

I exhaled slowly. 'Yes, I think so. I don't know why I'm so worried.'

Elswyth brushed her lips over mine. 'You're worried because your family is in danger. You'll feel this way until both Ashton and Willow are back within arm's length.'

'I don't like it,' I said crossly.

'Why do you think we stay so close to our bonded?' She pulled me gently away from the heartree's trunk. 'It's unbearable to be separated.'

'I'm *human*,' I argued. 'I shouldn't be feeling this.' I eyed her sideways as we walked through the Forest. 'Enough about me. How are *you* feeling?'

Elswyth shook her hair behind her shoulders; I glimpsed leaves and vines through its silver mass, and a blossom unfurled to rest on the top of one pointed ear. 'The bees told me I was being stupid,' she said petulantly. 'Apparently my mother has been speaking with them, and she reminded them of how many souls we have on board this ship. They said it was fine to be scared, but could I do it elsewhere, thank you very much, as they were sick of the flowers being dry of pollen.'

'Jerks,' I said cheerfully.

She laughed; the sound tied my stomach up in knots and made my heart lift. She laced her fingers through mine, and we walked to the hangar like two teenagers on their first date, stopping to exchange shy kisses.

Until I saw the hangar's huge doors, and I remembered what she'd distracted me from.

Juniper saw us walk in and rushed to Elswyth's side, her fingers flying furiously over her screen. 'They've picked up a Pod coming this way,' she said breathlessly. 'It's the First Guard's. I'm sure of it.'

'Has he sent a comm?' I said anxiously.

Juniper's face fell. 'Not yet,' she said, biting her lip. 'I've been trying to run a long-distance system check on the Pod for ten minutes, but it's not returning a proper reading, so if he tried to send a message, it might not have gotten through ...' She saw my face and trailed off. 'I'm sure the First Guard is fine. I'm sure he's fine, and he's brought Head Doctor Willow back to the ship.'

'Thank you, Juni,' Elswyth said quietly, gracefully polite when I couldn't even think straight. 'I'm sure you're right.'

The airlock hissed; I suppressed a squeak of surprise.

Juniper flashed us a panicked look, then dashed towards the airlock, where a Pod was being pulled into the hangar by the magnetic tracks lining the floor. I half-sprinted after her, dragging Elswyth with me, elbowing my way through the guards and engineers who'd been standing vigil in the hangar.

Pods were almost indestructible. But like any vehicle, they had weak spots.

Something had hit Ashton's Pod right where the cockpit glass stretched to meet the roof proper, right where the roof was weakest.

Right where Ashton's head would be as he piloted the small craft.

Elswyth choked back a whimper. I took her hand and squeezed her fingers as a team of mechanics used their odd mix of tools and stroking to trigger the Pod's roof to open, tearing away quantities of black moss that had grown over the damage. There was a shout as the roof slid back.

I took one look and spun Elswyth into my arms, pressing her face into my shoulder. She cried out in protest, but I held her, determined.

There was no way I would let her see *that*.

Ashton was still in the pilot's seat, but there was thick green blood *everywhere*. Even from a distance I could see the damage to his skull, the way his face wasn't quite the same shape it had been when he left. My mouth was dry with fear, with *grief*, and I forced myself to swallow, my throat aching. I buried my nose in Elswyth's hair, breathing her in.

'He's alive!'

I closed my eyes and held Elswyth more tightly.

'Willow isn't here,' she whimpered. 'Maeve, Willow *isn't here*. The doctor *isn't here*.'

'There are other doctors,' I whispered. 'Someone will help him. Cedar's the Second Doctor. Cedar will help him.'

'But not Willow,' she sobbed. 'Not the one who should.' She tried to pull away from me. 'I want to see him.'

I held her tight. 'Not yet. When they've bandaged him up. Not yet.'

She'd resent me for it, I suspected, but there was no way I was letting her see. I'd take her resentment, and I'd take the image of Ashton's caved temple, because Elswyth didn't need that seared into the back of her eyelids for the rest of her life.

'Come on.' I pulled her back through the crowd, realising we were in the way. 'He's here. He's home. They'll do everything they can. We'll see him once he's stable.'

Leaving him there felt all kinds of wrong. A hollow pit of sorrow and fear spun in my stomach, but I had to get Elswyth away before she saw him.

I pulled her all the way to the Forest, because I knew she wouldn't want to be anywhere else. She wriggled out of my hold once we got there, sprinting through the green to slump against her heartree and stare blankly up into the black of space. 'He can't die, Maeve.'

'I know,' I said softly.

'No, you don't understand. He *can't*,' she said fiercely. 'Do you know how old I was when Ashton became my guard?'

I shook my head.

'I was *fourteen*. A sapling. He was sixteen. And before he was my guard, he was my *friend*. He followed me from Tir. He could have stayed, could have joined the forces on our home planet, could have stayed closed to his mothers and fathers. But instead he left – left everything he knew – to follow *me*. To guard *me*.' She swallowed, brushing a hand across her eyes. 'He can't die, because he's been with me almost half my life. He can't die because I – because I –' She choked back a sob. 'He can't die because – no matter what happens between you, between *us*, whether we're together, whether we're a family or not – I don't know what my world looks like without Ashton in it.'

I slid down next to her, taking one of her hands in both of mine. I didn't know what to say. I refused to give her false assurances – I didn't know how *any* being, regardless how strong, could live through the injuries Ashton had sustained – but I didn't want to take her hope, either. Almost dispassionately, I watched the Forest shiver as it absorbed Elswyth's grief.

'Tell me how to help you, my love,' I whispered.

She turned and blinked at me, startled. '*My love*?' she repeated.

I shrugged. 'I've been getting this weird feeling.' I disentangled one hand and pressed it to my chest. 'Here.' I moved it down and splayed my fingers across the bottom of my ribcage. 'And here. I couldn't work out what the fuck it was. But I think you did, didn't you? You knew before I realised myself.'

'Yes,' she whispered.

I took a shuddering breath. The world slowed around me; every sound, every leaf in the Forest, took on an almost-painful clarity. Beside me, Elswyth's hair began to shine silver. 'I still need to find Tessa, and if she needs saving, I'll take her home. But I – but I –' I steeled myself, trying to find the strength to say the words I'd never said before, the words I thought I'd *never* say. Being their *karia* was one thing; *loving* was another, a *human* thing, the thing that was outside biology and magic – the thing that was a *choice*. 'I think I love you, Elswyth. Actually, I *know* I do.'

'Oh, Maeve,' she murmured. 'I think you were always meant to be here.' She pressed a kiss to my cheek. 'I love you too. I'll love you for as long as you'll let me.'

I swallowed. 'I think that might be forever.'

'Then forever it is,' she said simply, and lay her head on my shoulder once more.

A moment later, Elswyth began to sing. It was soft and low at first, a gentle, mournful melody, but as I listened, her voice gained power and I could feel the vibration of it through her slender form. The perfect sound – interspersed with clicks and growls – floated through the Forest; I rubbed my cheek on Elswyth's hair.

Then froze.

Around us, everything was *glowing*.

There was a barely-perceptible shiver of movement through the trees, though no breeze to cause it; the Forest was reacting to Elswyth's song. Trunks and branches took on a deep, warm light, and the leaves were lit the same colour as Willow's eyes. It looked like something out of a movie, and it was jaw-droppingly, unbelievably beautiful.

I held Elswyth close until her voice faltered and the song dropped away. The glow remained; we watched it slowly dim.

I didn't think I could speak.

Sometime later, Elswyth rose and pulled me to my feet. 'Come,' she said gently. 'It's been a big day.'

'You're magic,' I whispered to her. 'You beautiful, *magical* thing.'

She shook her head. 'I am whatever the universe made me,' she said. 'Nothing magic about it.' She laced her fingers through mine and held our hands up, studying them. 'Well,' she went on. 'Nothing magic but *this*, anyway. But this feeling. But *you*, Maeve.'

'The Human and the Hamadryad,' I said. 'That's what Ashton and Willow call us. Like we're a fairytale.'

She smiled and shook her head. 'The Human, the Hamadryad, the Doctor, and the Warrior,' she corrected. 'Not a fairytale. A *family*.'

ELSWYTH

WHEN THE SHIP ENTERED night mode, I waited patiently for Maeve to fall asleep, snuggling into her neck like I always did, breathing in the sweet musky scent of her. It took an hour or so for her body to relax and for her to give the adorable snuffling snore that signalled she was deeply asleep enough for me to move and not disturb her. I didn't mind the wait; I loved the quiet moments between us, the moments when I would open my eyes to see her studying my face, the moments where she stroked my hair like I was the most precious thing in the world, the moments where she whispered her secrets to me, and I gave her mine in return.

I kissed her cheek gently and carefully disentangled myself, rising from our bed to pull a robe over my slip.

'Where are you going?' Adair demanded, the moment I stepped out the door.

'None of your business,' I answered shortly.

He studied my face for a moment. I tensed, waiting for a cruel remark about Ashton, or a leer.

'Fair enough,' he said instead. 'But your mother will kill me if I let you go alone.'

'Is someone in the Forest?'

He nodded. 'Dale and Thorn.'

'You can come with me then,' I said ungraciously. 'But I don't know how long I'll be.'

He gestured with his staff. 'Lead the way, Lady.'

I tamped down my surprise and strode down the dim hall-way; Maeve's words must have actually had some effect.

I hadn't bothered with shoes, padding barefoot through the deserted corridors. The ship never fully slept, but it was quiet after Ashton's arrival. My mother had ordered Pods to the co-ordinates he'd entered into the system but had been unable to send, but only to observe; they should have been almost arriv-ing, and I imagined that everyone who was still awake would be glued to their screens, watching the livecast.

I couldn't think of anything worse. My imagination ran riot, seeing Willow's lifeless body floating in the depths of uncaring space, ejected after he served whatever purpose the Roth had taken him for. I choked back a sob, hurrying my steps.

It was odd being in the clinic without Willow; it seemed wrong, somehow. It had never been cold before, or sterile, but it was both now, without Willow's calm warmth. The ship's Second Doctor, Cedar, was dozing at Willow's desk, their waist-length hair caught back in an intricate braid. Cedar started in surprise and blinked at me as the door slid closed.

'H-Hamadryad,' they stammered. 'Lady. I wasn't expecting anyone else tonight.'

'I just want to sit with Ashton for a while. Is that all right?'

Cedar collected themselves and nodded, gesturing to Willow's examination room, just past the decontamination cubicles. 'He won't know you're there, just as a warning. But you're welcome to stay as long as you wish.'

I swallowed down my nerves, though I couldn't stop wringing my hands. *Courage*, I told myself. *Courage*.

Ashton lay in a medical bed, shirtless, the light blanket bunched around his waist. I took one look at him and my head began to spin; I turned around, fighting to catch my breath.

If he looked like this now, then I *never* wanted to know what he'd looked like when he got back. Maeve had been right to block my gaze.

One side of his face was covered with the fibrous green stitches used by Tirian doctors as a last resort. Our species generally healed so swiftly that sutures were entirely unnecessary; doctors only used them in the very worst of cases, where there was so much damage that the body didn't know where to heal first.

Ash's face was *covered* in them.

Cedar had shaved some of his beautiful hair, taking it from the temple downwards on the damaged side. The collarbone on the same side was covered in sticky, viscous healing paste, and the arm below was in a sling.

Tears slid down my face. He looked hurt, but even worse, he looked *vulnerable*, and Ashton wasn't supposed to look like that. He was always bigger than everyone else, always full of quiet confidence and sure strength. He'd been that way since we were saplings, my silent shadow, protecting me even when there wasn't a threat.

That Ashton wasn't here. Nor was the Ashton that stood vigil for hours beneath my hearttree, or the Ashton who had made Maeve cry out in pleasure in the green shaded safety of the

Forest. That Ashton had been chased away by this fragile one, this *broken* one.

I sat on the stool next to his bed. The bed was made of the same material as the Pod chairs, and it moulded around his body. He'd be comfortable and warm, at least.

'This isn't how it's supposed to be,' I told him blankly. He didn't stir. 'Even before you were First Guard of the ship, you were *my* guard. Do you remember when we were twiglets and we got lost in the home Forest? Our parents could hear us the entire time, but we were convinced we'd wandered into unknown territory, into another Forest's heart. You had your tiny spear, and I had my tiny knife, and you made me walk behind you because I was the Hamadryad, and I needed to be protected. You were so proud when you got us back to the village. Our parents laughed, but I ...' I took a shuddering breath. 'I was always grateful for you, Ash. I don't think I've ever told you. I'm grateful for every moment you've given me, every day you've spent beneath my boughs, every night you've watched the Forest to make sure I was safe. I'm grateful for every time you've tried to make me laugh, every time you brought me food, every time you sat with me in silence. You're part of my life, Ash, and the world doesn't feel *right* when you're not near me.'

There was no sign at all that he could hear.

'You'd feel better if Willow was here,' I whispered. 'He should be here. He should be the one caring for you. You'd recover for him. He wouldn't let you do any differently.'

I looked blankly around the room. Spore moss grew on the walls, and there was a single window looking out into the Forest. As sick rooms went, it wasn't a bad one, lined with calming green. But this was *Ashton*, who was larger than life by every definition. He shouldn't have looked smaller, diminished by his wounds.

I slumped down and let my forehead rest on the side of the bed, tears dripping from my chin onto the floor.

'He had this with him.'

I started, looking up at Cedar. 'He what?'

'He had this with him,' Cedar repeated, holding up something in their arms. Something vaguely rectangular, with wiring hanging out the bottom, covered in buttons that would usually be lit but were dull without power. 'It was in the back seat of the Pod. His prints are all over it.'

'A control panel,' I said stupidly.

'Mmm. The tech team said it's from a Roth dignitary ship.'

My mouth dropped open. 'Is that what he was doing? Boarding a Roth ship? *Without backup?*'

Cedar shrugged with difficulty, balancing the torn-out control panel in their arms. 'We'll hear from the reconnaissance team any moment now.' They made a slight face. 'This is heavy. Do you want it? It's already been through decontamination.'

I stared at the piece of the Roth ship. The piece of a Roth *dignitary* ship. 'Yes,' I said immediately. 'If Ashton thought it was important enough to bring back, then I want it.'

Cedar set it down on the other chair with a relieved sigh.

'How long will he need to stay here?'

The Second Doctor shrugged. 'It depends on how he improves over the next few days. If he gets worse, he stays here. If he gets better, he stays here.' Cedar paused. 'If there's no change, he can be moved and placed somewhere he can be monitored remotely.' They gave me a searching look. 'He couldn't go to his own room.'

I swallowed. 'So, if his condition doesn't change in the next few days ...'

'It's likely it never will.' Cedar gave me a sad, knowing smile. 'We're a funny species like that. We heal so swiftly – except when we don't. Head wounds are particularly fraught, and he sustained a blow that should have killed him outright. I rebuilt his skull and relieved the pressure on his brain and drained the blood that had pooled in the wound. I put his collarbone and his shoulder back together, and realigned his spines, but I can't wake him up until he's ready to wake. And Lady, I don't mean to be cruel – but he might *never* be ready.'

I nodded, then took up Ashton's hand. His fingers didn't give even a tiny twitch in response.

Cedar gave me a kind pat on the shoulder, then left me alone with Ashton. I dipped my head so I could rest my cheek against his hand, then looked across at the butchered control panel.

'You have to wake up, Ashton,' I told him. 'If only to explain what in the green gods' name you brought *that* back for.'

WILLOW

WE WERE LEFT ALONE for several hours, though I couldn't tell how many. Anna went back to sleep, a deep slumber that would do more for her healing than any painkiller would. Vesper gave me an unreadable smile and then *pretended* to sleep – starlings *did* sleep, I was sure, but his breathing was too even for true rest – which meant I was left to my own devices. I cleaned my equipment as best I could, using a bowl of water from the washroom and the travel spores I'd brought with me, then restored order to my bag, then spent the rest of the time counting the stars I could see out the tiny window.

I didn't mean to, but after a while, I heaved a bored sigh.

Anna gave a soft chuckle, surprising me. 'What would you be doing if you weren't here?'

I turned to her and smiled. 'I'd be in my lab. It's time to give the younglings on the ship their yearly vaccinations. They get annual shots for standard viruses, but I need to tweak it each time for the environments we're most likely to visit in the upcoming year. These ones need to be adjusted for the marine viruses common to Natare. It's a fair amount of prep work, not to mention getting through the shots themselves. Once the younglings are done, I move onto the adults.'

'What is your ship like?' she said, her voice wistful.

I told her what I could. Anna didn't seem like a threat, but caution had been drilled into me for years.

'A *forest*?' she said incredulously. 'There's a forest *on* your ship? Your ship must be enormous!'

Vesper gave a very awake snort. 'Doubt it,' he muttered under his breath.

I coughed. 'What's this ship like?' I asked, half expecting her not to answer.

'I haven't seen that much of it,' she said. 'Just the corridors when I was brought on board, and the Doctor's lab.' Her lips thinned. 'And the Prince's chambers outside this cell. I don't know why I've been kept in here.'

'My Captain often makes choices for reasons that are not immediately apparent,' I said. 'We come to understand in time. She has all the information, after all, and we see only part of the picture.'

'All the Prince can see is the body part he's thinking with,' Vesper muttered. 'Also very probably not enormous.'

'Thank you, Vesper,' Anna said tartly. 'You seem to have a lot of strong opinions about the Prince's body parts.'

I bit my lip.

'Do you have a family, Willow?' Anna smoothed her blankets. 'A partner? Children – *younglings*?'

I shook my head. 'No younglings,' I said, unable to keep the yearning from my voice. I had always wanted to be a father.

During one of our sessions in my lab, Maeve had told me – in no uncertain terms – that while she liked children, she had no intention of – in her words – *putting myself through that kind of physical, emotional, and mental strain*, which I supposed was fair enough. Elswyth, on the other hand, unconsciously brushed her hand over her stomach every time she saw a twiglet, her lips curling up at the sight of their chubby limbs and tiny features.

I let myself imagine it for a moment: Elswyth, her belly curved and full, spending time in the Forest under Maeve's watchful gaze and Ashton's protective glower. He'd be unbearable, I knew; no one would get within ten paces of Elswyth if she fell pregnant, regardless of who the father was.

Anna smiled. 'But you want them.' She glanced at the glass. 'I do, too,' she whispered. 'But I don't want to be *forced*. I want to have them with someone I love.'

I took her hand and squeezed it. 'That is preferable.'

'Do you have someone?' she said wistfully. 'Someone you love?'

I studied her for a moment, then opted for the truth – well, part of it, anyway. The Roth might have known which ship I came from, but there was no way I'd give them the names of those I cared about most. 'I have two someones. Maybe even three.'

'*Three?* Gosh. That's a lot of personality to keep track of. Most humans can't cope with one.' Her eyes darted towards Vesper, who sniffed and looked away.

'*Most* humans seem like fools,' he muttered.

'Four is a small family for Tirians,' I said, ignoring him. 'Most families are seven or more.'

'Family?'

I tried to think of what Maeve called it. 'A … A harem, I think? A female's group of lovers.'

She laughed nervously. 'Goodness. Lucky female.' She sobered. 'Wait. Does that mean that your someones, your … *family* … are waiting somewhere, wondering where you've gone? Are they worrying about you?'

I looked away. 'I hope they are.' I bit my lip. 'Yes. Yes, I think they will be worrying.'

She muttered something under her breath, then started to push herself from the bed.

'Anna?' I said, alarmed. 'What are you doing?'

She struggled to her feet, then moved to thump on the cell glass with her fist. I followed her, arms out to catch her if she fell. 'Tall, dark, and looming!' she shouted weakly. 'I want to talk to you!'

The glass immediately cleared, revealing the same huge Roth. 'You should be resting,' he said gruffly.

'Shouldn't you be flying this ship?' the starling muttered behind us.

'Willow needs to go home!' Anna said imperiously. 'You stole him to help me, and I'm helped. You need to send him back!'

The Roth crossed his arms. 'No.'

Anna mirrored his stance. 'You have to! You took him from his home, from his family. I understand that you can't send me back, but you can let Willow go!'

I watched her face, amused. She looked as if a stiff wind would knock her over, but when the Roth – twice her size – scowled, she simply scowled straight back.

The Roth glanced at me; I shivered under his jet-black gaze. 'He knows too much.'

'He knows nothing but this cell!' Anna insisted. 'He knows that Vesper is here, but Vesper really *is* a criminal –'

'Hey,' Vesper protested. 'There hasn't been a trial yet.'

'And he knows that *I'm* here, but –' she took a deep breath '– I am stating now, for the record, and for Willow to know, that I have *chosen* to be here, and I will not leave.'

'You *choose* to be here?' he repeated slowly.

'Yes.' Anna's hands shook slightly; she rested them on the glass. 'I am stating that I am here of my own free will. There. Willow knows that you are holding an intergalactic criminal –' she gestured at Vesper, who wrinkled his nose '– and you are *hosting* me as a *willing guest*. Let him go home.'

'A guest,' the Roth repeated flatly.

'A *guest*,' Anna insisted. 'An *honoured* guest of the Prince.'

He stared at her for a long, tense moment, then something in him deflated. 'I will ask the Prince.'

Anna held her chin high. 'Good.'

He gave a sharp nod. 'Fine.'

With that, the cell glass blacked once more; Anna staggered back. I caught her and assisted her back to the cot as she shook.

'You didn't really choose to be here, did you, Anna?' I said quietly.

She shook her head. 'It doesn't matter. You helped me, and now I'm helping you.' She gave a fierce frown. 'The Prince better pull his head from his royal backside and send you home.'

I coaxed her to lie back down and heaped the blankets around her. 'Even if he doesn't, thank you for trying.'

'You've always got to try,' she murmured. Her eyes fluttered closed; in moments, she was fast asleep.

'She said that once before,' Vesper offered, examining his hands. 'She said that trying and failing are far braver than never trying at all.' He glanced at the bed. 'Humans really are curious creatures.'

An hour or so later, I woke with a start as a loud growl echoed around the cell. I looked up, blinking rapidly, to see the same Roth had returned – and he'd brought a friend.

'Prince,' Anna croaked from the bed. 'I wish you wouldn't growl at me.'

'I was not growling at you,' the new Roth said petulantly.

He was as tall as the other, but more slender; where the first Roth had hair of a shining black that matched his eyes and was braided back from his face, the Prince was crowned in messy waves of auburn that curled around his ears and temples, waving around the protuberance of his backwards-curling horns. I didn't know much about Roth beauty standards, but he was handsome – albeit in a rather frightening way.

'If you were growling at Willow, then you can turn around and march right back out,' Anna shot back, pushing herself up on trembling arms.

The Prince stared at her, then rubbed his temples. 'Things were easier when I could not understand you,' he muttered.

Anna forced herself upright, her back painfully straight. 'Did tall, dark, and looming tell you what I said?'

The Prince considered her. 'He told me.'

'Let Willow go, and I'll consider giving you what you want.'

'You will consider it over dinner.'

Anna blinked. 'Dinner? With you?'

The Prince cocked his head. 'Is that not an Earth custom?'

She bit her lip. 'It's an Earth custom.'

'Then you will have dinner with me,' he said decisively.

'With *just* you?' she said, her eyes flicking to the first Roth.

The Prince gave a short, sharp nod.

'*Fine*,' Anna said. 'I will have dinner with you. But I am still *considering*. It doesn't mean anything.'

He gave a close-lipped smile. 'I will keep that in mind.'

'Just *please* don't make me eat the chicken again,' Anna said, as if she couldn't help herself; I eyed her sideways.

'No chicken,' the Prince said, his lips twitching.

'So you'll let Willow go?'

The Prince's answer took so long that I was sure he'd refuse. In the end, though, he gave a silent nod and turned his back, disappearing around a corner.

'Come with me now,' the first Roth said, gesturing to me.

I swallowed and turned to Anna. 'I'm going to leave more antibiotics and painkillers here, and the vitamins, and the food pouches, and a thermometer. Vesper, if she gets hotter than thirty-eight Earth degrees Celsius, give her the painkillers first, then another antibiotic shot. You need to drink more fluids than you think you need and keep up the vitamins. Wash the bite clean twice each day with water or an antibacterial spore wash – a *gentle* spore wash, not an industrial one. Any questions?'

Anna shook her head. 'Thank you, Willow.'

'You're welcome.' I stood, rifling through my bag, unpacking the things she'd need. I turned my back, purposefully making a rustling sound with the food pouches. 'Do you need help, Anna?' I whispered, as softly as I could.

She flicked a glance at the Roth, then back at Vesper.

The starling gave her a smile I couldn't read.

She pursed her lips. 'No,' she whispered back. 'No. Not if it means they could get hurt. I'll work something out.'

'I'll flag the ship regardless.' I handed her the food. 'I'll be thinking of you.'

She gave me a full, brilliant smile, and I could see why the Prince had been so desperate for his dinner. 'I wish I could see you again. I'd like to meet your family.'

I returned her smile. 'Stranger things have happened. Stay well, Anna.' I nodded at Vesper. 'Starling. I'll forget I ever saw you.'

'That would be ever so kind,' Vesper said. 'But if you happen to meet another starling who looks quite like this, please do feel free to let my twin know that I'd appreciate a rescue at their earliest convenience.'

'I'll keep that in mind.'

The Roth stepped forward and placed his hand against a scanner outside the cell. The glass slid open; I walked through, giving Anna one last small smile.

The glass slid closed behind me, and the wall wavered slightly; I imagined that from the inside, it was back to its impenetrable black. I looked up at the Roth, waiting for his instruction, and more than a little unnerved by his height and by the horns looming into the darkness.

He gave a slight sigh. 'I really am sorry about this,' he said, and he lifted his fist.

The world went black.

MAEVE

ELSWYTH HAD BEEN BY Ashton's bedside for *hours*.

I didn't have the heart to disturb her, so I'd left some food and water at the door and retreated into the clinic to annoy Cedar. The Second Doctor took it good-naturedly, putting up with my questions about the compounds they were mixing and what they did when they weren't in the clinic.

Cedar sparred, as it turned out. When I discovered that, we got along famously.

After I judged that I'd given Elswyth enough space, I slipped into the sickbay. Ashton did *not* look well, but at least Cedar had put his skull back together.

I pursed my lips. I would never forget the sight of his caved temple. My eyes sought the slight rise and fall of his chest to reassure myself that he was still alive. I watched the movement for longer than I cared to admit, then took a lock of Elswyth's shining hair between my fingers. 'How is he?'

Elswyth sniffed. 'I can't see any change,' she said hoarsely. 'He doesn't react when I speak, or when I touch his hand.' She wiped her eyes. 'You must understand that our injuries are usually healed within hours, even broken bones. This is ...' She trailed off. 'This is bad, Maeve.'

I pulled her against me, stroking her hair. 'He's strong. And he has a gorgeous female by his bed to come back for.'

'*Two* gorgeous females,' she corrected.

I squeezed her shoulder. 'What the fuck is the thing on the chair?'

She sniffed again. 'It's a control panel from a Roth dignitary ship.'

'Where did it come from?'

'Ashton had it in his Pod.'

'He stole a control panel? Why? What the fuck are we supposed to do with that?'

'It would have disabled the ship's systems,' Cedar called softly from the lab. 'Removed the relevant system brain, as it were.'

I stared at Elswyth. 'The dickhead messed up their systems and brought home a fucking *trophy*? Why? What the motherfucking ...' I blinked as I realised. 'Oh, if he doesn't die, *I will kill him all over again*. I shouldn't have told him that bloody story. *He brought back a fucking dragon's head.*'

Elswyth frowned. 'Story? Dragon ...' Her eyes went wide as she realised. 'Oh, Ashton. You gods-damned *fool*.'

I laughed. 'That fucker. Only Ashton would complete his quest but come back too injured to enjoy the spoils. It's poetic irony, or some shit.' I sobered. 'Anna would know.'

'Are we the spoils in that metaphor?' Elswyth took up his hand, lacing her fingers through his.

'I think we are,' I answered, watching him closely, but Ashton didn't stir.

A few moments later, Elswyth began to sing. She started off soft, a wordless, mournful lullaby that made me shiver and my skin break out in gooseflesh. The melody developed slowly, adding some words here and there until it morphed into something I recognised – the song she'd sung to the Forest.

Her voice rose, the notes so pure and lovely that my eyes began to prick with tears. I crossed my arms over my chest as her hair began to glow.

Then Ashton's began to glow, too.

He stirred on the bed, his skin lighting from within. Elswyth's voice faltered for a moment as she realised what was happening, then she continued her song, strengthening her voice until the notes filled the room. Cedar came to stand in the doorway, mouth hanging open; they rubbed their hands up and down their bare arms, shivering. Their hair began to glow, too, but softer than Ashton's.

Elswyth's song was for him, after all.

'Green gods,' Cedar whispered. '*Elya*. I've never seen it like this before.' Cedar looked down at their hands wonderingly, then clasped them together, almost in prayer, and lifted their eyes to fix on Elswyth. '*Lady*,' they said reverently.

Ashton gave a low, deep groan.

The proximity alarm began to sound. Cedar frowned, startled out of their wonder, then went to check the infirmary's main screen.

I followed them. 'What is it?'

'Fuck,' Cedar said. 'It's the stolen Pod.'

I felt a sense of deja vu as the Pod coasted into the hangar. Again, the cavernous space was crowded; again, Elswyth looked to be on the verge of tears; and again, I was feeling nervous, which put me in a punch-first-ask-questions-later kind of mood. Ashton hadn't woken up at the sound of the alarm, so we'd left him there after Elswyth fussed over his blankets.

She clung to my arm as the Pod settled down to a soft landing, guided by the automatic flight system, her fingers tightening around my bicep.

I kissed her cheek and willed myself to be calm.

The Pod slid back, and the engineers surged forward to help. A fair head emerged, and moss-green eyes sought mine from across the hangar, from through the crowd of Tirians.

Willow's voice was quiet, but its echo sent a shiver down my spine. '*Maeve.*'

Before I knew what I was doing, I'd broken away from Elswyth and was sprinting across the smooth hangar floor. I wasn't thinking, but my arms knew what to do, hooking themselves around his neck. My lips were sure, seeking his for a desperate, relieved kiss, a kiss he returned hungrily, his hand moving to cup the back of my head in the kind of tender, loving touch I hadn't experienced very often but had recently realised that I fucking *lived* for.

'Maeve,' Willow said again breathlessly as I broke away. He rested his forehead against mine and I *melted*, my legs trembling beneath me when it was *him* who'd just returned home from being violently kidnapped. 'Maeve.'

I laughed shakily. 'Fuck, I'm glad you're back.'

'Is the Lady well?' he said anxiously. 'She looks like she's been crying.'

I didn't think it was normal to love someone for asking about another female's health, but I did. I loved that he cared, loved that he'd asked, loved that his hand was still cupping my nape even as his eyes were on Elswyth, his expression concerned.

'She's as well as can be expected,' I answered. 'Willow?'

He dragged his eyes back to me. 'Yes?'

'You're mine,' I said.

'Yes.' He paused, and with his characteristic calm seriousness, said: 'Maeve, your eyes have changed. And ...' He ran his fingertips over the shell of one ear. 'By the green gods. What is this?'

'Not the most romantic *hello*, but not the worse one I've ever heard, either,' I told him.

He made a *tsk* noise, then pulled back and stared into my eyes. 'Maeve, your irises have green in them. And the shell of your ear is hardening. There are tiny points beneath the skin there. Can you feel?' He pressed gently down on the shell of my ear.

'I ... I think?' I faltered. 'Wait. What the fuck are you saying?'

'You've been on the ship for months. What if ...' He trailed off and bit his lip.

'Willow,' I said, as calmly as I could manage. 'Are you trying to tell me that I'm becoming Tirian?'

'No!' he protested. 'Well, maybe. A bit. If the change was gradual, I might have overlooked it. But Maeve ...This doesn't usually happen to humans, does it?'

'No. But I guess humans don't usually hang out with a bunch of space tree-elves,' I answered, pinching at my ear. 'Ouch.'

'I need to take some samples,' he muttered.

'You can scan me any time, Willow.' I took his hand. 'But first, there's something we have to tell you.'

ASHTON

'CEDAR DID WELL. BETTER than I might have managed. And whatever Elswyth did ... The scans show that his skull is healing, and his shoulder is almost fully set. All he needs is time.'

I frowned. That voice ... I knew that voice.

Loved that voice.

That voice was *impossible.*

I tried to lift my hand, tried to open my eyes. My fingertips fluttered against something soft.

'He's moving more.'

'Yes. Some of the movements will be involuntary, but it's possible that he's starting to respond.'

I can hear you, I wanted to say crossly. *I'm right here. Responding.*

'Maybe you should sing to him again, beautiful.'

There was a short silence, then the sound began again, the one that made the pain go away, the one that made me sleep.

I slipped back into blackness.

'Ashton, if you can hear me, I'm losing my patience.'

This voice was sharp and amused all at once. As if its owner was joking, but not entirely.

I shifted my fingers.

'I know you can hear me, elf-boy. I'm not made to wait in a sick room, Ash, and you're not made to be sick in one. So hurry up and heal so we can move you elsewhere.'

I wanted to wrap my arms around that voice. Or perhaps have it wrapped around me. Either way, I didn't want to be able to tell where that voice ended and I began.

'You're stressing Willow out,' the voice continued ruthlessly, 'and Elswyth needs daily healing because she's stripping her throat raw singing to you. The Forest is wilting again because it misses her. So pull yourself together, Ash. We need you back.'

I'm trying, I wanted to say. *I'm trying my best.*

'I know you're trying,' the voice said, as if she'd heard me. 'I know you'll be fighting with everything you have.' There was a rustle and the bed dipped, as if she'd sat down on the edge next to me. I tried to turn towards her – I wanted to bury my face in her lap and never surface – but all that happened was that my throat gave a low, rasping groan.

'There you are,' she said, satisfied. 'Hear me, elf-boy. We're here, and we're waiting for you. Willow is back, and we got your dragon's head. Come back. Come back to your family, Ashton.'

I tried. I tried to force my eyes open, tried to reach for her, but the black took me instead.

The next time I woke, the room was silent.

I listened for a few minutes. I could hear the soft inhale and exhale of my breath. Softer still, my heartbeats. From further away, muffled thumps and scrapes and shouted commands – the hangar.

I wrenched my eyes open, and this time, it worked.

I could see a moss-lined ceiling; with great effort, I turned my head to the side. There was a moss-covered wall, and an open door; a diffuse light spilled through. In my line of sight, a desk with a screen gone blank, and a fair head pillowed on crossed arms, a beloved face frowning in sleep.

'Will,' I whispered.

He stirred but did not wake. I forced myself to focus on his features, on his neat nose and lush lips and wide jaw. On the thorn-lined cheekbones I loved to kiss and the furrowed brow I wanted to smooth and the temples I loved to trace with a fingertip when I brushed back a silky curl.

I tested my arms. I bunched my fingers in the blanket, one hand after the other, then practised lifting each one. I could get each of them around an inch off the bed before I had to let them fall again.

'Not good enough,' I croaked.

I gathered every ounce of strength I had, then wrenched one across my body, the momentum turning me half on my side.

Good. With both hands braced on one side, I could push against them.

I pushed myself up, then collapsed immediately down. I growled, the sound rasping and raw, tearing my throat, and tried again, leaning my weight forward as I did.

My torso slid off the bed, leaving me half-on, half-off the sickbed.

I grunted, my hands hitting the cold lab floor. I swung my hips so the rest of my body would follow – and ended up in an ungainly heap.

At least I'm out of the bed.

'Ashton?' Willow's voice was sleepy and amused. 'What are you doing?'

I tried to rearrange my twitching limbs. 'Getting up.'

'And how much success would you say you're having?'

I bared my teeth. 'I'm out of bed, aren't I?'

'Here.' Willow bent down and scooped an arm around my back, getting me into a sitting position with some difficulty. 'Green gods, you weigh more than an oak. Back up you go.'

He hauled me back up onto the bed but left me sitting on the side. I was naked and the lab was cool; I shivered, so he pulled my blanket around my shoulders.

'Will –'

'Shh,' he soothed. 'Your throat will be raw. Are you hungry? Thirsty?'

I shook my head. 'They took you. They took you, and I left you there.'

'Don't talk nonsense,' he said. 'You didn't leave me anywhere.'

'I knew which ship you were on,' I rasped. 'I took down the other, but I *left* you on that ship.'

He stroked my face. 'And why did you leave me, Ash?'

'To get backup, but –'

'Yes, because taking down *two* ships would have been rather pushing your luck, I'd imagine.' His thumb skimmed my lip in a featherlight touch. 'Do you know what happened on your way back?'

I shook my head, then winced as pain bloomed over my temple. I lifted a hand to find it covered by a leaf bandage.

'Don't touch that.' Willow took my hand away. 'A reconnaissance drone captured footage of it. The Roth ship started shooting blindly when the crew realised they were going down. They hit the Pod's shield and one of the larger asteroids at the same time. The direct strike from the ship destroyed your shield, and the asteroid was blown apart at the same moment. A fragment ricocheted and hit the side of the Pod. The force caved in its side.' He swallowed. 'Along with your temple. Cedar put you back together, but Ash ... It's been weeks now. We weren't sure ...' He pressed a soft kiss to my forehead. 'We weren't sure that you'd come back.'

'Weeks?' I said hoarsely. 'How many weeks, Will? How close are we to Natare?'

He sniffed. 'Three,' he whispered.

Panic shot through me. 'Three *months*? At normal travel speed? I've been sleeping for an entire *month*?'

'No, Ash. Three *weeks*. We're three *weeks* out from Natare.'

I pulled away and stared at him. 'That can't be true.'

He gave a shaky laugh. 'You have no idea how pissed Maeve is that you've been unconscious all this time.'

'She's angry?' I said anxiously.

'Not *with* you. She's just impatient for you to wake up. And Elswyth has been singing to you every day, and it drains her *elya*, and she gets weepy when she's tired, and when she's weepy, Maeve goes on the warpath towards anyone who so much as looks at El sideways, and –'

'*El*?' I interrupted.

He flushed a lovely dark green. 'She likes it,' he said shyly.

I swallowed, my heart suddenly in my throat, my stomach twisting with jealousy; whether it was for Willow getting time with them, or them getting time with Willow, I couldn't say. 'You've been with them this whole time.'

He snorted. 'Don't start that rubbish. They've been *here*, by your side, every moment of the day, and I've been here at night. You haven't been left behind, Ash. You just weren't conscious to appreciate how much attention you've been getting.'

I exhaled, my arms all but shaking with relief.

'Elswyth got your dragon's head,' Willow said casually. 'She's put it in the family room. Maeve built a shelf for it and everything.'

The family room.

Yearning shot through me, so strong that my cock stirred. 'You've been staying there?'

'Yes.' He took my chin in his hand and gently forced me to look at him. 'I've moved your things there, too. I didn't organise them for you because fuck, Ash, your shelves were a mess, but I moved everything. Tell me if I did the wrong thing.'

I stared at him. 'Maeve agreed?'

He laughed. 'Maeve suggested it. Well, when Maeve *suggests*, it's not really a suggestion. It was more like she said *it would be good if Ash's things were in here when he wakes up*, and then she gave me a look, and next thing I knew I was elbow-deep in your unwashed uniforms.'

I gave a wheezing laugh, then winced when pain spread through my skull.

'Right,' Willow said, and before I could protest, he'd gently pushed me down and settled my blanket around my body. 'We'll try this again tomorrow.'

I struggled weakly. 'Don't go.'

'I'm not going anywhere.' He touched my cheek. 'You risked your life for me. I'm not letting you out of my sight ever again. When you're back on rotation, I'm going with you every time you launch a Pod.'

My eyes fluttered closed. 'The Captain will have words to say about that.'

'She's welcome to say them. Whether I choose to listen is a different matter entirely.' His fingertips stroked my skin. 'Sleep.'

I slept.

I woke to a dull *thump*.

'For fuck's sake, be *careful*,' Maeve hissed. 'You're not carrying in the shopping. He almost *died*. If you hit his head, Adair, I will hit *yours*.'

'He's fine, Maeve,' Willow said soothingly. 'It was the hover mechanism of the bed. His head is fine.'

Maeve muttered something under her breath.

'The next part will be the hardest,' Willow went on. 'We're going to get him from the sick bed to the real bed. We're going to –'

'I can do t'm'sel,' I slurred, annoyed.

'Oh, yes?' Willow said politely. 'Because I had to dose you with painkillers after what you pulled last night, you were moaning so loud in your sleep. Can you open your eyes, Ashton?'

I tried to open them.

'Mmm. That's what I thought. Now be a good patient and let us get you comfortable.'

My head spun as they lifted me. I was shifted and lowered gently back down; someone grunted at my weight. The bed beneath me wasn't the sick bed; instead of compounded moss, I was lying on sheets and a soft mattress.

'Fucking hell, Ash. I thought this bed was huge, but you take up three quarters of it.' Maeve's voice was amused.

'I did warn you,' Willow muttered. 'I can sleep in my room, if –'

'Absolutely fucking not,' Maeve said sharply. 'You're mine. You're not going anywhere.'

I groaned. 'Pu' me ba' in the sickrum.'

'Shh,' Willow said.

'I don't mind snuggling.' A softer voice came from my side; I turned to it like a flower towards the sun. A finger touched my cheek.

'Lady,' I croaked, and tried to reach for her.

'Shh,' Elswyth chided, taking my hand. 'Be calm, Ashton. We've moved you to the family room for the rest of your recovery, but if you push yourself too hard, we'll need to move you back. You don't want that, do you?'

'M'not a saplin',' I slurred crossly.

'No, you're not. But you're on enough painkillers to fell an oliphant, and your body is still healing. So be a sensible male and go to sleep.' She caressed my fingers. Sleep.'

I did.

'I can get up.'

Maeve crossed her arms. 'You're not getting up.'

'I want to get out of this bed, Maeve.'

'Well, you can't, elf-boy,' she snapped. 'Deal with it.'

'How about *sitting* up?' Elswyth coaxed, trying to keep the peace.

Maeve considered it. 'Fine. He can sit up.'

Elswyth moved to help me; I stopped her with a look, struggling to get myself upright. It took a few moments, but I managed it, slumping back against some pillows, panting.

'There we go,' Maeve crooned. 'Now we can snuggle.'

I stared at her. 'Snuggle?'

'Please tell me you know what that means.'

'I know what it *means*,' I muttered. 'In theory.'

Maeve and Elswyth exchanged a look.

'Willow and I have been sneaking around for three years,' I said defensively. 'There wasn't a lot of time for *snuggling*, and even when there was, it wasn't ... restful. We were too afraid we'd get caught.'

'We'll have to teach you, then,' Elswyth said mat-ter-of-factly. She climbed onto the bed next to me. 'Maeve harassed the communications engineers until they built a feed to Earth media, so we get human content on the comms stream now. Some of it is pretty good.'

Maeve snorted. 'You have a low bar, beautiful. Reality TV is not *pretty good*.'

'I like all the emotion,' Elswyth said, unfazed. 'Can you get the snacks?'

Maeve bustled around the food processor, fiddling with the programme until she had enough *popcorn* and *chocolate* to feed a small army. She laid it within arm's reach in front of me, fussing with the tray and with my blankets until I snarled at her.

'Grumpy,' she muttered.

'It is my job to fuss over *you*, not –'

'Yes, yes, we know, you've told us,' she said impatiently. 'And when you can walk, Ashton, you can do your job. For *Elswyth*, not me, just so we're clear. Fuss over me and I will fuss back with my fists. I don't need that shit and nor do I want it.'

'You are our *karia*, you need –'

She climbed onto the bed and silenced me with a swift, fierce kiss.

My mind blanked the moment her lips touched mine.

'The film is starting,' she said, breaking away and sitting beside me like nothing had happened. 'Shh.'

Every inch of my skin was tingling, hyper aware after the quick caress of her lips. My cock twitched under the blankets; I casually shifted my arms into my lap to cover it. Elswyth leaned against me, resting her cheek lightly against my healing shoulder, and Maeve mirrored her on my other side, linking her arm through mine.

I could smell both their scents, Elswyth's alluring floral and Maeve's assertive musk. My mouth watered and I swallowed nervously.

This was ... *nice*.

They were warm and comfortable by my sides, and their combined scent went straight to my cock. Elswyth's silver hair was tickling my skin and Maeve's fingertips were absently tracing patterns on my forearm. I took a shuddering breath.

'Are you all right?' Elswyth asked, concerned.

Maeve glanced at my stirring crotch and laughed. 'He's fine, beautiful. What did you choose for us to watch?'

Elswyth pressed a button, and an Earth melody filled the room. I wrinkled my nose. It was relatively gentle compared to some of the other so-called *music* Maeve had subjected us to, but it was still somehow too *loud*. There were too many instruments and too many sounds, and they all happened too quickly.

The screen showed a green Earth landscape. 'Oh, this is Anna's favourite,' Maeve said. 'She talks about it all the time.'

'Where are the trees?' Elswyth said, wrinkling her nose. 'Why is there so much green but no trees?'

Maeve snorted. 'That's grass. It's a plant, too. Humans are obsessed with it. And this is a period film, so there's a *lot* of grass. And rolling hills. And roses, and white dresses, and lingering looks.'

Elswyth touched her ear. 'Willow said my translator isn't broken, but sometimes I'm not sure.'

Maeve rubbed her cheek on my shoulder, laughing, then took up my hand, lacing her fingers through mine. My heart lurched. 'Just watch. It'll make more sense later.' She paused. 'Or not, maybe. I don't really get these films, to be honest.'

There was a soft *beep* from outside the room, and the door slid open. Willow walked in, then stopped short when he saw us. 'Oh.'

'Want to watch a movie with us, doctor?' Maeve purred.

Willow flushed his lovely deep green blush, then ran his hands through his waving hair. 'You did this on purpose.'

'We just wanted to watch a film,' Elswyth said innocently.

'You coming in is just an added bonus,' Maeve agreed.

Willow glared at me. 'Were *you* part of this?'

'Part of what?' I said, bewildered.

Willow threw up his hands and stormed to the bathroom, muttering crossly under his breath the whole time. The door slid shut behind him.

Maeve and Elswyth waited until the patter of the water shower sounded faintly, then collapsed into howls of laughter.

I frowned. 'What's so funny?'

'Poor Willow,' Maeve said, clutching her stomach. 'He's too noble for his own good.'

'He decided that he would wait for you to be better,' Elswyth explained.

'Wait?'

'For kissing, and ... more than kissing,' Maeve said huskily. 'He decided to be all virtuous and decent and self-sacrificing and wait until you were ready, so you wouldn't feel like you'd been left behind.'

'But Maeve hasn't been making it easy for him,' Elswyth added.

Maeve snorted. 'Not just me, Miss-flouncing-around-in-her-underwear. He's been taking so many cold showers I'm surprised the ship hasn't had to harvest more ice.'

'You know what he's *really* doing in there,' I said thickly.

Elswyth frowned at me. 'What he's *really* doing?'

'The shower won't be cold.'

Maeve gave a slow, dangerous grin. '*Mmm.*'

'What?' Elswyth said, confused.

'He's jerking off,' Maeve said.

Elswyth flushed. 'Right now?'

I settled back on my pillows. 'Right now. His hand will be on his cock, and he'll be thinking about you two – and maybe me – while he moves it up and down his shaft. His head is especially sensitive, so he'll –'

Elswyth smacked my thigh; I could almost feel the heat radiating from her cheeks. '*Ashton.*'

Maeve gave a husky laugh. 'Who knew you had such a dirty mouth, Ashton McCarthy? I like it.'

Ashton McCarthy. Not Ashton Unclaimed. Tirians usually took their *karia's* first name to denote their family status, but I wasn't about to complain; I liked the way my new name sounded.

'It can be as dirty as you want.'

'Mmm,' Maeve hummed again, stretching and unfurling her body in a graceful movement. She climbed over my lap to seize Elswyth's mouth in a long, nuzzling kiss. My cock throbbed painfully, but I was content to watch as she pushed Elswyth down on the bed and thrust her hand into her pants.

My Hamadryad whined, pushing her hips up to meet Maeve's touch. She glanced at me and flushed, but evidently wasn't bothered by my presence. I listened to their panting, my own breath coming fast. Dragging her eyes back to our *karia*, Elswyth unzipped Maeve's jeans and paid her back touch for touch; Maeve cried out as Elswyth's fingers found some sensitive spot.

I groaned softly.

It only took a few moments for Maeve to make Elswyth fall apart; she threw her head back, panting and whimpering as Maeve coaxed her through her climax. When her breath had calmed, she returned the favour with a single-minded focus that was at once arousing and slightly terrifying; Maeve didn't seem to mind, blooming a minute later with a surprised laugh and a moan that sent shivers through my entire body.

The door to the bathroom slid open, and Willow walked through, his hair wet, his lovely chest bare. His eyes went wide as he took in the females lying entwined on the bed, Elswyth's hand still thrust down the front of Maeve's jeans.

'For fuck's sake,' he muttered, and turned around, heading straight back into the bathroom. The shower started up again a moment later.

Maeve laughed again, the sound deep and satisfied. 'This is so much fun.'

'Ash. Ash. *Ashton*. Wake up.'

Something soft trailed down my chest. I groaned, fighting off sleep. Hair brushed over my belly; a tongue traced wet circles around my hip.

'Will,' I said hoarsely.

'I'm going insane. I can't stand you being so close when I can't touch you. Can I?'

His fingers pushed the blanket down my thighs and found my hardening cock. 'Mmm-es,' I managed. I cleared my throat. 'Yes. Please. *Yes*.'

'Thank the green gods,' he muttered. 'Stay still.'

His lips closed around my swelling head. He sucked; I swore, my hips twitching of their own accord.

'Stay *still*, Ashton,' Maeve warned. Her voice was heavy with sleep and desire. She sat up. I could see her silhouette in the darkness; it must have been hours until the ship's day cycle was due to begin. She pushed her hair from her face, her eyes on Willow as he stretched out between my legs.

His mouth came off me with a wet *pop*; he turned his attention to my shaft, working it up and down with his tongue then, once it was wet enough, with his hand, his fingers skirting around my burl.

'Will,' I said again, groaning.

'He's not allowed to come, Willow,' Maeve said sharply, watching intently. She reached out and trailed her hand over my stomach. 'That part is for me.'

'Oh, *green gods*,' Elswyth whispered from my other side, watching Willow's movements. 'That should be illegal.'

Maeve laughed. 'Come here, beautiful.'

Elswyth hopped from the bed and crossed to the opposite side as Willow took up a slow, methodical attack of tantalising teasing, lavishing me with short, hard licks and small sucks, not enough to take me anywhere close to climax, but enough to make me almost painfully aroused.

Maeve arranged Elswyth on her lap facing me, her back against Maeve's chest. The Hamadryad was wearing a sleeping shift and apparently nothing else; Maeve pushed her knees apart and began exploring unhurriedly between her legs. It was too dark for me to see anything in detail, but I watched Elswyth's head fall back on Maeve's shoulder, saw Maeve bite her lip, and I could hear the sounds as Elswyth grew wet and then wetter, and savour her tiny cries as Maeve began to work her faster.

Willow surged forward and took me fully down his throat.

My groan echoed off the walls. 'If you don't want me to come, that is not a good idea,' I grated out.

His mouth slid off me with a wet sucking noise. 'So soon?'

'Fuck you, Will, I've been unconscious for months.' I reached down and caught his chin, then drew him up for a kiss. He planted his arms either side of my head and took my mouth gently, careful not to jostle me. I ignored the stab of pain in my shoulder and chest and slid my arms around him, almost weeping at the slide of his skin on mine, at the hard press of his thick cock on my stomach. 'Green gods, I've missed you.'

'I love you,' he whispered. 'Don't ever do that to me again.'

I kissed him as hard as I could manage, parting my lips to let him fuck his tongue into my mouth. I yielded before him, moaning when he rubbed his cock against me, seeking friction.

'Oh, *fuck*,' Elswyth sobbed, then cried out; I turned in time to see her shudder and slump back against Maeve, who murmured a handful of nonsense endearments and gave her a satisfied kiss.

'We're not done yet, beautiful,' Maeve murmured. 'Will, can you take her?'

Willow gave me a last possessive kiss, then rolled away from my body and scooped up Elswyth in one graceful movement, rubbing his cheek against her hair as he held her in his arms. He was entirely naked, so there was no way I couldn't find the sight erotic, but it was more than that: the way he cradled her was tender, his embrace at once gentle and protective.

I rubbed my chest, over both my hearts.

'Gorgeous, aren't they?' Maeve murmured to me, her voice admiring. She bent and kissed me, nipping at my bottom lip. 'Now, you need to stay still, Ashton. If you start to move, I'll stop.'

'Stop what?' I started, but my voice faltered as Maeve swung a leg over my hips and straddled my thighs.

She gave me a questioning look. 'Yes or no?'

'Fuck, yes,' I breathed. 'Yes, Maeve.'

'Good.' She took up my cock with both hands, pumping my shaft loosely with one, tracing the precum already leaking with the pointer finger of the other. 'I suspect we're already bonded in every way that matters, but there's no harm in making sure.' She hummed and lifted her hips into position, teasing me with the lightest touches of my head along her slit. 'This might take a little while. I'm used to something smaller.'

'Stop stroking my ego and fuck me,' I said.

She laughed. 'Tell me what to do again and I'll play with Willow instead.'

I snapped my mouth shut.

'Thought so.' She dragged my head through her wetness; I bunched the sheet in my hands and bit my lip, then made a strangled sound when she sank down.

Despite what she'd said, she took me in one smooth movement, panting when I bottomed out. She braced her hands on my chest. 'Fuck, Ashton. *Fuck*.' She laughed again. 'I can't fucking breathe.'

I was holding my own breath, so I understood. She was warm and wet and soft inside, and so fucking *tight*; it felt like my cock was held by a vice. Her slightest movement around me sent waves of pleasure through my body; when she clenched her internal muscles, I bucked my hips.

'Stop that,' she panted. 'I mean it. If you do anything that could damage your healing, I will put you back in that sickbay myself.' She paused. 'Also, I need some time to adjust. Stay still.'

'Can I touch you?'

She bit her lip, then nodded her assent. 'Only if it doesn't hurt you.'

I reached up and skimmed her shoulders, dancing my fingers down her arms and then back up. I took a lock of her hair between my fingers and let it slide over my skin. I traced the shape of her breasts, small and perfectly shaped, her nipples a dark pink in the dim room. I teased them to hard peaks, gently kneading the soft flesh then plucking at her nipples; she wriggled on my cock, making both of us cry out. I spanned her waist – my hands could circle it, she was so small – then grasped her hips. I rocked her slightly forward, then back.

'Fuck, fuck, fuck,' she chanted.

I kept one hand on her hip, encouraging her to start moving in small, easy rolls. Her eyes fluttered closed and her lips parted as she rode me; the sight alone was enough to make my body tense in readiness.

Not yet, I begged myself silently. *Not yet.*

Her internal muscles clenched and released around me, and a fresh wave of pleasure rolled through my body. My cock pulsed inside her, the pressure so much it almost skirted pain. My head throbbed, and the base of my shaft felt ready to burst.

I tipped my head back, groaning. '*Maeve.*'

'Fuck, Ash, are you getting *thicker*?' Maeve panted. 'What is –' she broke off with a high-pitched whine.

My burl was throbbing like it had its own heartbeat. It was throbbing and swelling and waves of sensation were radiating from it, spreading up to my head and down to my sac, and every time Maeve moved, it pressed against a patch of roughness inside her, and –

'Fucking *hell*,' she whimpered. 'Fucking hell. What the actual *fuck*. Ashton, if you don't make me come this second, I'm going to –'

I slid my hand between her legs and pressed down softly on her bud.

She shrieked; her slick walls clenched me in strong, even pulses. Her nails dug into my chest as she rode me through her climax, her hips wild and careless, taking me deep and fast. 'Mine,' she managed, panting. '*Mine*.'

I exploded into her, snarling her name. Everything went white as pleasure made my entire body tense, every muscle hardening until the waves stopped crashing and I relaxed, panting.

She rocked through my orgasm, moaning. 'Never – done it – bare before,' she panted. 'Like – it.' She bent down and kissed me hungrily, devouring my mouth until I cupped her face in my hands and the kiss changed to something softer and sweeter. She rolled her hips as she kissed me, then slipped off my cock, snorting at the wet sound.

'Oh, *fuck*,' she said, inspecting me. '*That's* what that was. I forgot about your burl.'

I reached down to touch it, and inadvertently made myself moan. 'Fuck. Tell me I can do that again every day until I die.'

She laughed. 'Maybe not *every* day,' she said. 'I'm not into period sex. But most days, sure. It's not going to be a hardship.' She smiled, her eyes hooded. 'Now, Willow. You've been waiting so *patiently*.' She collapsed onto the bed next to me. 'Your time has come, doctor.'

Willow gave Elswyth a swift, sweet kiss on the cheek; she slid off his lap and settled next to me, then reached out with a tentative hand to touch my chest.

I covered it with my own as Willow crawled over Maeve, his expression intent.

Maeve grinned up at him. 'I bet you last all of two seconds,' she taunted.

'I'll take that bet,' Willow said, and kissed her.

Elswyth whimpered at the sight, her fingers tightening under mine. I lifted her hand to my lips and brushed a kiss over her knuckles. 'Is all well, Lady?'

'I didn't know,' she whispered. She rubbed her free hand across her chest. 'I didn't know how *right* this would feel.'

Willow growled as Maeve hooked her legs around his hips; Elswyth and I watched as he thrust home.

Maeve's eyes closed and her teeth sank deep into her bottom lip. 'Fuck,' she moaned.

Willow always knew exactly where to touch, exactly where to kiss, exactly how to move. I knew what it felt like to be under his hands. But seeing him with Maeve was something else entirely. His hips rolled, smoothly and unhurriedly, and with every forward thrust Maeve cried out. He dipped his mouth to the hollow of her collarbone, tasting her skin before moving lower, mouthing at one hard nipple. Her knees tightened around his hips and she panted, hooking her feet over his back as he swapped between her hard peaks, licking and sucking and nipping until she was chanting his name. When Maeve dug her nails into his back so hard I could see the green shadow of blood, he took her wrists and pinned them above her head. A moment later, vines grew down from the wall and wrapped around Maeve's wrists, leaving her open and fully pliant beneath him.

'Green gods,' Elswyth whimpered. She tore her gaze away, looking down at me. 'I, ah,' she started hesitantly, 'I don't think

I'm ready yet. But do you think maybe one day you would want that? With me? If Maeve is all right with it?'

'You don't – need my – permission,' Maeve gasped, as Willow thrust into her. 'He's – ours. Mine. Yours. Willow's. Do whatever – you want.' She paused, then moaned, then bit her lip. 'With – in – reason, and with – ongoing – consent, of course.'

I reached up and touched Elswyth's cheek. 'Whatever you want. Whatever you need. Whenever you need it. I am always yours to command.'

My Hamadryad pressed a kiss to my palm.

Maeve moaned. '*Willow*. These burls – are – something else. *Willow*. That. There. *Yes*,' she hissed, and Willow snarled as she arched her back, coming with a scream.

Willow's back muscles clenched, and he swore as he emptied himself inside her, collapsing sideways and pulling her with him once he was done, swapping their places so that Maeve's head was pillowed on his chest.

'*Oh*,' Elswyth said breathlessly. 'I *definitely* want that.' She bit her lip. 'Maybe sooner than I thought.'

'Well,' Maeve said a few moments later, once her breathing had calmed. 'That was nice.'

'Nice?' Willow growled.

'Satisfactory,' Maeve said, her taunting grin a flash of white in the darkened room. 'Pass level. Three stars –'

She shrieked as Willow dragged her down the bed and buried his face between her legs.

Elswyth laughed and snuggled into my side. I pulled her closer, my hearts feeling so full they could burst. 'I am *not* going to be the one washing the sheets,' she said into my chest.

I kissed her head. 'Next time we should do this in the Forest,' I murmured. 'Much less to clean up.'

'Under my heartree,' she said with a shiver, beginning to glow. 'Yes. In the Forest, where we belong.'

EPILOGUE

MAEVE

IF YOU SQUINTED A bit and didn't mind that the ocean was the wrong colour, Natare looked a bit like Earth. The landmasses were smaller and seemed to be grouped into archipelagos, which explained why Willow had mentioned there wasn't much agriculture. He said the cephalopods practised mariculture instead, farming kelp and fish and other sea creatures.

Tessa is somewhere down there.

The Captain had confirmed that the ship Tessa had left Earth on had landed on Natare two weeks ago. I'd chafed at the wait – *surely we can land now?* I'd begged several times – but because of *diplomacy* we had to wait until we were officially invited to land. The Queen of Natare was tardy on the invite, which made me anxious, and when I got anxious, I got all kinds of annoyed.

Ashton and Willow took turns fucking me to try and make me calmer, which I wasn't sad about. That kind of reward wasn't exactly giving me an incentive to change my behaviour.

'All good?' Ashton murmured, taking up position next to me. His hair was braided back, showing the patch on one side where it had been shaved. He wore his official First Guard uniform, a forest-green tunic embroidered with gold thread over leathers. He looked all kinds of delicious, and for a moment I considered skipping the landing party entirely and dragging him back to the bedroom. The look he shot me – all hunger and arrogance – said that he was thinking along the same lines.

'Don't you dare,' Willow said, standing on my other side. 'Maeve has come across multiple galaxies for this moment.'

'Spoilsport,' I muttered, pouting. He was in uniform too, his wavy hair brushing his shoulders, and he looked so beautiful that my insides went all melty. 'Where's Elswyth?'

'On her way,' he said, studying the ocean from the hangar viewing platform. 'She couldn't decide what to wear. She's the Captain's daughter and our Hamadryad, after all, and she wanted to look the part.'

I smiled. 'I can't believe she puts up with us.'

'Sorry, sorry,' Elswyth said, skidding to a stop behind us. Her cheeks were flushed green with exertion and a few strands of carefully-pinned hair had escaped an elegant twist to frame her face. Her dress was a cold-tone pearl that picked up the shine of her hair and made her eyes glow.

'Fuck, you're beautiful,' I breathed.

She flushed further, like I hadn't said the same thing a thousand times, like she hadn't been riding my face a few hours before. 'You are, too,' she said shyly.

I'd borrowed a dress from Juniper and had taken some care with my makeup, scrounging ingredients with Willow's help until we'd concocted something that approximated foundation, blush, eyeliner, and mascara. Some of the other Tirians had stared at me, but I didn't care what they thought. I wanted extra armour for this battle.

And Elswyth liked it, which was pretty much the end of the story.

We divided into Pods, with some grumbling from Ashton about applying for a four-seater family craft. A half-hearted argument later, we were seated.

'Breathe, Maeve,' Elswyth reminded me.

I exhaled. 'What if Tessa's hurt? What if she's –' I choked off that thought.

'What if she's not?' Elswyth replied sensibly. 'What if she's perfectly fine? What if she's *happy*?'

'Then I don't have to convince your mother to do an immediate U-turn, which is preferable,' I joked. 'I brought it up the other day and she just said *Do you think the Tirian fleet revolves around your wishes, Maeve*? But I'm pretty sure she was just annoyed that I beat her at poker.'

'*That's* why she was in a bad mood,' Elswyth muttered. 'She kept going on about forgetting what the aces were. I didn't know what she was talking about.'

My anxiety skyrocketed as the Pod's automatic launch sequence began. I hadn't been in space since my first trip, and my hands dug into the chair beneath me as we shot from the peacekeeping ship and into the black, then began to break atmosphere.

'And breathe *out*, Maeve,' Elswyth said sternly.

'You're spending too much time with Willow. You've even got the tones perfect.'

She gave a visible shiver, blossoms shifting in her hair. 'He was ordering Ash around the other morning while you were sparring with Cedar. It's ... *nice*, isn't it? Listening to him?'

I burst out laughing. '*Nice* is not the word I'd use. But yes.' My core clenched in remembrance of the last time he'd ordered *me* about. 'Nice. *Very* nice.'

She was silent for a moment. 'I can't believe how lucky I am. How lucky I was to find you.'

Warmth spread through my chest; I rubbed my hand over my heart. 'I'm so grateful you did,' I whispered.

A vine of arcadia blossoms climbed over Elswyth's shoulder and down to my hands, twining around my wrists.

'*Breathe*, Maeve.'

'Breathing,' I said.

Elswyth reached up to press a light above her head. 'We'll land in a moment. Do you remember the itinerary?'

'Welcome, food, Roth discussion, food, break, food, sleep,' I recited. 'A few days of general schmoozing, lots of eating, discussing why the Roth are bad, and trying to find Tessa.'

'And are you ready for it?'

'No,' I said honestly. 'What if she's not here? What if I never find her? What if I *do*, and I have to say goodbye forever?'

'I don't know,' Elswyth said after a moment. 'But we'll be here for you, no matter what.'

I stroked one of the arcadia blossoms on my wrist. 'I know you will. And I love you for it.'

The Pod made a whirring noise as it lowered towards the ground.

'In and out, in and out,' Elswyth reminded me.

I squeaked as we landed on the designated pad and the Pod roof slid back.

Natare's atmosphere was almost the same as Earth's, so we didn't have to worry about breathing. The landing pads were like long, unnatural jetties, jutting straight into an expanse of green-blue sea. It was breathtakingly beautiful; the water shone with reflected light from the planet's small suns.

I'd already been warned not to put so much as a toe in the sea unless I was given the okay by one of the cephalopods. Apparently, the water was full of aquatic nightmare fuel, although I was pretty interested to see how they compared to Earth's own sea-based prehistoric monsters.

'You look amazing, Maeve,' Elswyth whispered as we climbed out and straightened our dresses. I tucked a strand of shining silver hair behind her ear, and she adjusted one of my borrowed earrings, a beautiful concoction of woven rose gold.

I took her hand.

Make sure you mark your family, the Captain had warned me. *The Queen of Natare enjoys trying out different species.* She'd paused. *She usually eats them afterwards.*

I mean ... That was kinda badass, as long as it wasn't *my* Tirians she was trying to eat.

Maybe I'd feed her Adair.

Ashton had landed right behind us, and he and Willow climbed out of their Pod, Ashton with a green flush darkening his cheeks.

'What the fuck were you two doing?' I demanded, curious.

'Willow decided it was an appropriate time to tell me all about what you three did yesterday when I was reporting to the Captain,' Ashton said grumpily.

I grinned. 'Oh.' I nudged Willow in the side with my free elbow. 'You are surprisingly sadistic. You know that, don't you?'

Willow's lips curled up. 'I can't help that I always notice details. Lots and *lots* of details. About you and Elswyth, specifically. I thought Ashton would enjoy it.'

'I did,' he grumbled. 'That's the problem.'

Ashton tried to subtly adjust himself beneath his tunic – without much success; he was lucky the tunics weren't tighter – and they both flanked us as we waited for the Captain to alight. She didn't take long, climbing out of her Pod in a dress much like Elswyth's, her badge of rank pinned to her breast, her hair held back with a circlet of Nataran wild pearls that she'd chosen specially for the occasion.

We followed the Captain and her bonded off the landing pad and towards a massive sea-green pavilion, decorated as if it were catering for a ridiculously expensive wedding. Large flowers had been arranged in bunches and to drape down as if the pavilion were half alive; a heavy floral scent filled the air.

'Sea lilies!' Elswyth said, delighted. 'A different kind to the ones on Tir. How beautiful they are!'

I took Willow's hand and squeezed his fingers, then exchanged a glance with Ashton. I knew we were all thinking the same thing: *They don't compare to you.*

The pavilion was packed with beings, including a very liberal sprinkling of humanoids wearing navy blue, high-necked uniforms that were clearly military.

Ashton tensed as he took them in. 'Nataran soldiers in their humanoid form,' he murmured. 'Where's your knife, Maeve?'

'I have one in each boot, elf-boy. And one in my bodice, just as an FYI.'

'I cannot *believe* I find that arousing,' Willow muttered. 'I'm supposed to be a pacifist.'

'You can get it out for me later,' I said cheerfully. 'Preferably with your teeth.'

One of the Nataran soldiers shot me a startled look; Elswyth cleared her throat.

I grinned at the fair-haired guard. 'Right, the super fancy, super formal, super important diplomatic thing we're doing right now. I have officially stopped talking about tits.'

The crowd shifted as Elswyth's mother walked through it; either the other beings knew who she was, or her general demeanour of *get-the-fuck-out-of-my-way* was working its usual charm. She was heading for a fuck-off *huge* throne that looked to be entirely made of some kind of shining, silver-toned metal that shifted colour slightly as I stared at it, as if it were shimmering. There was a fair-haired female sitting upon it comfortably, inclining her head every now and then, with sapphire-blue eyes that shone even from a distance.

I didn't stare too long at her eyes, though, once I noticed the tentacles.

'Fuck me,' I muttered under my breath, taking in the blue-green limbs coiled loosely over the sides of her throne. I cleared my throat. 'Um. Wow.'

Elswyth's hand found my arm. 'Maeve.'

'Yep, sorry. I've stopped staring,' I said, continuing to gawk from the corner of my eye.

I mean, *tentacles*.

'Not the Queen,' Elswyth said impatiently. '*Look*.'

As the Captain and her family moved to speak with a blue-skinned female dressed in a long, diaphanous gown of gold, I caught sight of someone standing next to the Nataran Queen's throne.

Someone who had wild, ashy-brown curls and wide green eyes; someone whose hair was caught back in what looked to be suspiciously like a *crown* and whose emerald-green dress was stretched tight and proud across a belly that was clearly growing something else inside it.

I staggered. Elswyth kept me upright as Willow wrapped an arm around my waist. 'Tessa?' I whispered.

Ashton loosed a long, soft growl that stopped the conversation around us dead.

'Tessa?' I repeated, my voice wavering in the sudden silence.

The green eyes fell on me and widened. The goblet she'd been holding dropped to the floor.

'She's pregnant,' Elswyth breathed.

'*Maeve*?' Tessa screeched.

'Green gods,' Willow said.

Tessa started down off the throne podium. The dark-haired man with the built shoulders appeared out of nowhere – *literally just appeared* – to help her down. She hissed, but after a moment, leaned her weight on him a little as she walked with difficulty towards us.

Tessa would rip my hair out if I called it *waddling*, so I tried to forget the word existed.

'Maeve, what the *fuck* are you doing here?' Tessa cried.

I strode forward and enveloped her in a tight hug, keeping well away from her belly. 'I came to find you.'

Tessa pulled back and stared at me. 'You did *what*?'

'Next time, leave a better note.'

She let out a startled laugh, then sniffed, her eyes welling with tears. 'I can't believe you came across the fucking *universe* to find me.' She caught up one of my hands and pressed it to her damp cheek. 'God, I'm going to ruin my makeup. Wait – why the *fuck* are your eyes green?'

I waved a hand. 'Long story.'

'Tessa, starlight, please don't cry again,' the black-haired man coaxed. 'Mor is going to lose his shit.'

'Last time it was his fault, the asshole,' Tessa said crossly, wiping under her lashes.

'He didn't know it was the last block, *elyn*, I promise.' A red-haired beauty appeared at Tessa's side – walked up, not appeared from thin air like the black-haired one – and handed her the pocket handkerchief from his fifties-style suit like a perfect gentleman. 'I'll make you more.'

'I know you will, handsome,' Tessa said, dabbing at her cheeks. 'And if that dickhead *touches* it, he's sleeping in the pit for the rest of his fucking *life*.'

'The last block of what?' I said warily.

'Peppermint chocolate,' Tessa said matter-of-factly, as if this was a perfectly normal conversation to be having, and we weren't on an alien planet for an intergalactic peace summit with a whole range of non-human beings staring at us. 'It's all I want to eat, and Morgan –'

'Tessa?' The call came from across the pavilion.

The black-haired man rolled his eyes. 'Your father is insufferable,' he said to Tessa's belly, smoothing her dress over the swell. 'It's my turn next time, and I promise I will behave *much* better.'

'You're both getting the snip,' Tessa told him. She turned to the red-haired man. 'Not you, Cy. You're perfect.' She patted his cheek.

'Because I can't get you pregnant,' he muttered.

'It's a definite plus, yes.'

'You'd make very beautiful babies,' I offered, deciding to roll with the chaos.

Tessa groaned. 'Aster has already been researching how to make it happen. Don't encourage him. He has it in his head that they all *get a turn*.' She gestured at her stomach. 'Like this is a ride at some fucking fairground.'

'That *is* the equitable way,' I said with a grin. 'I take it these are your new dresses?'

'Dresses?' the dark-haired man repeated.

Tessa snorted. 'They're rather less *new* now, and sometimes I think about returning them,' she said archly. She took the red-haired man's hand. 'Not you though. This is Cy, the love of my life who can do no wrong.'

Cy blushed a lovely deep pink and gave me an adorably awkward smile.

'And Aster, who is all right sometimes.'

The black-haired man I'd seen at Advena grinned and offered a jaunty wave.

'*And* you're about to meet Morgan, who is going the right way for a thorough stabbing,' Tessa concluded. 'Unfortunately for me and my sanity, I love all three of them more than is sensible, so the stabbing will only happen in my imagination. Probably.'

'Tessa?' came a rumbling growl, and a blonde man pushed through the crowd to our side, tall and broad enough to give even Ashton and his shoulders a run for their money. 'I can smell you crying.'

Tessa raised an eyebrow at me, as if to say *see why I want to stab him?*

I was enjoying myself immensely, so I gave him a shit-eating grin. 'That was my fault. I made her cry.'

His blue eyes focused on me and narrowed, and a deep, animal growl escaped his chest. Before I could blink, Ashton had pushed forward to stand between us and was growling right back, his hand hovering over the knife at his hip.

I laughed out loud.

'Idiots,' Elswyth muttered, loud enough for them all to hear.

'Morgan,' Tessa snarled. '*Stop that.*'

The blonde man stopped growling and eyed us suspiciously, then sniffed. 'Oh. She's your housemate. From Earth.'

'And you just growled at her, you asshat,' Tessa muttered.

Morgan looked utterly unrepentant. 'Welcome to Natare.'

Tessa snorted, but Aster just grinned again. 'This is already better than I imagined,' he said.

I glanced to the side. Elswyth was looking around with a slight frown and Ashton's hand was still rather close to his knife, but Willow was staring at Aster as if transfixed.

'Do you have a twin?' he blurted.

Aster blinked, surprised. 'Yes,' he said, studying Willow warily.

'Vesper,' Willow said carefully.

Aster's expression clouded. 'That's right.' His golden eyes narrowed. 'You don't know him *professionally*, do you?'

'In a manner of speaking,' Willow said calmly. 'I'm a doctor. I was kidnapped by some Roth to heal a human in their ... care. Vesper was sharing her cell. He was fine,' Willow added hastily, when Aster's brow furrowed. 'He was chained with dark matter, but he was cheerful enough. He told me that if I ever met his twin, I should let him know that a timely rescue wouldn't go astray.' Willow paused. 'He did admit to fairly serious theft, though, so I'm not sure if I should have passed the message along.'

Aster exchanged a long look with Morgan. 'I see,' he said eventually. 'I'll keep that in mind. Thank you.'

Tessa's eyes were travelling over Ashton and Willow; when Elswyth met her stare, Tessa offered a friendly smile. 'Something you want to tell me?' she said to me.

I took Elswyth's hand. 'Tessa Wilding, these are my loves Elswyth, Ashton, and Willow.'

Tessa's smile grew wider. 'It's a pleasure to meet you.'

'The human Vesper was with. *Vesper* hadn't hurt her, had he?' Aster interrupted. His deep voice was tinged with worry.

'Anna? No, she'd been –'

Tessa and I rounded on him at the same time. '*Anna*?'

Willow blinked at me, startled. 'Yes, didn't I mention her name?'

'No, you didn't,' I said, with a calm I didn't feel. 'Anna is the chef at Advena. She's tiny and blonde and pretty –'

'And she has blue eyes,' Willow finished.

I stared at Tessa. *That would explain the radio silence*. 'Fuck.'

'You said she was on a *Roth* ship?' Tessa said, her brow creased.

'Yes, but –'

The noise of the crowd rose, then dropped to a low, frightened murmur.

'What the fuck?' Aster muttered, turning around.

Morgan was looking up at the sky. He gave a low, savage growl, and between one blink and the next, he went from having two well-muscled legs encased in uniform dress pants to having eight sucker-lined tentacles disappearing beneath his fancy jacket.

Those tentacles were a bright, agitated red, and within another heartbeat, Tessa and Cy were encased in a nest of them.

I followed his gaze upwards.

'Oh, green gods,' Elswyth said.

Even from a distance, I could see that the ship hovering over the sea was spherical; light from the two small suns glinted off its silver hull.

Ashton stiffened and pulled his gun from the holster at his side, keeping it next to his thigh.

'Roth,' Willow whispered.

Every weapon on the ship was trained on the pavilion.

To be continued ...

The *Advena Abductions* series will continue with Anna's story,
Dark Space.

Notes on the Text & Acknowledgements

During my Honours year, we studied a poet called Andrew Marvell.

Marvell was a metaphysical poet, and perhaps best known for his *carpe diem* poem *To His Coy Mistress*, but I was more interested in his work *The Garden*. As with all of Marvell's poems, the work offers a range of readings and interpretations; he was a writer who delighted in double – or sometimes triple – layers of meaning, so much so that it is often difficult to pin him down. *The Garden* is certainly packed full of things to think about, but with my smutty mind being what it was (and still is), I wrote my final Marvell essay on his use of the colour *green*, and included a discussion of what seems like outright dendrophilia in a number of *The Garden*'s stanzas. (On the narrator's part, of course; we all know that art is not the artist!)

> No white nor red was ever seen
> So am'rous as this lovely green.
> Fond lovers, cruel as their flame,
> Cut in these trees their mistress' name;
> Little, alas, they know or heed
> How far these beauties hers exceed!

Fair trees! where'se'er your barks I wound,
No name shall but your own be found.

When we have run our passion's heat,
Love hither makes his best retreat.
The gods, that mortal beauty chase,
Still in a tree did end their race:
Apollo hunted Daphne so,
Only that she might laurel grow;
And Pan did after Syrinx speed,
Not as a nymph, but for a reed.

I'll let you make your own meaning from this, but for me, there's a lot going on here to suggest that the garden – and trees – are not *just* trees, if you get me, especially given the assertion that they are more beautiful than women, the pun on the word *wound*, and the following stanza, which talks a lot about fruit (including peaches; make of that what you will, emoji fans), and the garden *ensnaring* the narrator with flowers (ie. the garden is a willing and active participant in this tryst). Marvell could, of course, be having a laugh – which is especially likely given his consistent tendency to obscure meaning, and the poem's irreverent tone – but this isn't the only poem of his to refer to plant life in an amorous way, and there is a certain satisfaction in thinking about A Very Important Metaphysical Poet writing about fucking (actively consenting) trees. I was also curious about the notion that Apollo hunted Daphne *so that she would shift into a tree*, not because he wanted her in her original nymph state, so I went back to Ovid's *Metamorphoses*.

If you haven't heard the story, it features the unfortunate nymph, Daphne, who wanted to stay a virgin, but caught the roaming eye of Apollo (who was less inclined to let her stay that way). She fled from his chase, praying to the gods for death – or to change her body – so that she might escape him. The gods, in their wisdom, decided that a laurel tree was the go.

> Scarce had she made her prayer when through her limbs
> A dragging languor spread, her tender bosom
> Was wrapped in thin smooth bark, her slender arms
> Were changed to branches and her hair to leaves;
> Her feet but now so swift were anchored fast
> In numb stiff roots, her face and head became
> The crown of a green tree; all that remained
> Of Daphne was her shining loveliness.

> And still Apollo loved her; on the trunk
> He placed his hand and felt beneath the bark
> Her heart still beating; held in his embrace
> Her branches, pressed his kisses on the wood ...

Now, it might just be me, but it certainly seems like Apollo isn't *that* sad about Daphne's sudden shift into a tree, and he certainly keeps up his non-consensual attention afterwards, embracing her branches, groping beneath her bark, and kissing her ... wood.

But Hollie ... What the holy heck is your point?

All this is my roundabout way of saying that when I needed a new species of alien to sweep Maeve off her feet, something to do with trees made a lot of sense – to me, at least. (And if there's anyone in your life who snipes at you for reading smut, you can tell them that your smut has Very Serious Literary Allusions – and also, as Maeve would say, to fuck right off. (If you really want to double down, buy them a copy of *Fanny Hill*.)

Hamadryads are a real thing (insofar as a mythical creature can be *real*). Both Dryads and Hamadryads are types of nymph from ancient Greek myth, originally associated with oak trees. While the Dryads lived in and around trees generally, Hamadryads were bound to particular trees in such a way that they lived and died *with* it (the prefix *hama* means 'together', which may have been used to indicate the nature of the Hamadryad's bond to their particular tree). The concept of the heartree is inspired both by this, and by the idea of the 'mother tree', which is *also* real (and absolutely worth an internet search). As far as I can tell, the science behind the mother tree theory is debated, though the idea itself is wonderful.

Obviously, I have played fast and loose with these sources of inspiration, and none are intended to be a direct parallel, but I hope this gives the novel a little more context for you.

Maeve is a special heroine to me. When I was sixteen, I heard the term *bisexual* for the first time, and my world suddenly made a whole lot more sense. (That's the power of words, friends!) Unfortunately, my formative years took place in the 90's and 2000's in a small rural city, and the popular sentiment seemed to be that bisexual women either didn't exist, or (conversely) existed solely for the male gaze. We do exist, of course, and decidedly not for the pleasure of misogynists, but that awful notion – coupled with being told *you're just confused, you're just greedy, you need to pick a team, I just don't think you're like that* and losing friendships because of homophobia – had me holding my tongue about my sexuality until much later in life. I prefer the term *queer* now; I know that word is loaded for many people, but I feel like it fits me better. Maeve is *not* me, but rather, she's the kind of person I wish I'd had the courage and opportunity to be when I was younger – brave, unapologetic, and entirely comfortable in her own skin.

I didn't write acknowledgements for *Count Down*, because I was quite stressed at the time and forgot about it entirely; I'd like to offer an extremely overdue (and heartfelt) thanks to Michelle and Erika, both of whom beta read the novel. This time around, I will *not* forget. Thank you so much to my tiny village – to Kelly, John, Hannah, and Erika for beta reading this, and for your general support and expert cheerleading. I can't tell you how much I appreciate the time and energy you give; you're all fucking magical. Thank you, too, to all the readers who took a chance on the *Count Down* ARC – you have no idea how much it means to authors when strangers not only decide to read your work, but like it. I know that *Into Orbit* is a little longer, and a little different, but I hope you'll love reading about Maeve and her space tree-elves as much as I have loved writing them.

Excerpt from Andrew Marvell's *The Garden* taken from *Andrew Marvel: The Complete Poems,* Penguin Classics Edition, Penguin Books, London, 2005.

Excerpt from Ovid's *Metamorphoses* taken from the A.D. Melville translation in the Oxford World Classics edition, Oxford University Press, New York, 1998.

Also by Hollie Hartwright